I0524803

LADDIES AND GENERALMEN

by

Paul Gubbins

Published by New Generation Publishing in 2012

Copyright © Paul Gubbins 2012

First Edition

The author asserts the moral right under the Copyright, Designs and Patents Act 1988 to be identified as the author of this work.

www.newgeneration-publishing.com

 **New Generation Publishing**

It is, of course, a sociological truism (Kant, 1964; Misthaufen, et al, 1987) that society comprises splashers and the splashed. Among the splashers might be found, in modern society, a disparate mix that reaches across the social spectrum and might include royalty, arms dealers, lawyers and plumbers (Klempner, 1981). These people belong to an elite that would readily 'stick the heads of those around them into the water-butt of life and hold them there' (Narrenschiff and Mankasklap, 1983: 177). Nevertheless, as might be expected, it has been estimated that some 94% of the world's citizens (Dubinde, 1985a) belong to the splashed. Many of these, of course, are found in underdeveloped and developing countries. There is, however, increasing evidence that more and more people in such countries are aspiring to join the elite to which Narrenschiff and Mankasklap refer. Nowhere is this truer than in China.

From the unpublished doctoral dissertation of Arthur Brush.

1

Anne Hathaway's cottage was playing hard to get. So too was the Tower of London. As for the castles and cathedrals and quaint market towns which, according to the tourist guides, comprised England's fair and pleasant land, there was no trace. Instead, all Wang could see, nose snubbed against the scratched and greasy window of the Airbus A320, was cloud; grey and leaden, tugging sullenly at the wings of the aircraft as it lumbered towards Cramcaster International Airport.

Gateway to the North, the website said. Wang had chuckled when he looked up 'gateway' and understood its meaning. What could the British know about gateways? China was the place for gateways. Gateways, flanked with sturdy square towers: gateways in the Great Wall, gateways in the ancient city of Xi'an, where the Silk Road began, and with walls so wide that two chariots could pass with ease. Quite definitely, China was the place for walls. And gateways. All of which were now far behind him, on the other side of the world.

Wang sighed, and glanced nervously at the luggage locker. All was well. Despite the groaning and creaking of the aircraft as it wrestled with the clouds, the locker remained firmly shut. At least for the moment, the case was safe. Wang was unsure whether to be relieved or disappointed. The case, and in particular its contents, was an embarrassment, but Uncle Peng had insisted. This is the way things are done, the old man said, and Wang had no wish to offend. His uncle had been good to him, raising him after the pit explosion that claimed his father's life and his mother's wits. He had shared with him the secrets of his trade – bicycles and, in particular, their repair and maintenance. Surely the

5

nephew would follow in this noble calling. But no. Wang was bright: his teachers, with party approval, directed him towards further schooling, university and now – the highest honour – postgraduate study abroad.

Uncle Peng had taken great delight in travelling with his nephew to Beijing to take in the marvels of the new China. At Beijing airport – a place of wonder for the village bicycle man – Uncle Peng was astonished to learn that luggage is removed from the traveller and put in the hold of the aircraft. This cannot be, he told Wang. Surrender one case, if you must, but this must remain with you. You know its worth... sealed as it is with the sweat of honest toil.

Wang half-hoped the case would be deemed too large to pass as hand-luggage and would be confiscated. True, this might cause problems at the other end, but a telephone call, an email, would doubtless resolve any difficulties. At this point, old China prevailed over new. Uncle Peng waved a pinkish 100-yuan note at the official who, after carefully examining it, stuffed the money into his pocket and declared the case to be hand-luggage. On the plane, it occupied the best part of an entire locker. During the stop-over in Charles de Gaulle the object attracted no attention: a partial strike, it seemed, had rendered security insecure so that Wang, plus case, had been waved onto the A320 like royalty. Not, he supposed, that royalty was likely to carry its own case. Not when the heir to the British throne – as Wang had discovered from a magazine article – had a servant to squeeze toothpaste onto his brush.

The aircraft tannoy crackled into life and, concentrating hard, Wang deduced the plane was about to land in Cramcaster. Yet clouds still swirled outside his spy-hole, that oval of perspex which seemed but a larger version of one of those lenses in a hotel-room

6

door giving a crazed, hall-of-mirrors perspective onto the corridor beyond. Wang knew about hotels. He had worked in one in Beijing, after leaving the village, and before university. Wang was responsible for re-stocking rooms with the bath-robes, shampoos, soaps, notepads and pens removed in copious quantity by Western tourists in whose own countries, the supervisor said, such luxuries did not exist. Wang thought this unlikely but, to preserve his job, said nothing.

He pressed his nose to his spy-hole once more and peered into the cavorting murk. All he could see were sumo-wrestler rolls of cloud. There was none of the honeyed late-summer welcome promised by the British Council or, indeed, by the enthusiastic lady from the postgraduate office of Cram Vale University, on a Chinese freebie. Britain wasn't supposed to be like this.

Something cold and clammy reached into his brain and squeezed hard. Perhaps this wasn't Britain. Perhaps at Charles de Gaulle he had boarded the wrong flight. The few staff in evidence at the airport seemed harassed, over-stretched, perhaps hadn't checked the boarding card properly. Why, he might be heading not for Cramcaster... but where? Some place for which almost certainly he had no visa, where the case would be opened, examined, and its contents produced in evidence of... what? These days... terrorism. What a fool he'd been to let his uncle have his way! He'd be arrested, flung into prison, eventually deported: the shame, the ignominy. He reached to adjust the air jet above him, to feel a flow of cooling, calming air on his forehead, but it appeared not to be working. No panic, he told himself. You've come this far...

As if in confirmation, at that moment the Airbus – staggering and lurching like a Beijing drunk, and shuddering fit to catapult him into the row in front – recovered and, with a triumphant bellow of its engines,

7

locked itself in furious combat with an element as unrelenting as the cloud had been pliant. Tarmac, Wang realised. A runway, an airport. He gave a sigh of relief and peered again from his window. The gloom had lightened and, as the plane howled to a halt, he made out a building, and another, and men with orange clothing, walking, marching. Orange. Surely not. That bay place... where the CIA took terrorists and did unspeakable things. No... there must be some mistake...

'Mesdames, messieurs...' an Air France voice cackled. 'Laddies and generalmen, we'll come to Cramcastair...'

A ripple of relief, Wang thought, passed through the aircraft. Cramcaster. He turned to his neighbour, a smartly-dressed woman of a certain age wearing several layers of make-up and an expression that told everyone she ought to be in club class, and mouthed the three syllables that spelled liberation from the CIA and the prison whose name he couldn't remember.

'Cram-cas-ter...?'

'Oui, oui,' the woman replied, looking for the first time at her fellow passenger and feeling uncharacteristic pity for the moist and jaundiced creature next to her – l'opium, n'est-ce pas, c'est ça le plaisir des chinois – and confirmed with a curt nod: 'Cramcastair.'

Wang's face lit into a smile wide enough to embrace Tiananmen Square.

'You very kind,' he told the woman. 'And now you please tell me... what mean generalmen? And "we'll come to Cramcaster"... why no present perfect... how textbook teach?'

The woman, whose English was limited, frowned. It was possible the young man was asking her to convey opiates into Britain. Despite an occasional flutter at

8

Chantilly races, Madame's interest in quadrupeds did not extend to mules – still less drug mules.

'Non, non,' she bristled. 'Je regrette...' Then, having unfastened her seatbelt, she folded the copy of Le Monde she had been reading and tucked it into a neat but copious bag.

Generalmen, pondered Wang, resolving to key this mystery into his electronic dictionary as soon as an opportunity arose. Then he recalled immediately, to his annoyance, that the device was in the other suitcase. Generalmen would have to wait.

2

It was not only generalmen that had to wait, but also lesser men and women from the Paris flight. When Wang arrived some half an hour later at the baggage hall to collect case number two – containing, among other things, the universal bicycle repair tool Uncle Peng had insisted he take, on the grounds that no-one should travel without one – the Air France Paris carousel was idle. When it eventually jarred into action there was, like a damp Chinese New Year, much disappointment. It was apparent the go-slow or whatever in Paris meant the aircraft had left without its full complement of cases. At least half the passengers from the Paris flight found themselves luggage-less, silently wishing they had heeded maternal advice to put clean pants and a toothbrush into the hand-luggage. A moment of uncertainty followed as the carousel clanked to a halt. A dishevelled youth, wearing a Cram United shirt, shuffled to the start of the carousel and ranted at the black rubber thongs which, in more active moments, lashed with unbridled sadism each piece of emerging luggage. Embarrassed by the football shirt – which, like a medium on a spirits' day off, was trying vainly to communicate with the other side – the dispossessed shuffled in awkward silence, as if they themselves were to blame, towards a grubby window with a sign above it which proclaimed, in stark capitals, Luggage Claims.

Clutching the case he had carefully prised from the aircraft locker, Wang followed, obeying some inbred travellers' lore that here, behind this window, lay the means to conjure bags out of – appropriately – thin air. Yet, something was wrong. It was the sign: Luggage Claims. Evidently, the window was involved with bags, baggage, suitcases, and whatnot. The word 'luggage'

10

was not a problem. But the present tense verb – third person singular, the S-ending – tagged to 'luggage' was puzzling. Luggage claims. Luggage claims what? Surely 'claims' was a verb... a transitive verb... needing an object. A noun, a pronoun. But where was this object? Wang looked round, expectantly. Perhaps... another sign, another wall. Luggage claims progress in realisation of five year plan? Luggage claims triumph in war against imperialist aggression? Luggage...

'No hyphen,' a voice said. In Mandarin.

Wang span round, for a welcome moment believing himself back home.

'Haaar...' he gurgled.

'English... they hate hyphens. Almost as much as they hate the French. Or Germans. Everyone, really. I keep seeing signs saying: Police Speed Cameras. I ask you. Why should police speed cameras? It must play havoc with the settings. A case of indecent exposure, don't you think?'

Wang didn't think. His head had dislocated itself from his body and was preparing to enter orbit round a planet inhabited by speeding cameras and policemen snapping each other in suggestive poses.

'Haaar...' he gurgled again.

'Strictly,' Wang's mentor continued, 'there should be a hyphen. Luggage-claims. And speed-cameras. But nobody bothers. Too much effort. Everything's too much effort in England, and not just grammar. I mean, just look around. But everyone understands. Everyone being the English, that is. Because, of course, for the English, there isn't anyone else. Except perhaps the Americans.'

Wang was about to gurgle a third time, but thought better of it.

'Qi Liang,' the mentor introduced himself, and extended a hyphenated arm towards Wang. 'First time,

11

I take it. Here. In Britain…?'

Wang nodded. Qi was older than Wang, perhaps by about ten years. He was what might be called new-China – European-, American-, Japanese-China. But not China-China. Definitely not China-China. For a start, Qi was tall, a good head taller than Wang: by Chinese standards, China-China standards, that is, he was almost freakishly tall. But no-one would call Qi a freak, certainly not to his face. Qi, with his sharp suit and shiny shoes, exuded confidence, exuded… Wang groped for a description… exuded direction. That's what it was: direction. Qi knew where he was going; indeed, looking at him, had probably got there already. It was likely, thought Wang… and stopped. Qi was looking at him with a slight frown. It seemed something was expected of Wang, who suddenly remembered.

'Haa…' he stifled a gurgle. 'Wang Ti. Honoured to meet you.' And Wang, in response to Qi's still outstretched arm, extended his own in greeting; noting, as hand met hand, that Qi's was smooth and unrumpled, like the suit he was wearing, and unlike most of the hands attached to Wang's friends and acquaintances.

'My first time. Here… in Britain,' said Wang. And began to gush: 'A great privilege, a great honour, to study for an MBA in England at a leading university…' He checked himself. That was the second time in almost as many moments he had used the word 'honour' or some form of it. Qi would think him a fool, an imbecile, unable to express himself without resort to repetitive and time-worn clichés.

'Haaar…' he gurgled, resorting to a repetitive and time-worn cliché, albeit of a personal kind, and withdrew his hand, which was signalling urgently to his jet-lagged brain that it was time to retreat from Qi's

12

lotioned and scented grip.

Qi seemed not to notice Wang's discomfort. 'Oh,' he said, with easy indifference. 'A student.' Then, with more urgency: 'Come. Let's get this case business sorted.'

Wang was amazed. Surely no case belonging to someone as suave, as certain as Qi, would have the temerity to go missing and force its owner to queue at some pokey little window to seek redress?

'You don't mean your bag has gone missing as well...?' Wang began.

'Story of my life,' Qi said. 'When you're on and off planes as much as I am, it's an occupational hazard. Did you know there's a whole industry... you'll like this, studying business... a vast growth industry devoted to returning lost bags?'

Wang's eyes widened.

'Armies of people in vans and taxis all over the world, getting cases to their rightful owners. I tell you... these days there are more people in the airline business driving vans delivering lost bags than flying planes. Funny, that, if you think about it. But it could be useful. For you, I mean. If you want a part-time job – don't all students? – you could do no worse than come down here and get taken on as a driver. A white-van man, as they say in English.'

'Can't drive,' said Wang. 'But perhaps a bicycle and trailer...'

Qi snorted. 'This isn't China,' he said. 'In England bicycles are for kids or cranks. Or trendy politicians. Normal people... forget it. And as for not driving... don't worry about it. The first qualification for van-driving in this crackpot country is not being able to drive.'

Wang smiled, feebly. He felt the conversation was passing him by, striding off down a rutted, pitted trail

13

still waiting for road-menders to plug the holes with sense and meaning: he knew if he followed he would end up, face down, in a puddle of misunderstanding. Absence of electronic wizardry, the dictionary, could not be blamed. Nevertheless, something seemed lost between the Mandarin tongue of Qi and the Mandarin ear of Wang.

A sheet of paper was pushed into Wang's hand. 'Here,' said Qi. 'Fill this in. To get your case back. Then give it that man over there.'

Wang looked around. The elegant French woman who had sat next to Wang on the plane, now with a face as black as storm clouds over the Great Wall, had just handed her form to the official. Not her... not her case too? thought Wang, shocked – as with Qi – that even the high and mighty could be laid low by something as demeaning as an errant suitcase. Such a thing would never happen in China. If luggage belonging to a party official, someone important, went missing... why, heads would roll. Literally. Clearly in the West, death, the great leveller, the great egalitarian – and a good communist – had a powerful rival: the missing suitcase, whose absence cut across class and affected all in the same way. On the other hand...

''Ey... you. Yer... that's right. You. I'll 'ave that form, thank you very much.'

Wang gazed in the direction of the voice. It was the official who, having committed to wanton memory the finer points of the topography of the retreating French woman, remembered he had a job to do – collect as many soddin' forms as possible and bugger off for his break.

'Yer... over 'ere. Want yer bag back, don't you?'

Indeed, Wang did want his bag back. Holding his non-missing case carefully in one hand, and clutching the form in the other, he moved cautiously to the

14

official, who snatched the paper from Wang's hand.

'What's this? You 'aven't filled it in.'

Wang felt his tired eyes watering. Words, English words, rattling like stones beneath boots on a mountain track, dislodged themselves from his subconscious to fall inchoate into an abyss of inarticulate gloom. He would have liked to explain that the official hadn't given him time to fill it in, had jumped to a false conclusion that the form was already complete, had insisted in no uncertain terms that he come over... but it was no good.

'Haaar...' he managed, and a tear trickled down his cheek.

'For God's sake,' the man said, not unkindly. ''Ere... I'll fill it in.'

Wang blinked and tried to compose himself.

'Okay. Yer case. Tell me about yer case. I mean...'

'Back,' choked Wang. 'Back and...'

'Yer, yer... it'll come back,' the man said. 'Always do. Well... for the most part. Now if you tell me what it was like...' He stabbed at the form on which Wang, through brine-filled eyes, could distinguish certain shapes – bricks, mobile phones, chocolate bars – all of which, on closer examination, appeared to have straps, handles and occasionally wheels. Though why chocolate bars should have wheels was beyond Wang's understanding. Qi was right: this was crazy-land, and Wang wanted to go home.

'Just show me what yer case looked like. 'Ere... it's not difficult,' the man said, looking at Wang's puckered face and immediately realising the stupidity of his last statement. 'See 'ere... did yer case look like this,' – stab – 'or that,' – stab – 'or...'

'Yes, yes,' said Wang, feeling a response was appropriate. 'Like that... and that.'

'Okay,' the man sighed, putting a cross next to a

15

picture of a case with as much resemblance to Wang's as a worm to a rattlesnake. 'Good. We're makin' progress.'

'Yes, yes,' said Wang, relaxing slightly, and wiping away his tears. 'Progress.'

'Right,' said the official. 'And now the colour...'

'I tell already,' said Wang, mangling his tense and his verb. 'I tell... back.'

'You'll get it back...' the official began, and stopped. A door creaked opened on a cobwebby chamber in the recesses of the man's mind. 'Ah,' he said. 'Black.'

'Yes,' said Wang, feeling real progress was indeed being made. 'Back. And big. Big trunk. Like elephant,' he added, attempting his first English joke with a real-live Englishman.

The real-live Englishman stared at Wang with a mixture of pity and wonder. 'Tell me,' he said, and scratched at a boil on the back of his neck, 'tell me... 'ow many elephants can you get in a mini?'

Wang furrowed his brow. 'I sorry...?' he said, as the confidence painfully acquired over the previous exchanges took fright and bolted. 'I sorry...?'

'Never mind,' the man said, sharply, and noted 'black' on the form. 'And now just give us yer name and address.'

Wang complied. 'Wang Ti,' he said. 'P.O. Box 49, CN 100028...'

'For God's sake,' the man snapped. 'Not yer address in bleedin' wherever. We're not sendin' yer case 'alfway round the world to where you've just come from. What do you think this is... Cook's bleedin' tours for cases?'

The tide of tears, in slow ebb, executed a quick turn and began flooding back, fast, salty, stinging, towards Wang's eyes. 'Haaar,' he began, in uncomprehending

16

anguish, suddenly aware a small queue had built up behind him. Eyes impatient, non-saline, bored into his head, maggots into a rotten apple, for his head was rotten; it was tired and confused. There were things crawling in it which shouldn't be there, unexplained things, things which required gizmos and liquid crystals – but gizmo and crystals were in Paris – the electronic dictionary, his life-line, key to an unspellable language in an unspeakable society...

'I think,' said a voice behind him, in Mandarin, 'the gentleman means your address in England. That's where the case'll be sent... that's where you need it.'

'Haaar,' gurgled Wang, choking back his frustration and turning to see Qi gazing benevolently on him. The address, obviously, the Cramcaster address; of course, how stupid... and he flashed a brief smile of gratitude at Qi.

'Address,' Wang said, turning back to the official who, by his contortions, and by the furious working of a hand at the back of his neck, appeared about to detonate his unexploded boil. 'My address... you want.'

'Too right, chum,' said the official with a grimace, as the hand went about its business.

'Address,' repeated Wang, fatuously. And then, slowly: 'Address... haaar... address... all papers... in case...'

'Open it then,' the man ordered, as a none too salubrious paw emerged briefly from the centre of operations to motion at Wang's other case. 'Open it.'

'Haaar...' wailed Wang. 'Address... in other case. Stolen case...'

'For cryin' out loud,' the man exclaimed, squeezing hard at the offending pustule. 'You don't mean... argh!'

'Haaar...' echoed Wang, believing for a brief and joyous moment they were joined in common language.

17

'Gotcha. Troublin' me for days, that little bugger,' the official said, removing a victorious hand from his neck, examining it, then wiping his fingers on his trousers. 'Always get 'em this time of year. It's the pollen. And global warmin' doesn't 'elp. Too many bloomin' aeroplanes. Now... where were we?'

'Allow me,' said Qi, moving alongside Wang, only too happy to let someone else take charge. 'The address... here...' and Qi fired off a round of strange syllables which seemed to satisfy the official but which made no sense to Wang, apart from the word Cramcaster.

'What... what's going on?' Wang addressed Qi in Mandarin. 'What are you doing...?'

'Sign,' said Qi. 'There... at the bottom. No... not his pen. Not the one he's been fingering. Use this.'

Qi drew from his pocket a shiny metal ballpoint, clicked it open, and handed it to Wang. 'Just sign.'

Wang obeyed. He was too tired to question further, any self-assertion or resistance beyond him. As he handed over the completed form he felt he was surrendering a part of himself, but he didn't care. Perhaps that's what you do in foreign countries, Wang told himself: you surrender yourself, or at least part, in order to survive.

He felt a hand in the small of his back. It was Qi... Qi, steering him past idly chatting customs officers, past bored people awaiting friends and relatives, and messages saying Amikaro Plc or Car For Mr Schneckenfresser; Qi guiding him past a waiting England.

'All the English ever do is wait,' Qi said. 'Wait to cast off the past and find a future. So welcome to limbo-land. Welcome to Britain.'

18

3

The taxi into which Qi bundled himself and Wang at the airport chugged its way towards the city centre along a damp and dowdy dual carriageway. An odd term, thought Wang, who could see no carriages, little realising he was being conveyed in licensed hackney carriage number 2241 registered to a Mr Shabbir Ahmad Khan. As Wang tried to identify some of the smells that clung to the upholstery of Mr Khan's cab, Qi thrust into his hand a card with a Cramcaster address on it and told him to get in touch in a couple of days, when his luggage would have turned up.

Wang was still troubled. 'I haven't got my papers, my registration letter, the address of the residence where I'm supposed to be staying. They're all in the other case. What do I do... where do I go?'

Qi was reassurance itself: Swiss Re or Munich Re or any of the large insurers' insurers would have snapped him up had they been sitting that damp September day in the back of Mr Khan's taxi. Qi told Wang not to worry. He said that the university would have Wang's name on record, that as soon as he showed up the computers would produce the relevant information, including accommodation details, and that Wang could supply any missing documentation as soon as the case arrived.

'Besides,' said Qi, 'things could be worse. At least you've got one of your cases... at least half your stuff. Imagine the state you'd be in if everything had gone missing.'

Qi was right. If both cases had gone... well, he might just as well have given up there and then and slunk back home. Except he couldn't: he had to remain in Britain at least a month before he could invoke his open return to China.

The dowdy dual carriageway had been joined by several other roads feeding into it and, as custom dictates, had shrunk to an even dowdier two-lane thoroughfare to accommodate the additional traffic. The journey took them past rows of what appeared to be shops, though their windows were either shuttered or adorned with slogans, generally incomprehensible. 'Snack's Fag's Booze' caught Wang's attention, in particular the apostrophes. There was something odd about them. Wang knew about apostrophes; indeed, prided himself on his understanding, having sat through countless classes on them, completing ream after ream of apostrophe worksheet, and finally being examined, with commendable success, on their application. But here... even though he had a vague idea of the meaning of 'snack', and no notion at all of 'fag' or 'booze', these apostrophes didn't look right. He thought he might ask Qi. He would be sure to know, but on the other hand he had already prevailed enough on Qi – and besides, he didn't want to appear any more of a peasant dunce than he probably did already. Instead, he turned to peer once more through the window of Mr Khan's cab.

At least not all the buildings were scruffy. One or two were quite imposing, or had been in their time. There were a couple of banks, an office block or two, and a rather fine edifice with a flag outside. This was presumably government-owned and probably the headquarters of the local Communist party. Except the Communist party didn't exist in Britain... or did it? Wang was too tired to recall, and instead tried to focus on the changing streetscape beyond the taxi window. There was what looked like a school, but which could have been police or army barracks; an art gallery, ditto; a couple of Chinese restaurants, which looked like nothing back home; and also Indian restaurants which for some reason, as the taxi lumbered past, prompted Mr Khan to wind down the window and spit into the Cramcaster drizzle. Wang closed his eyes to reflect on this custom, wondering why he had never been taught it in his Introduction to English Culture class... and the next thing he knew, Qi was shaking him, telling him to wake up.

'We're there,' Qi was saying. 'The university.'

Wang stirred himself, and sat up. The taxi had stopped outside a half-timbered building, brightly lit, which could well be the cottage belonging to Anne Hathaway he had tried to spot from the air. Closer inspection, though, revealed it to be a McDonalds, and Wang felt a twinge of disappointment.

'Not there,' Qi said, seeing the direction Wang's head was turned. 'There...' and he pointed to a flight of steps leading to a glass-fronted building with double doors and, above them, a sign: Registration.

'There you go,' said Qi, leaning across Wang to open the taxi door for him from the inside. 'This is it. Quick... and best of luck.'

Wang's stammered thanks, as he manoeuvred himself and the suitcase out of Mr Khan's cab, were drowned by a savage hooting from buses, lorries and vans trying to circumvent the road-block that licensed hackney carriage 2241 had suddenly become.

'How much...?' asked Wang from the pavement, but already Qi had slammed the door and, with a smile and a wave to indicate no payment was needed, had signalled to Mr Khan to resume the interrupted journey. With a jolt the taxi plunged into the traffic, splashing Wang from a muddy puddle, turned a corner, and was gone.

21

4

'Sorry,' the welcome desk student said. 'No mention of you at all.'

This was her fourth attempt to conjure Wang from the massed megabytes of Cramcaster University's database.

'Look,' she said, pointing at the screen, and Wang leaned over the desk to peer at the flickering names. 'Several Wangs... umpteen Wings and Wongs... but no Wang Ti.'

'Mistake,' said Wang. 'Big mistake.'

'Quite possibly,' the girl sighed. 'It wouldn't be the first today. Overload, you know. The system can't cope.'

Wang wasn't sure if he could, either.

'Of course,' the girl continued, 'it would help if you had your letter of acceptance. Then we'd have a reference number. We could probably find you from that. But, as it is...'

Wang catapulted himself into yet another colourful and largely unintelligible account of someone called Mr Key, or Mr Kiwi, and hair part and low gauge, which the girl deduced might have something to do with airport and luggage. She regretted she had reminded him about the letter of acceptance and wondered, as she found herself floundering, if at that moment her boyfriend Dave was having it off with her best mate Estelle.

'Ah,' she said, momentarily shelving her suspicions about Dave, who in fact was in a pub with her other best mate Jasmine and wondering if he could pull. 'Excuse me... Mr Andrews,' she called, beckoning her supervisor, and cutting Wang off as he reached the point about Qi filling in his, Qi's, address on the form he, Qi, had given him, Wang, to retrieve the missing

22

case.

Jim Andrews was passing on his way to the toilet to read the current Golfing Monthly (concealed in a brown A4 reusable envelope marked 'Internal Mail Only'). He was not best pleased. That was the trouble with taking on these students at admission time... hadn't a clue what they were doing, always wanting help, getting things wrong. Even simple things...

'Yes, Amanda?' he said tersely.

'It's Liz, actually,' Amanda-Liz replied, equally tersely.

Andrews glared. This was wasting good Golfing Monthly time. And what did he come to work for, if not to escape the nagging and niggling which was his lot at home? And now...

'I wonder if you could give me a hand,' Amanda-Liz said. 'Something seems to have gone a bit wrong.'

'Hurmph,' grunted Andrews. Golfing Monthly had obviously landed in the rough. On the other hand, the girl was quite pretty. Mischievous eyes. And a nice nose. Delicate. Can't see her legs, though, because of the table. Tables should have glass tops. What did she say her name was?

'I can't bring up any information on this student,' Miss Eyes-and-Nose said. 'He doesn't seem to be in the system.'

'Right,' said Andrews, about to dazzle, leaning close to the girl – a scent of young and forbidden flesh gave him a momentary thrill – to drag her computer keyboard towards him. Then, to Wang, 'What did you say your name was?'

'Haaar... name. Wang Ti. From China,' reported Wang, and added, as an afterthought, 'sir.'

'Ah... I see,' chortled Andrews, anxious to make his mark as a wit with this rather gorgeous young thing in his charge – why hadn't he noticed her before? 'I see.

23

All the tea in China, eh?'

Amanda-Liz Eyes-and-Nose looked away, into a hazy distance where Dave and she lay naked and entwined on a sandy, sun-kissed beach, about to...

'Tea in China...?' repeated Wang, puzzled.

'Lots of it,' said Andrews. 'Lots of tea in China, eh?'

'China tea. Very good,' said Wang dubiously, wondering if this were an English pleasantry akin to the weather or football or something equally dull. Perhaps now the real conversation would begin.

Andrews spotted the glaze in Wang's eyes and, having failed to elicit the desired admiration from the object of his new-found affections, decided to press on. 'Tell me your name,' he said, imperiously.

'I say name,' said Wang and, to assist the man, whose defective memory singled him out as a professor of distinction and repute, repeated loudly and distinctly, 'Wang Ti.'

'Wang Ti,' Andrews savoured the sound, rolling it round his tongue as if it were a syllabic coffee cream, as a second opportunity to reveal his comic talent unexpectedly presented itself. He cleared his throat. 'Any relation to Mr T?' Pause for effect. Then, for good measure, in throaty cod American, 'I ain't gettin' on no plane. Not with no crazy man.' Further pause for adulation. None was forthcoming. A note of desperation in his voice. 'The A Team. B.A. Baracas. B.A. The big guy. You must know B.A...'

Wang did know BA. Indeed, yes. Here, at last, was solid ground, something familiar, his reason for being, and Wang resolved to exploit it. 'BA. Beijing University... bachelor. Soon MBA... master... English university. Please.'

The girl giggled. My God, thought Andrews, she's laughing at me. Not with me... at me. He fixed her with

24

a steely stare, causing her to giggle all the more. A film of perspiration was forming on his forehead, and he realised the clown, the Chinaman, the cause of his discomfort, was watching him too. Wang was looking pleased, having established in a single utterance his qualifications both earned and yearned. Smug bastard, thought Andrews. I'll have you.

'It's no use giving me an initial,' he said. 'I mean... T. I can't identify you just from a letter.'

'Letter in case,' said Wang. 'Case in Paris.'

'Bugger the letter,' snarled Andrews, wishing he were in Paris. 'I need your surname... your s-u-r-n-a-m-e,' he added, emphasising every letter.

The girl giggled again. Who the hell took her on? Andrews wondered. Some oaf from the student union. He'd have his balls with a six iron...

'Excuse me,' the girl said, gazing with obvious schadenfreude at her supervisor, who winced, 'but I think you'll find Wang's his surname. In China it's the other way about.'

Andrews glared at her. The girl was enjoying herself, at his expense. Too cocky by half. Shouldn't be at university. Should be a barmaid, a hairdresser. Of course, he told himself, that's probably where she'll end up. Most of them do, these days, even with degrees.

'That'll do,' he snarled. 'I know perfectly well about Chinese names. It was just a joke... the A Team. It's a poor do if you can't take a joke.'

'Isn't it just?' the girl said, coming as near to a sneer as a 20-year-old can. And, before Andrews could respond, she added brightly: 'Look. We're not getting anywhere with the computer. I'll give the business school a ring. Mr Wang's an MBA student...' – Wang nodded enthusiastically – '... so they must have a record.'

The naivety of youth, Andrews told himself. There was as much chance of the business school – any school – keeping records as there was of the British National Party forming the next government... though, come to think of it...

'Just what I was about to say,' Andrews lied. 'Excellent. That'll sort it.'

So saying with a nod, and salvaging what he could of his battered dignity, he turned his back and stalked off.

'Excuse me, Mr Andrews,' the girl called after him, picking up a large and suspiciously heavy brown envelope from her desk. 'You've left your magazine. Sorry... papers.'

The supervisor wheeled round, ready to let fly with an oath more usually encountered in the rough next to the sixth hole, but seeing the look of sweetly-smiling innocence on the girl's face thought better of it.

'Thank you,' he hissed, snatching the envelope from an outstretched hand. Then, illogically – the refuge of the beaten boss whose contribution to productivity has been nil – 'Get on with your work.'

Liz grinned at Andrews's retreating pride. And grinned at Wang, who grinned back, though he was not sure why. She began to leaf through an internal telephone directory on her desk to look for the business school extension, when a thought struck her.

'Tell me,' she said to Wang. 'You don't by any slight chance remember the name of the admissions tutor... the person who sent you your acceptance letter...? I mean... perhaps you've spoken to this person on the phone? Or emailed...?'

A distant bell tinkled in Wang's tired memory. 'Haaar... email,' he said. 'I email... write professor... nice man.'

'Good,' said Liz. 'I don't expect you remember his

26

name?'

'Haaar...' said Wang, thinking hard. 'Long name. Queer name. Not normal name. Not... Smith.'

'Well... that helps,' said Liz, instantly regretting her rudeness, which Wang, furiously engaged on a search-and-find of memory files containing MBA, failed to notice.

'Haaar...' he triumphed, causing Liz to jump. 'Pendegrass. Professor Pendegrass. Nice man. He write me... welcome, he say, at university.'

'Thank you. That's very helpful,' Liz said, picking up the phone, and motioning in the direction of a monstrous fake-leather couch which looked as if it had escaped from Las Vegas. 'Why don't you go and sit over there while I see what I can do?'

Wang bowed his gratitude and, moving to the monstrosity, fell into its shiny embrace – where within seconds, his suitcase next to him, he was fast asleep.

Poor sod, thought Liz. Why do they do this? And she dialled the number of the business school.

5

Some two hours later Wang, with suitcase, emerged from the Cramcaster University student welcome area into a damp British late-summer afternoon. Commuters and others, heads down, umbrellas up, scurried past on their way home at the end of the working and shopping day. Wang found the scene strangely reassuring, strangely familiar: for a moment he found himself back in Beijing, watching the home-going crowds stream into the central station, though here there was something missing. Wang racked his brain, momentarily refreshed after its nap on the couch in student reception. Bicycles: that was it. Where were the bicycles? What was it Qi had said... bicycles were for cranks and trendy politicians? Wang shook his head in disbelief, and thought of Uncle Peng. No work for a cycle repair man in Cramcaster; indeed, these days, there wasn't much in China. Times were changing: the future was cars, motorcycles. It flashed across Wang's mind that perhaps, once he had got his MBA and was earning serious, Western-style money, he could set his uncle up in a small garage and help him move with the times. But his uncle was too set in his ways, too old to change. Besides, that was the future: in the meantime, there was the small matter of the present.

The welcome desk student, Liz, in conjunction with the business school, had done her best. No, the business school told her, there's no Professor Pendegrass here – but there might have been a Pendegrass, or something like it, on work-experience at some time. And no, we don't keep files on every work-experience kid who passes through the office. As for incoming MBA students; sorry, the computers are playing up, been like it for days, you know how it is; but we'll try and get hold of Dr Jamieson, the MBA admissions tutor; wait,

28

we'll come back to you.

Liz waited. Eventually, as Wang snoozed on, the business school rang back. Can't get hold of Dr Jamieson, he's working from home, always does when the cricket's on, even when it's rained off. But you're in luck because someone said there was a Pendegrass in business studies at the poly – sorry, Cram Vale – best ring there and check.

Liz thanked the business school, adding that she hoped their computer problem would soon be resolved. She then rang Cram Vale University, asked to be put through to their business school, was told it was called the school of management, and found herself speaking to the school administrator. Indeed, the administrator said, Mr Pendegrass is responsible for MBA admissions; he's currently in a meeting, but if you give me a second while I access the files... yes, here it is: Wang Ti, from China, due to arrive today.

'I'll send him over,' Liz said, and explained how Wang was obviously confused between Cramcaster University and Cram Vale University. An easy mistake, said the Cram Vale administrator, adding – a little frostily, Liz thought – that it wasn't just foreigners who got confused.

'I'll tell him to take a cab,' Liz ignored the last remark. 'If he leaves now he might just make it,' and put the phone down.

Wang, however, once on the street, had other ideas. The thought of subjecting himself for a second time that afternoon to more humiliation from bureaucrats and computers did not appeal. He was hungry, tired, and his limbs ached from excessive exposure to economy airline seating and the Cramcaster University couch. Moreover, he was still trying to unravel the fact that the city had two higher education establishments, and that Qi had pitched him from the taxi at apparently

29

the wrong one.

Haaar... Qi. Wang fished in his pocket and produced Qi's card. The words in English, while meaning little, were clearly an address. Wang gazed at the writing and wondered. Qi had been kind, had invited him to visit. The fact that the suitcase would not yet be there was irrelevant: Qi meant him to call, perhaps not so soon, but under the circumstances... anyway, what was the alternative? A hotel would be expensive and, even though Wang knew he had money enough for a night's accommodation, the spectre of Uncle Peng rose before him, chiding about extravagance and wanton Western ways.

No. It was Qi or nothing. But how to reach the address on the card? Wang had no wish to exercise his English, already sorely tried that day, on public transport. And Mr Khan's taxi, which most ungraciously – surely an ill-omen – had splashed him, did not encourage Wang to hail a cab. He would be far better walking; it would help clear his mind, and at least the suitcase, though bulky, was reasonably light. But which direction...?

Wang summoned what remained of his flagging courage. 'Excuse you,' he said, to a tall, middle-aged woman wrestling with a folding umbrella, who had just come out of the building he had left a few moments before, and he waved Qi's card under her nose. 'You tell me please where I go.'

The woman paused, looked at Wang, looked at the card, and frowned. 'Compton Park,' she read. 'Hmm. You need a bus. You need the interchange...'

'No bus,' said Wang. 'No bus. Walk.'

The woman frowned again. 'It's a long way,' she said, doubtfully, surveying Wang and his suitcase. 'How about a taxi?'

'No bus. No taxi. Walk,' repeated Wang.

30

The rain began to fall, heavier than before. There was no point in prolonging the discussion if the young man was determined. 'That way,' she said, indicating the direction Qi's taxi had turned. 'Along there. You come to a main road. And then you just... sort of... keep going. More or less a straight line. But it's a long way. A very long way,' she cautioned.

'You very kind,' said Wang. 'Very kind. Thank you.'

He turned to go. But not before the woman had thrust her umbrella, still not fully open, into Wang's free hand. 'Here. Take it,' she said. 'You might need it.'

'Haaar...' gurgled Wang, in surprise.

The woman smiled briefly and, turning, strode off into the rain. That poor boy, lost in a strange city, was someone's son. And her own, on a gap year, now in Argentina – or was it Chile?

'Haaar...' said Wang and, practised as he was, deftly flicked the umbrella open above his head. It was good to hear the rain bouncing off the black fabric, just like it did at home.

Across the street, the lights of Anne Hathaway's McDonald's reminded Wang he was hungry. But no. He told himself he would not eat. Not yet. A long road lay ahead of him. His own, very own, long march.

6

'So,' Brush said, 'and what's your view?'

Pendegrass blinked. The professor was staring at him, in apparent expectation of a response. Apart from the fact that Pendegrass was yawningly conscious of his lack of afternoon nap, and that he hadn't taken in a word of what his head of school had been saying, he had, at that moment, no particular view at all. Except, it occurred to him, the view across the Cram Vale University playing fields. The view from the window of Brush's professorial suite on the ninth floor of Wole Soyinka was far more impressive than from his own modest office a floor below; besides, Pendegrass's window faced inwards, towards the campus, contemplating not fields but the architectural pick-n-mix of the average British university. Pendegrass thought he might venture a joke to the effect that he had rather a pleasant view, but immediately thought better of it. Professor Brush was not noted for humour. Nor, indeed, Pendegrass for wit.

He blinked again. 'I suppose,' he said warily, 'it all depends.'

'Just so,' said Brush, relieved the buffoon appeared to be with him. That was the thing with Dozy Pendegrass. You never knew. The fool was always half asleep... tried to blame the university, the electronics department, the experiments in magnetic levitation in the basement of Wole Soyinka. Sick building syndrome, Pendegrass said. Bunkum. The only one afflicted was Dozy... though, come to think of it, the handful of students Brush encountered during the academic year all seemed pretty lethargic, despite the fact that most of them ended up with firsts. Brush frowned, and ploughed on.

'Of course... you understand it would help the

32

school's finances enormously. I mean... point-two of a salary might not seem a great deal, but when faced with the shortfall, you'll appreciate it's not insignificant.'

'No, no... exactly,' Pendegrass agreed. Then, picking up on shortfall, added, 'Of course... postgrad admissions are holding up well, all things being equal.'

It was the professor's turn to blink. 'I'm not really bothered...' he began.

'We'll meet targets,' Pendegrass continued. 'No problem. All the same... quality. That's different. I mean... the Chinese students. Nice people, hard-working... but generally incapable of putting together a coherent English sentence...'

'Sod English,' Brush said, irritated. 'And be grateful for the Chinese. Bums on seats, that's what counts... overseas bums with overseas fees. But back to what I was saying...'

'Ah,' said Pendegrass. 'Of course.'

'It's the VC's wheeze... not mine. But I support it wholeheartedly. And, as I say, point-two of your salary would come from central funding, not from the school, which helps our finances. And you wouldn't actually have to do a great deal...'

'I wouldn't...?' enquired Pendegrass hopefully.

'Hardly. I mean... I suppose... some sort of introduction. The VC's PA would provide all the details. All you have to do is put it together and deliver it.'

'Deliver it...?' asked Pendegrass, wondering if he was about to be pensioned off to the Royal Mail.

'That's right,' Brush interrupted. 'Just a couple of minutes. Of course, we'd have to vet it beforehand. Not that we don't trust you...' Brush cackled insincerely.

'Of course not,' said Pendegrass, still puzzling over the part allotted him in the professorial drama about to unfold.

'I think it's rather good. Adds dignity. Sometimes I don't think we make enough of graduation. The ceremony... the tradition... goes down well with punters. Leaves a good impression, encourages them to sign up to the alumni appeal.'

Pendegrass raked an overgrown patch of grammar-school Latin, and wondered if alumni should be alumnus. Lynne Truss, she of grammatical certainties, she who urged felt-tip war on self-important capitals and grocers' apostrophes, would surely know. Alumni suggested plural, but surely the appeal was made to an individual. And what was an alumnus, anyway? It sounded like something in the garden. In addition, he had no recollection of Caesar crossing the Alps with cohorts of alumni or abandoning them in winter quarters to shelter from ablative absolutes, deponent verbs, or other linguistic barbarians that invaded Latin textbooks. Yet another of life's conundrums, Pendegrass thought. Or should that be conundra? Oh, Lynne, guide me, counsel me...

'Well...?' said Brush, jerking the erstwhile Latinist back to the present. 'A decision now... or next year?'

'Hold on. I don't quite see how graduation fits in...'

Brush rolled his eyes heavenward. He was wrong; the clot clearly hadn't taken in a single word.

'Look,' he growled. 'Graduation. The university orator welcomes the...'

'Orator...? You mean... talking?'

It was on the tip of Brush's tongue to say, no, it was serving drinks at the degree ceremony reception, but thought better of it, since the idiot would doubtless believe him. And, he seemed to recall, the man was teetotal.

Pendegrass opened his mouth as if to speak, but promptly shut it again. A goldfish, Brush thought, and about as much use. In fact, running a university

34

department was like keeping fish: constantly flinging academic ant eggs at staff, trying to keep them happy, and hoping they'd eat the eggs and not him. The difficulty was getting them to bite, like the Dozy Fish now, gaping at him across the table.

'It's quite straightforward,' Brush said, possessed of only the vaguest idea what the vice chancellor had in mind. 'All you do is... er... a sort of warm-up speech. About the university. Then introduce the principal guest...'

'I'm not used to talking in front of hundreds of people. Bigwigs. Parents. Anyway... I've enough on my plate with postgrad admissions.'

Brush ignored the last point. 'Marvellous opportunity. Think about it. You could introduce the Earl of Cramcaster... great patron of this university, gives a lot of time and money...'

Something clicked in Pendegrass. 'Hold on. You want me to stand up, in front of all those people, and sing the praises of...'

'Absolutely,' said Brush, pleased that at long last the oaf had cottoned on. At this rate he might yet get that point-two of a salary paid from central, rather than school, funds; this would give him another couple of grand to play with, which meant he could order the new office carpet and the executive desk. Also...

Something was happening to Pendegrass. The man had stood up and, for a creature noted for lassitude, was displaying unaccustomed animation. Moreover, he was talking: rapidly, excitedly, slightly incoherently.

'The Earl of Cramcaster...' he croaked, 'one of our richest landowners... owns half the town...'

'I won't deny he isn't well off. So what? He's been very generous to the university...'

'Half the county... all that farmland out towards the coast... that's all his.'

35

'Half the county's a bit of an exaggeration. And I don't see...'

'That's just it,' Pendegrass was hopping from foot to foot. 'I couldn't. Not him. I mean... I won't.'

For the second time that afternoon, Brush blinked at Pendegrass.

'The Nazareth and Ewesbottom Repentant Sinners...'

'The what...?' Brush shrank back in his chair.

'The ancestors of the Earl of Cramcaster exploited our founding fathers, charging exorbitant sums to erect our humble places of worship on Cramcaster lands. And the rent... rising fivefold, tenfold, year after year. Is it not writ in the scriptures that charity...'

'Oh my God,' Brush groaned.

'No need to blaspheme. But what I'm saying... the Earl's ancestors were crooks, and the Earl himself.... born with a silver spoon in his mouth... is no better. That's a terrible role model for our students. There's no way...'

Brush shut his eyes, and his ears, and allowed the tirade to play itself out. Ten minutes later he was alone in his office. He had never seen Dozy Pendegrass so excited, so enthusiastic, so... awake. The professor put it down it to the male menopause. Either that, or the religion Pendegrass espoused. Religion did strange things to people.

Brush picked up the phone on his desk. 'No calls, please,' he told Michelle, his secretary. 'Research. Vital I'm not disturbed.' Then, prodding testily at his computer keyboard, he was relieved to see his saved game of spider solitaire, interrupted by Pendegrass's arrival, unfurl across the screen.

Excellent, he grunted happily, a professorial pig with electronic truffles, and, after a moment's deliberation, settled into his fourteenth game since

36

lunch by carefully placing the queen of hearts onto the king. The afternoon, he told himself, was not entirely lost.

Meanwhile, back in the familiarity of his own office, Dozy Pendegrass was asleep – exhausted, as members of the school of management would put it, from a brush with Brush – or, in Pendegrass's case, from his uncharacteristically spirited attack on a university benefactor. In this he had surprised himself with his passion and eloquence, to the extent that a period of calm and contemplation, as befits a leading member of the Nazareth and Ewesbottom Repentant Sinners, was required. Nevertheless, Pendegrass reflected, before drifting away to dream of earls suspended by magnetic levitation over serried gowns of graduating students and suitably suited parents, perhaps on the basis of today's performance he wouldn't have made such a bad orator after all.

7

Wang's very own long march was proving longer than expected. The instructions from the umbrella lady to follow the main road and then 'sort of' keep going, proved more 'sort of' than going. Indeed, much of the going seemed to be coming and, in particular, coming back. The roundabouts were to blame: though smaller than in Beijing, they seemed to have more exits, and to split what might have been a straight road into several separate and confusing ways. They reminded Wang of the spokes of a bicycle wheel, and he thought of Uncle Peng. For a moment he wished himself back in China, even in his uncle's remote and backward village. Its hardships, its tedium, seemed suddenly paradisiacal compared with the dreary, litter-strewn unfamiliarity which now enveloped him.

Choking back tears – not tears, Wang told himself crossly, but drops of rain gusting beneath the umbrella – he forced himself to focus on finding Qi's house. Here he would be greeted with food and shelter and, even more welcome, a friendly voice and sympathetic ear. He could gather his strength to venture forth the following day and present himself at the correct university to meet his tutor, the estimable Professor Pendegrass. No doubt the professor would be worried. Perhaps even offended. In China, failure to attend an important appointment would be construed as impolite, an insult. Indeed, because of this slight to a professor of rank and repute, the university place might have been withdrawn, reallocated. Surely not: then the dream would cease, a nightmare begin. Wang shuddered, and clutched his case tighter to him.

Compton Park. It had to be here somewhere. He looked for a sign, some indication as to direction or distance, but none was apparent. Indeed, had he not seen it written down, or did not possess a card on which was printed, clearly and boldly, Compton Park, he might have believed the place unreal, as unreal as Alice in Wonderland which one of his British Council teachers – a Lewis Carroll fan – had encouraged them to read. 'Good preparation for England,' the man had told them. 'Probably, apart from Monty Python, the best.' Wang couldn't recall pythons in Alice in Wonderland but remembered thinking Britain must have enormous rabbits. After all, if a young girl could go down a rabbit hole... yet none of the cultural briefings he had received before coming to England ever mentioned outsize rabbits. As it happened, a rabbit hole at this moment would be most welcome. It would offer refuge from the incessant drizzle and be drier than the pavement where passing cars splashed him from Cramcaster's puddle-pitted roads. Furthermore, on the Alice principle, it might lead directly to Qi's house.

All the same, despite the invisibility of Compton Park, Wang felt he was learning. Learning by example, and by application of that example: the very reason, he reminded himself, he had come to England. So it was that, trudging past a parade of shops, and following the example of Qi's taxi-driver on the journey from the airport, he spat – with mucus and venom – at an Indian restaurant. Wang was congratulating himself on his successful observance of an important English custom, and was readjusting his mouth after its unexpected expectoration, when two darkly-hooded creatures stepped out of the rain and murk and barred his way.

Clearly, judging by the uniform – black top, hood over face – and by the demeanour – hands in pockets, no doubt clutching a weapon, and slouching, with easy indifference – the pair were police officers, who could be relied on to direct Wang as speedily as possible to Compton Park.

'Haaar...' began Wang.

'Why you insult restaurant?' said one of the officers.

'Bay of Bengal... very fine,' the other put in.

'We see you,' the first continued. 'Disrespect. Big time. You now say sorry, or else...' and a mouth, filtering flavours foreign to Wang, caused him to recoil.

'Haaar... Compton Park, please you,' Wang said. 'This way... right way?'

'Say sorry,' the second policeman said. 'Our uncle... run good restaurant. Win award. You spit... unclean. Unhealthy. Not good for trade.'

'Haaar,' said Wang, at last recognising a word he knew. 'Uncle... my uncle... bicycle man. Good man...'

The single punch to the mouth laid Wang out flat. Somehow he managed to keep hold of his case which, in the split second when he realised he was about to receive a face-full of fist, began to rise, like a shield, to protect its owner. Too late. Knuckles, hard and bony, smashed into an upper lip, spattering skin and blood, and rattling an incisor to its foundations.

'Haaar,' Wang groaned, writhing on the pavement as a boot thudded into his thigh, while the case took the brunt of another blow. Beatings... police beatings were to be expected, a fact of life; but so soon after arrival in the land of the British Council, Shakespeare and Her Majesty the Queen? Uncle Peng told how he had once been beaten, in the bad old days, for alleged infringement of his street trader permit. A bribe, apparently, had spoken louder than any protestation, and settled the matter immediately. So, if Wang could just open the case...

Then... a siren, flashing blue light, car engine. A hurried voice, to Wang: 'Honour satisfied. No hard feelings. Bay of Bengal... good. You come. Most welcome'; then footsteps running, fading; car doors; another voice, deeper, almost a growl, and a fatuous,

40

regulation: 'You alright, matey?'

Wang was not alright. The left side of his mouth was raw and bleeding and, as his tongue explored the damage, he felt a front tooth wobble.

'Bugger's been beaten up,' another voice said, again stating the obvious. 'We'd better...'

'Yeah, yeah,' rasped the first voice. 'You do that.'

Wang, still clutching his case, began to stir, in an attempt to get up.

'You stay put,' the gravely voice said, pushing Wang back onto the cold, wet pavement. 'Until the paramedics get here and we know what the damage is.'

But Wang had begun to writhe and wriggle. The dampness seeping through skimpy trousers into an equally skimpy backside was more uncomfortable than the throbbing emanating from his mouth.

'Haaar,' Wang said. 'I pay.'

'You what?' said PC 6239 Chester, known to colleagues on account of his voice as Gruff, and easing his hold on Wang. 'You play?'

'Lots. Very happy... make you happy. I show.'

Gruff frowned. It was obvious this foreigner chappie was trying to tell him something. He trawled his brain to recall if Cramcaster United had signed any players from Asia. The fellow didn't look like a footballer, didn't have the build; on the other hand perhaps he was fast, a master of the swift pass, moving the ball upfield. Best be careful. The fact that the fellow seemed to want to give some sort of demonstration, as well as his increasingly desperate pavement gyrations, suggested, even to the policeman's procedural mind, that apart from the obvious injury to the mouth there was probably nothing substantially wrong: no broken bones, no blocked airways, no obvious damage to other parts of the body. Gruff extended a hand and helped Wang to his feet, pointing him in the direction of the waiting

41

police car.

'No car,' said Wang, starting to fiddle with the case to which, it occurred to the officer, he seemed to be attached. 'No. No car. I pay. I pay good.'

'Ah... I'm getting the message,' said Gruff, beginning to be impressed and adding, as a precaution, a deferential 'sir'. 'It's an expensive vehicle, and...'

'I pay. Good money. But no car.'

'Good money... you can say that again,' said Gruff, becoming more and more certain of his ground. 'Very good money. I mean... you premier league people make more in a week than us lot in a lifetime. Mind you, I'm not saying you don't deserve it. And the flash cars. Not at all, sir. I mean... the skill. And all that training. Isn't that right, Den?'

PC Denzil Dutton, collar number 6957, having radioed for paramedics, had stepped from the police car to rejoin his colleague.

'Quite a celebrity we have here,' said Gruff, who prided himself on his detection skills and harboured ambitions of a career in CID. 'One of United's finest. The gentleman's been telling me about all the big money he makes. And,' he added with a flourish, to impress Dutton, 'it transpires he's had his vehicle nicked.'

'Oh,' said Dutton, who was not the least interested in football, but who restored Morris Minors as a hobby and was into cars. 'What? Porsche? Ferrari?'

'Haven't quite got round to details yet, have we, sir?' said Gruff, addressing both Dutton and Wang. 'The gentleman's still in a bit of a state of shock. But if we can sit him comfortably in the car...'

'No car,' said Wang, starting to move off in the opposite direction. 'Compton Park. Go.'

'Your vehicle was stolen from Compton Park?' Dutton began, taking out his notebook.

42

'Compton Park. Compton Park,' Wang said gratefully, rejoicing in the familiar words.

'It's very damp out here, sir,' Gruff said. 'If you'd just step inside the car, while we wait for the paramedics, we can sort this out in a jiffy.' And, taking Wang by the arm, he began to lead him to the car.

Wang, though, convinced that jiffy was slang for car, was having none of it. Keeping a tight grip on his case, he shook himself free from the officer and began to trot in the direction he had been going before his way was barred outside the Bay of Bengal.

'Hey up,' said Dutton, exercising highly-trained police powers of observation. 'He's doing a runner.'

'It's that smack on the face,' said Gruff, lumbering after the fleeing Wang. 'Poor sod. It's affected him. Big style.'

Gruff, owing to a regular diet of canteen pudding, chips and mushy peas, was no athlete, but his burly figure caught the fugitive after a couple of paces. Wang – unfed, exhausted, burdened with a bulky suitcase, and with a face pulsing and pounding like a disco dance-floor – felt the sweaty palm of the law on his collar, and realised flight was useless.

'I pay. Big pay,' he groaned, as Dutton and Gruff forced him into the back of the car and slammed the door.

The two policemen were still trying to extract Wang's name and details of the stolen vehicle when, a few minutes later, the paramedics arrived.

'Hello,' said a green-clad being, which reminded Wang of a cucumber, as it opened the door of the police car. 'I'm Vikki. What's your name?'

'Haaar…'

'Harry,' said the vegetable. 'That's lovely. Now… if I can just take a look… oh, dear… that's a bit nasty.'

'Harry's a footballer,' Gruff told Vikki. 'United.

43

Probably not the first team, but…'

'A footballer,' said Vikki, dabbing at the wound to stop the bleeding. 'Well… you've probably been in worse scrapes on the field.'

'Money,' said Wang, unaccustomed to being addressed by a vegetable. 'Money. Money…'

'Many scrapes. I thought so,' said Vikki, whose colleague was shining a light into Wang's eyes, which made him wince. He felt the beam bore into his pupils, then beyond, past pain and weariness, into his brain, where it diffracted in a starburst of clarity. It was obvious: first the police beating, then torture… torture at the hands of shadowy state operatives who would extract, along with his teeth and fingernails, whatever secrets they sought. But Wang had no secrets. He knew nothing, possessed nothing, apart from a degree in Business Studies from the Guang Hua School of Management at the University of Beijing and a Cambridge proficiency certificate in English, of which he was particularly proud. Beyond these sterling achievements, Wang was ordinary. Surely no-one could be intent on beating or torturing the nephew of a humble bicycle-repairer…? But perhaps that was it. Yes. Qi had said at the airport that bikes in England were for kids or cranks. These people thought him a crank, a lunatic. They had found Uncle Peng's universal bicycle repair tool in the other case and had come to hunt him down as… as what? A deranged subversive. A bicycle-riding menace to society, whom… yes… they would brand as insane, and then torture until he recanted. And agreed to drive a van… a white van: that's what Qi had said. Oh, Qi was so right: this place was indeed crazy-land. But Qi would know what do to… Qi… and suddenly salvation loomed large in Wang's jaded mind, as a familiar word penetrated his mind.

'Hospital. We'll get you to the hospital, Harry,' the vegetable was saying. 'Just to get you checked over.'

Wang knew about hospitals. For a start, he recognised the word, which had featured – ominously – in the mandatory survival English course taken before coming to Britain. More importantly, however, he knew hospitals were run by the state and secret police as an adjunct to the prison system, where dissidents were branded as lunatics and incarcerated 'for their own protection', and drugged, tortured and generally abused in a way that made that American prison whose name he couldn't remember look like a seaside holiday resort – which George Bush probably thought it was.

'No hospital,' Wang insisted, squirming on the back seat of the police car, as he began to fish inside his blood-spattered jacket. 'No hospital... no.'

'What's he doing?' said Dutton, who had never entirely swallowed the footballer story, and thought Wang might be reaching for a weapon.

'Haaar,' said Wang, triumphantly, pulling out his wallet and brandishing it at the officers, before removing a business card, which he handed to Gruff.

'Qi Liang,' Wang said. 'He good man. He know.'

'You really ought to be checked over at the hospital, Harry,' Vikki was saying. 'It's just a precaution...'

'It says his name's Qi Liang,' Gruff pronounced the words slowly, and with difficulty, making the first name sound as if it were 'queer'. 'Lives up on Compton Park...'

'We know that already,' Dutton sneered. 'He said so.'

'Didn't know any footballers lived on Compton Park,' Gruff said. 'I thought they all lived in the stockbroker belt...'

'I thought he was Harry,' Vikki said, hurt that her first-name familiarity seemed to have misfired. 'But I'd

45

still like to get him to hospital...'

'No hospital. Compton Park,' Wang said. 'Please you.'

Vikki sighed. A trip to the hospital with Harry, or Queer, or whatever he was called, would be useful. A cup of fresh tea in the cafeteria would slip down nicely, especially on a damp night like this. But no-one could be forced to attend casualty: the wishes of the patient were paramount.

'Okay,' she sighed. 'But I think it's a mistake.' She stood up and walked over to her car, where her colleague handed her leaflets and other papers. She took them back to Wang.

'Read these,' she said, thrusting them at him. 'They might come in useful. If you get any additional pain... if this mess round your mouth doesn't start healing up... then that's where you go. The hospital. And there's a map.'

'Haaar,' gurgled Wang appreciatively, sensing that a trip to the internment centre, in its guise as a hospital, was now optional, rather than inevitable. It all seemed too easy. In China there would have been no choice. He would have been hauled away and perhaps, many months, many bribes later, released: flotsam on the foreshore of new democracy. He shuddered, and reached out to make sure his case was still on the seat beside him. Clearly, the name of Qi had exercised some sort of magic, some sort of mystical power which caused all to yield before it. At the airport it was obvious Qi was no ordinary person but, if proof were needed, proof beyond all doubt had now been delivered. But who exactly...?

Wang became aware things were happening around him, that the cucumber – or was it an unripe banana? – and its light-shining assistant were backing off, humbled, defeated.

46

'Okay, boys,' Vikki was saying to the two policemen. 'I've done my bit. He's all yours. And best of luck.' With that, she turned her back – abruptly, it seemed to the watching policemen – on Wang and stalked to her car. She got in, slammed the door, and the vehicle drove off at speed.

'What now?' Dutton said.

'Well,' said Gruff. 'It's not everyday we have the company of a premier league star. I think… I mean, it's only ten minutes or so… we might perhaps…'

'Yeah, okay,' Dutton said. 'See Mr Queer safely home. Though I'm still bothered about this stolen vehicle…'

'Forget it,' Gruff said. 'At least for now. Poor bugger can hardly string a sentence together. After what he's been through.'

Gruff turned to Wang on the back seat of the police car. But Wang, for the second time that day, had opted out of proceedings and, cradling his case, was already fast asleep.

8

Dusk, aided and abetted by storm-clouds stealing across the skies, was already falling when the police car drew up at the address in Compton Park printed on Wang's card. The house, or rather, mansion, was in darkness, and for a moment Gruff thought they were mistaken.

'Doesn't look much like a footballer's house. Thought they went for something more modern... more flashy.'

'Looks okay to me,' Dutton said. 'I mean... look at all that security.'

It was true. The building, a Victorian villa which had probably been built for a mill- or colliery-owner, was surrounded by a brick wall topped by metal fencing. Behind double gates – which, thought Dutton, would not be out of place at a prison, or a palace – a sweeping gravel drive led to a porticoed front door, and beyond. The drive disappeared round the side of the building, where the front of a transit van, or minibus, could be made out.

'Bet there's CCTV,' said Dutton, pondering what a pile like that would cost, and wondering if there were former stables round the back which could be converted into workshops for repairing Morris Minors.

Gruff turned to the dormant Wang on the back seat of the police car. 'Wakey wakey,' he bellowed, jabbing at Wang with his fist. 'Home sweet home.'

Wang grunted, giving little indication of either wakefulness or sweetness.

'Help him out of the car,' said Dutton. 'Poor bugger's obviously had it.'

Together the two policemen hauled Wang, still attached to his case, onto the pavement, where they stood him up, dusted him down, and steered him towards a keypad set into the brickwork by the front gates.

'Right, matey,' said Gruff. 'Over to you.'

Wang blinked at him, blinked at the keypad, and blinked at the enormous house behind. If this was where Qi lived... why, Wang's first impressions had been correct. Qi was obviously a high-ranking party official, at least a secretary, responsible for hundreds, if not thousands, of party members and workers...

Wang was aware of alien tones obtruding on his thoughts.

'Look sharp,' Dutton was saying. 'Don't want to catch our deaths out here.' Wang turned to his erstwhile captors, now liberators, and blinked again. 'The code,' Dutton said, pointing at the keypad. 'Then you're in. And we can be getting along.'

Wang turned to the keypad. It appeared to have escaped from a computer, or an oversize mobile phone; there were buttons on it, presumably to be pressed. Perhaps it was an electronic dictionary – how thoughtful to place a dictionary, like a phone box, on the street, for passing foreigners, what a wondrous idea – but the characters on the buttons were not Chinese, and there was no monitor, so how could the translation be spelled out? In addition...

'Poor sod's forgotten the code,' said Gruff. 'It's that knock on the head. Left him queer.'

'It would,' said Dutton. 'That's his name.'

'Here,' said Gruff, elbowing Wang to one side. 'Let me. I mean... if there's anyone in...'

'Bound to have staff,' Dutton said. 'A place that size. A butler, at least.'

'A woman, more like,' Gruff said, pressing the button marked 'attention'. 'They all have them, these footballers. It's WAGS. W... A... G... S... women and good sex.'

49

'I think it stands for...' Dutton began, when the intercom crackled into action. A stream of sibilant syllable assailed Gruff's ears.

'Bloody hell,' he said, stepping back. 'What's that?'

'Haaar,' said Wang, who recognised the dulcet tones of home enquiring merely who was without. 'I speak...'

Gruff, having recovered himself, was having none of it. 'This is the police...' he snarled back into the intercom, which clattered cacophonously before falling suddenly silent. At the same time security lights flicked on, painting house and grounds in a polar whitewash lacking only sleds, sleighs and Santas.

Wang had caught the anxious words in Mandarin 'It's the police,' and, given his own experience with the authorities in Britain – a beating, attempted institutionalisation in an asylum, and possible kidnap in a police car – he sympathised: the voice was right to be anxious.

Meanwhile Gruff was stabbing a fleshy finger at the keypad as if rapping a report on an ancient Imperial. At the same time he was lambasting the intercom, telling it – and most of Compton Park – in stentorian tones that the police were outside, having brought Mr Queer home; that Mr Queer, having been involved in a serious incident, needed entry at once; that Mr Queer's injuries were such that the club coach, the physio, and very possibly the manager, should be informed; and that Mr Queer was greatly distressed because his vehicle had been taken. At this point, Dutton nudged him.

'Hey up,' he said, pointing to the house. 'Something's going on.'

Something was indeed going on. The front door had opened, only to close again from the inside, after emitting a suit – too flimsy for the time of year – buttoned around a middle-aged man of Chinese origin.

The suit looked towards the group at the gate, glanced at the sky and, clicking open an umbrella, began crunching across the gravel towards them. In the brilliance of the security lights the rain flickered like sparklers from the black umbrella, and hope illuminated Wang's gloom.

'Ni hao,' said Wang, as the suit reached the gate. 'Hello.'

The suit shot a disdainful look at Wang whose optimism, having fizzled in, fizzled out like an off-centre Catherine wheel.

Gruff, pleased to have a person to harangue rather than an intercom, launched into his inventory, now well-rehearsed, of incidents, entry codes, football managers and missing vehicles. Dutton, not to be outdone, enquired about the make of vehicle and the registration, adding that without this information the aforementioned conveyance, taken without authority contrary to section 12 of the Theft Act 1968, would not be recoverable, and we wouldn't want Mr Queer to be deprived of his motor, now would we, sir?

What sir might or might not have wanted, however, remained as opaque as standing orders at a police conference. The only indication that sir was human, and not robotic, was a frown that rumpled an otherwise expressionless countenance. At that moment it seemed to Wang, observing the scene with mounting despair, that time once more was stopped; it was an irrelevancy, replaced by primeval, protoplasmic silence, pricked only by the patter of raindrops on the black arch of the umbrella.

And then...it was too much for Wang. Something snapped inside him; deference and humility, willingly offered with passport and visa the moment he set foot in the paradise the British Council had promised, fragmented in fear and frustration. With a roar he

51

charged at the gate, thrust his arms through the bars, and poured out his tale to his countryman. He spoke of police brutality, the mental asylum, the warder who shone lights in his eyes; told of the suspect universal repair tool and of Uncle Peng; recited the calamity of the missing papers and the university that would not accept him, despite his Beijing degree and the Cambridge proficiency certificate; and described how, at the airport, Qi had taken him under his wing, and...

At the mention of Qi the suit, or robot, or humanoid – whatever it was – jerked into life. Raising a brisk hand to staunch Wang's volubility, it reached into its pocket and produced a phone. Then, punching the instrument with its thumb, it turned away, so the ensuing conversation, brief but animated, was indistinguishable. Snapping the phone shut, it turned back again, and went to the wall, disappearing from view. A moment later the gates swung open and an invisible voice, in Mandarin, called: 'Enter.'

Wang needed no second bidding. He was through the gates like a coursed hare, leaving the two hounds who had harried him thus far open-mouthed. As the gates slid shut behind Wang, the voice emerged.

'Thank you,' it intoned, addressing the policemen. 'All well. Goodnight.'

'Just a moment,' said Dutton. 'What about this missing vehicle?'

A brow briefly wrinkled. An expression, which in humanoid circles might pass as a smile, flitted over a face. 'Thank you. All well,' the voice insisted, in a tone which suggested further attempts at communication would be as fruitful as procreation with a eunuch. And, sweeping Wang under the cupola of the umbrella, the Chinaman led him across the gravel to the front door which, as the pair approached, opened expectantly. As soon as they disappeared inside the house and the door shut, the security lights went out; and the evening, forced cruelly into the shadows by the harsh brilliance, heaved a sigh of relief into a passing breeze, and resumed its crepuscular advance.

'Bugger me,' said Gruff.

'I'm not happy about that stolen vehicle,' said Dutton.

'No rush,' said Gruff. 'He can report it tomorrow. Anyway... he's more important things to worry about. He needs to get himself sorted if he's going to be match fit.'

'There's something not right about this...' Dutton began, moving towards the car and tugging open the driver's door.

'You're telling me,' said Gruff. 'All that messing around and we never got the bugger's autograph. But we've not lost the chance. I mean... he owes us.'

9

About the time Wang was deposited at the mansion in Compton Park, a car pulled up outside a restaurant in suburban Cramcaster. A professorial figure released itself from the vehicle and strode across a damply glistening pavement which, some half-hour before, had hosted briefly Wang's recumbent form. The figure entered the Bay of Bengal.

'Ah, Mr Professor, sir,' a voice greeted the arrival. 'Please...'

'Uncle indisposed, sir,' another voice said. 'But we serve our distinguished guest...'

'Most distinguished guest, Mr Professor, sir...'

'The usual,' Brush said, easing himself into his customary seat. And added, with a satisfied smirk, 'Just me. Mrs Brush will not be dining this evening.'

Indeed not. Councillor Mrs Rosalind Brush, chair of the neighbourhood regeneration review and scrutiny committee of Cramcaster City Council, was engaged on council business. At least, Brush assumed she was. That's what she had said, not that Brush paid much attention. If it wasn't the council, it was something else. A school-governorship, Townswomen's Guild, fund-raising for the Schizophrenic Animal Dispensary or the Campaign for the Reduction of Antisocial Practices. The woman was never at home – or, if she was, she was invariably about to leave. Brush wondered why she didn't up sticks entirely and set up residence under a committee table. Then she could pop up at the appropriate moment, sign some minutes, move an agenda item and raise a point of order, and finally slip back below the table to the nether regions of any other business. Perhaps, he sometimes thought, all this was a charade. Perhaps there was no Schizophrenic Animal Dispensary, no Campaign for the Reduction of

54

Antisocial Practices, still less any committee or sub-committee to service these phantom organisations. Perhaps Mrs Brush had a lover: that might explain why she claimed exhaustion when finally she arrived home, rarely before the hour when regional television news emitted its final hurrah of sport and weather. A secret love life might also account for the fact that sexual intimacy between the professor and his wife was as frequent as pack-ice at the equator. These days, the only spice in Brush's life came on a plate in the Bay of Bengal. Not that Brush was bothered: if his wife had a lover, several lovers, a council cabinet of lovers, that was fine. It got her off his back, allowed him to pursue his own interests, his own ambitions and, in particular, his academic research.

Perhaps, as Brush admitted in his more despairing moments, the term 'academic' was stretching things. After all, research into spider solitaire could hardly be considered intellectual. Or could it? People undertook research on all sorts of themes. The significance of the lute in mediaeval love-making; the development of the toothbrush; the musicality of insects, with special reference to bees. Besides, the patterns Brush believed he could detect in spider solitaire involved mathematics of the higher kind. That Brush was not strictly a mathematician was neither here nor there: he knew enough about statistics and algorithms and probability to plot the seemingly random sequences in which the cards fell, and to note in these a certain logic.

If he could get to the bottom of this, if he could crack whatever code governed the mysteries of spider solitaire, then he could write the definitive handbook on the game. The Secrets of Spider Solitaire, if published in time for Christmas, could well prove a nice little earner. That would make Councillor Mrs Rosalind Brush sit up. A published author – not just of the occasional scholarly article, but a Christmas best-seller. Why, he could probably retire on the proceeds, would never have to keep angling for that deanship that always evaded him, and never have to put up with the idle halfwits it was his misfortune to work with.

Like Dozy Pendegrass. A dead loss: if not a dead loss, then certainly a dormant one. The man's ability to nod off was legendary: he fell asleep not only in meetings but also, it was rumoured, while lecturing. Brush felt that was something of an urban myth – surely the fellow would fall over and wake up? On the other hand, knowing Pendegrass, probably not. The only thing with which the fool could be entrusted safely was postgraduate admissions. This required minimal effort, since the MBA programme at Cram Vale was invariably over-subscribed, generally by mildly impecunious foreign students unable to afford more prestigious institutions such as Cramcaster University, but desperate for some reason for a British degree. All this was fine, but their enthusiasm for learning was invariably in inverse proportion to their quaint and idiosyncratic English. Not their fault, but Pendegrass had a point: their grasp of language...

'A beer for Mr Professor, sir,' a voice broke in. 'Compliments of the Bay of Bengal. Uncle sadly indisposed... delay in kitchen. But rest most assuredly, Mr Professor, sir, we do everything that is needful to bring food to table most swiftly.'

There was a place, Brush thought, for quaint and idiosyncratic English. The Bay of Bengal was one of them. Whether the postgraduate school of a British university was another was debatable. On the other hand, it was quaint and idiosyncratic English, or rather the users, that kept the whole place financially afloat. Without overseas fees...

'Fine,' Brush said. 'Always worth waiting. You do

56

the best you can.'

The best you can. With an absentee wife, nitwits like Pendegrass, and teaching rooms stuffed with foreign students barely able to communicate, that was all one could hope for.

Brush sighed, sipped his beer, and dreamed of the time when he would be rich and famous thanks to The Secrets of Spider Solitaire.

10

They were leaving. Yet they told him to stay. It isn't time, they said. It isn't time. But it had to be. If they were leaving the plane then, surely, it had to be time? Except... the plane was still flying. At least, it was bouncing around. And something was pushing him down. A hand. Gentle, but firm. A steward. Flight attendant. Whatever. Perhaps it was emergency procedures. In the unlikely event of landing on water... but he wasn't on water. And the voices kept saying: It isn't time. But what time was it? If it was dark here then it would be light in Beijing, because Chinese time is ahead. Or behind. One of the two. So if it was six here then it would be... would be... if he could look at his watch he could work it out. His watch was on his wrist, but they told him not to worry – it was early, he should sleep, they'd all soon be gone and it would be quiet. But it wasn't quiet. They were milling round trying to get their cases, which were missing. In his case was... he couldn't remember. But it was important. Very important. He needed whatever was in it to get the case back. Without it, no case. But if the case was missing, so was the... the pen, that's what it was. The pen to write the address where the case should be sent. A special pen, because Qi had given it him... but where was Qi? He'd left the plane, too, bailed out, and... that's right... they were floating, drifting, all of them, downwards, towards Anne Hathaway's cottage, where someone was serving fries. It was the man from the British Council, grinning from ear to ear, dressed like Ronald McDonald. Welcome to Crazyland, he was saying. Welcome to Crazyland...

**

58

Wang woke with a pressing need to empty his bladder. He sat up, and immediately smashed his head on something hard. The sky had fallen in: it was the end of the world, he was dead, would never again see Uncle Peng or split with him a cooling beer. But... skies don't fall in. Wang cursed his stupidity and peered into the gloom. He was in a room; heavy curtains blocked the light, but he could make out beds. He forced his eyes to focus. Bunk beds. A room full of bunk beds. He was near the floor, in a lower bunk, which accounted for the crack to his head. The room was some sort of dormitory. Perhaps... a school. But why? Then he remembered. Uniforms, a journey in a police car, security, a gatehouse. That's what it was. A prison. He'd arrived in Britain, the police had picked him up, he'd been thrown in jail. And yet...

He needed desperately to relieve himself. From his recumbent position he flung back the bed-cover and swung his legs outwards and downwards until his feet found floor. The surface was cold, hard, and his toes twitched upwards, signalling desperately for readmission to the still-warm bed. The signals emanating from his bladder, however, demanded a more urgent response.

Wang staggered to his feet, trying to ignore the chill invading from below and the throbbing occupying his forehead. The room, he rapidly discovered, was lavatorially challenged: no toilet, no urinal, not even a wash-basin that might, in extremis, serve in lieu. All it contained were bunks and, along one wall, metal lockers. Wang groped his way to a door and, with momentary hesitation, pulled it open, blinking at the watery sunlight that greeted him, and stepped into a narrow corridor with rooms on one side and windows on the other. As the door clicked shut behind him, Wang realised he was wearing just his underpants. It crossed his mind to go back into the room, retrieve his shirt and trousers; but when he tried the handle, and pushed at the door, he found it unyielding. What if someone came and found him half-naked? But the house was quiet. There was no-one around. And his bladder, sorely tested, was clamouring for relief.

Emitting a low moan, and hopping, rather than walking, he set off to his right along the corridor. The first door he tried was shut, apparently locked; likewise the second and the third. None of the doors bore any identifying feature, neither number nor name, certainly nothing to suggest what he knew the Americans call a comfort station. He reached the end of the corridor and turned the corner. Another passage, slightly wider, slightly newer – an addition, perhaps, to an older building – stretched before him. More doors, more windows – not barred, Wang noted, which was encouraging, suggesting his prison surmise was wrong – but now was not the moment to deliberate. Wang needed to pee: achingly, cripplingly, agonisingly. He needed to release, to let go, to experience that bliss of standing, legs apart, with half-closed eyes and head tilted slightly back, exhaling, as the still-spraying member sprinkles itself like a fountain of old, with splashes of its own flow bouncing off the playful porcelain. Oh, rapture; and Wang shut his eyes in brief but happy anticipation, only to open them and, on the point of retreat, to behold an object which, he was convinced, had not been in evidence when he first looked down this second corridor.

A vase. An enormous, ornamental vase. Yes, thought Wang, bearing down upon it, there is a god, a god of urination; more potent than any town god, or martial god, or any of the other gods that joined him too infrequently along life's way. Why no-one had told him of this god seemed unfair, both on himself and the

60

deity, but now the vase – decorated with a reddish spiky flower and a yellow bird nesting on what looked like grapes – was in Wang's trembling hands, lifted from table and lowered to floor, there, and perhaps for the first time in a venerable and ancient existence, to serve nature, not art. Indeed, as Wang relieved himself into it, lustily, deliriously, directing a steaming stream into its dark and mysterious interior, it was likely the vase had never been so appreciated nor its true worth understood. And if anyone had emerged from any of those doors, or happened along the corridor and seen him, Wang would not much have cared. Not even Qi, or the odd little man in the suit who opened the gates and let him into the... the what? this place where he found himself... would have brought a flush of shame to Wang's countenance. After all, it was their fault there was no toilet in the room where they left him, no directions as to where he might go. Yes, they were to blame... not that he could imagine telling Qi to his face that he was responsible.

As Wang stood there, poised over the vase, he recalled he had read that urination was like sex or, since passing water is essentially a solitary activity, masturbation. Peeing, apparently, particularly when the need is strongest, is one of the most satisfying sensations known to humankind: one of those delectable moments when a powerlessness so powerful possesses the practicant that all else is cast aside. Yet peeing is not a pleasure that poets praise or novelists narrate. Statistically more frequent than sex, and arguably as vital, albeit for different reasons, weeing remains a curious last taboo in an otherwise self-indulgent and hedonistic world.

Wang had puzzled over these words. Now, however, he felt he was beginning to understand; at least in part, for the reference to sex remained obscure. Any mention of sex brought him out in a sweat. It involved women, or so he had been led to believe, and women were a mystery. They tended to flutter their eyes, to whisper among themselves, to giggle, and were best avoided. What was more, Wang had learned, it seemed the business of sex could be conducted between men. This, however, struck him as even more fraught. There were some things, he told himself, best left alone. Sex was one of them. At any rate until his studies were over. And he had got himself a decent, well-paid job, perhaps with a Western firm operating in the new and burgeoning China. Then, perhaps...

With a sigh of contentment, he shook the last droplets into the vase and persuaded his still-throbbing, slightly aching organ to take refuge in his underpants. Intending to place the vase back on its table, and return at a convenient moment to empty it, he bent to pick it up. He had already partially lifted it from the floor when his eye caught something soggy poking above the surface of the cess. Peering into neck of the vase, he realised what he could see were banknotes.

In his amazement, he felt the vase slipping from his grasp. Only through luck did his hands lock more tightly to ease it to the ground. Then, tilting the vase so the interior would catch the light, he examined the contents again. He was right: money. Loads of it, by the look of things: not just the odd note but wads of the stuff, in rolls, and soggy, already curling at the edges. How much he'd no idea. These were English banknotes; larger, of a different hue, than those back home. Wang felt vaguely something had to be done: he couldn't just leave the money to stew in his own urine. After all, it belonged to someone: to Qi, probably, who apparently distrusted banks as much as Uncle Peng and believed always in the virtues of ready cash. But that was crazy. Qi was a man of the world, a businessman; a

62

generational age but an ideological lifetime removed from the rustic bicycle repairman. No, there had to be another reason. It must be... and Wang gasped. It was obvious. If this were indeed a prison, or police station, as he first thought, then the money would be from bribes. Payment for charges dropped, statements amended. That was the way things worked; that's what the money was. The realisation filled Wang both with hope and fear. Hope, in that he too had the wherewithal to bribe his way out; fear, that if he were found responsible for the ruination, no, desecration of a huge cache of banknotes, there would be no way he would ever be in a position even to attempt to bribe his way out.

Quite how Qi fitted into all this was unclear, but that was not Wang's immediate concern. On impulse he thrust his hand into the neck of the vase to salvage the money – surely he could somehow clean it, dry it out – but his hand, despite its delicate proportions, caught in the even more delicate neck of the vase and refused to extricate itself. A low wail issued from Wang's lips. He would be discovered, semi-clad, with his hand stuck in a possibly priceless vase containing a bladder-load of piss and a quantity of sodden, and by now worthless, banknotes. There would be no excuse, no mitigation, no mercy: he, rather than the money, would be hung out to dry. In despair he placed his free hand on the vase, just below the neck, to steady it, and tried twisting and turning the other in an attempt to free it. In vain. He wondered if he could stir or agitate the contents to create a sort of wave to lubricate the trapped hand and let it slide to safety: the vase, though, proved too cumbersome to shake in this way. In frustration, and as a last resort, he gave a mighty tug at the stricken hand. There was a sharp crack as a piece of rim broke from the vase and crashed to the wooden floor, where it shattered. Wang groaned, immediately withdrawing his hand from the now enlarged, albeit flawed, aperture, and flinching from the stench which had been temporarily corked by his bruised and battered hand.

At that moment a voice wafted along the corridor. 'Mr Wang... our esteemed guest. Is that you?' Footsteps could be heard, faint, but nevertheless approaching. In panic Wang seized the vase, replaced it on the table, turning the broken part of the neck to the wall, and kicked the shards of porcelain beneath it. He felt something prick his foot, and winced; and set off, limping, albeit briskly, in the direction of the voice. Where the two corridors joined, the older and the newer, he turned the corner and collided with the besuited gentleman, the humanoid, who had admitted him the previous evening.

'Haaar,' gasped Wang, almost bowled over by the impact.

'There you are,' the man said, giving the student a strange look and, Wang thought, wrinkling his nose. 'I thought I heard signs of life.'

'Haaar,' gasped Wang again, wiping his hand on the back of his underpants. 'I was... er... looking for a toilet.'

The man frowned slightly, but at once recovered his composure. 'Along here,' he said, leading Wang past the dormitory he had vacated what seemed an eternity ago and pausing at the next door along. 'If you'd turned left, instead of right, you'd have found it.'

'Haaar,' said Wang again, and thought for appearances' sake he should go in.

'When you've done, come down. Stairs are along here. I can find you something to eat. And I've got your clothes.'

Wang blinked. 'Not in here...?' he began, motioning towards the dormitory.

64

'You needn't go in there,' the humanoid intoned. 'Not now. Besides, it's locked. Security. We've somewhere else for you. More congenial. Now... in you go. I'll see you downstairs in a minute.'

More congenial, thought Wang, entering a washroom with several toilets and showers. Congenial might mean anything. If they discover the money... the vase... but at least he knew where to empty it. And clean the notes. And... pain shot through his foot. Wang looked down and discovered blood on the floor; moreover a faint trail led from the door. He bent down and, with difficulty, pulled a shard from his sole. The blood flowed more freely. Wang, hopping, grabbed a handful of loo paper and, stuffing it underneath his foot to staunch the flow, used it as a mop to wipe the incriminating trail which, in fact, served only to smear the blood more widely over the floor. What if he had been bleeding outside, in the corridor? What if the man with the suit had noticed? What if...?

The man with the suit had noticed. Outside the bathroom door, he had seen not just one but several spots of blood on his otherwise immaculate carpet. He stared at the stains in disgust, and thought for a moment. That carpet would need cleaning, possibly replacing. Mr Qi was so particular, adamant there should be no dirt to encourage disease which, in turn, might impede the smooth running of the business or, worse, cause the authorities to investigate. Anything for a quiet life. But the blood was curious. Why their guest should bleed was a mystery. A mystery which, like all mysteries, would no doubt resolve itself in time. And with patience. Yes, with time and patience, the suit reminded himself, heading downstairs, the mulberry leaf becomes silk.

11

'I'm sorry,' said Wang. 'I don't get it. I mean... this set-up here. What... who...?'

Wang, fed, dressed in the previous day's clothes, which had been washed and ironed, and wearing a clean pair of underpants somehow procured for him, was sitting in a cavernous kitchen in the company of the suit, who had introduced himself as Mr Wu, Qi's right-hand man in Cramcaster. On closer acquaintance the man was more affable, more accommodating; altogether less humanoidy. As well as providing Wang with a bowl of soup, strengthened with slivers of what tasted like chicken, he had treated Wang's injuries: not just the damaged mouth but also the bruise ripening on his forehead, cracked against the upper bunk. He had looked, too, at the flayed flesh and slight swelling around Wang's hand, but said nothing. Nor had he examined Wang's foot. Instead, he had treated the face with a pungent, but not unpleasant, lotion, which he told Wang to rub in. 'All in a day's work,' Mr Wu said. 'We're used to things like that around here.' Wang felt immediately better; calmer, more relaxed; and, tucking into his food, he began quizzing his host.

Mr Wu told Wang that Qi was in import and export, that this involved considerable travel, which was why Qi had flown in yesterday but had left a few hours later following a business meeting.

Wang wasn't satisfied. He wanted to know what sort of import and export, wondering for an awkward moment if it might be vases, but Mr Wu was noncommittal. 'General commodities,' he told Wang. 'This and that.' Then Wang enquired about the house: why it was so large, why it had dormitories, why there was laundry suspended on racks from the ceiling of the kitchen, and why Mr Wu was preparing rice and sauces

66

and other foods that simmered on cooking ranges of the type he had seen in the Beijing hotel where he had worked. Wang said at first he thought he was in some kind of prison, whereupon Mr Wu allowed himself a brief smile; then Wang added it seemed more like a hotel, or hostel, rather than a prison, because of all the beds and the food and the laundry.

'You might say that,' Mr Wu said, expertly chopping greenery of some sort – Wang thought parsley – and tossing it into one of the pots. 'A hostel. Yes. Mr Qi has many people working for him, in different capacities, who need to be housed. Looked after. One big, happy family, you might say. And that's my job.'

Wang wanted to know how many people comprised this family, where they came from, and whether he had already met some of them in the dormitory when he was half asleep. Mr Wu cut short Wang's interrogation and told him, not unkindly, that he was too inquisitive.

'Save all this curiosity for the university,' he said. 'Curiosity, in the wrong place, can be dangerous. It can lead to unpleasantness. Embarrassment. We wouldn't want that, would we?'

Wang, thinking of porcelain vases doubling as chamber pots, and a cache of soiled and soggy money floating therein, took the hint. Quite right: embarrassment was the last thing he wanted. Instead, picking up Mr Wu's reference to the university, he changed tack.

'I ought to get along to the university,' he began, pushing aside his empty bowl and wriggling off the stool on which he was perched. 'I need to register. And find out...'

'Waste of time,' Mr Wu said.

Wang stared.

'You'll never make it. No way.'

Wang wondered if he had missed something.

Insurrection, riot, revolt; tanks on every street corner; the army out in force to restore peace and democracy. Had the British risen up against their capitalist masters? Against the bankers who, Wang knew, had brought the country to its knees? If so...

'Seen the time?'

Wang looked blank.

'Almost half past three. Even if you set off now...'

'Half past three? It can't be.'

Mr Wu nodded towards a clock on the wall behind Wang. 'You've slept the best part of the day. You were exhausted...'

A wave of panic washed over Wang. 'They're expecting me. It's all arranged. If they think I'm not coming, they'll give my place away...'

'Hardly,' Mr Wu shrugged, slicing carrots as if practising karate. 'As I understand it, they take people weeks after the start of classes. That's when the school leavers, hoping to get jobs, realise there aren't any. And they don't have conscription. No wonder the place is the mess it is.'

Wang frowned. He wasn't sure what point Mr Wu was trying to make, though he was probably right about the university: by the time he got there, everyone would be going home. Besides, all the paperwork he would need was in the other case which was... where? Still stuck in Paris, perhaps. Or inside one of those white vans Qi had told him about, the significance of which he had forgotten. Wang cursed to himself: why had his uncle insisted he bring two cases? If he had brought just one he could have kept it with him all the time on the plane. Then he wouldn't be in his present pickle. He could have moved into his hall of residence straight away, had a decent night's sleep, been up bright and early to meet his professor and perhaps even bought a couple of textbooks to begin studying. Instead he was miles away from the university, holed up at Qi's house... actually, it was Qi's fault. If Qi hadn't put him out of the taxi at the wrong university then, even without his case, he might have been able to sort things out. Okay, not entirely Qi's fault... he couldn't be blamed for the case. But mixing up the universities... and there was something else Qi had blundered over. What was it? Oh, yes, the toilet. Not making it clear where to find a loo, which in turn... suddenly Wang remembered the vase and, in particular, its contents, and it occurred to him if he couldn't go to the university he could at least return to the first floor corridor and clear up what he would find there.

Yawning loudly – the exaggerated, fake yawn yielding immediately, and somewhat to his surprise, to the genuine article – Wang announced that he was still tired and thought he should retire to the dormitory. Mr Wu was having none of it and said, on the instructions of Mr Qi, that Wang was to be shown to his own room at the top of the house where he could stay as long as he liked until his university accommodation was confirmed.

'Mr Qi seems to have taken quite a shine to you,' Mr Wu said dryly, and with a disdainful sniff. 'The master says the room we gave you is no place for a scholar. Of course, last night, you weren't expected. And I'd no way of knowing you weren't like the others. Therefore...'

'Mr Qi is too kind,' Wang stammered. 'But there's no need...'

Mr Wu fixed Wang with a stare that suggested there was every need. Obviously, if Qi decreed the dormitory unsuitable, that was an end to the matter. An alternative would indeed have to be found.

In fact, as Wang had to admit a few moments later, when Mr Wu opened the door to a top floor bedroom, the alternative was a vast improvement on the dormitory. The room was neatly furnished, with a single bed, and reminded Wang of a hotel room. He was also pleased to see his luggage at the end of the bed, including the errant case which must have turned up during the day. He was disconcerted, though, when Mr Wu – a little sardonically, Wang thought – indicated the en suite. 'No need to get taken short,' Mr Wu said, pointing his sentence with the disdainful sniff the student had come to expect. He was further put out when told a meal would be brought him in his room.

'Why can't I eat with the others?' Wang asked. 'It would be nice to meet them properly.'

Mr Wu pursed his lips. 'Scholar's privilege,' was all he would say. 'Enjoy it while you can.' Wang was again struck with the idea that this house, or hostel, was indeed a sort of prison. He had been segregated, to be held in solitary confinement, to be fed apart, away from the others. Why? What was going on in Qi's house?

Wang might have had an idea if, an hour or two later, he had heard a minibus growl across the gravel below his window and disgorge a cargo of tired and dusty workers. He might have caught snippets of conversation in his own language – a plague on the rain, on leaking boots, a curse that the mobile slum they'd just left still had no working heater, banter that the evening meal would be yesterday's leftovers – as his countrymen trudged into the house. Wang, though, was impervious. Tiredness, or possibly boredom – his room offered little in the way of distraction with no books, no radio, no television – had fallen onto the bed, where sleep had overcome him.

Tiredness, boredom and, following a foray to the first floor to seize the vase, dispose of its contents in the en suite, and somehow wash and dry the money, bewilderment. Bewilderment, that the vase on the table

70

at the end of the corridor was not the one which had so fortuitously served him earlier in the day. Bewilderment, that the vase he now beheld was as perfect a specimen as anyone might wish: gleaming, lustrous and, above all, whole. No chips, no cracks, no breaks; certainly no urine and certainly no money, and never a whiff of either.

Wang was nonplussed. He staggered back to his room, wondering if he had somehow imagined the events at the end of the corridor. He flung himself onto the bed, and tried to make sense of things. It was all surely a dream, or nightmare; soon he would wake and find himself back with Uncle Peng, sharing a beer, talking of inner tubes and sprockets and brake blocks. In the meantime, as sleep overcame him, he found himself on a bicycle, pedalling furiously, as people and buildings flashed past in a blur, but he was getting nowhere. Getting nowhere at all...

12

Dozy Pendegrass was exhausted. Even though, as he freely admitted, exhaustion was his customary state, on this particular morning he felt especially drained. It wasn't so much that one of the new postgrads – an eager Chinese girl, with large, piercing eyes framed by even larger spectacles – had taken up the first hour of the morning with her insistence on course handbooks, reading lists and timetables, none of which Pendegrass could coax from his computer. It was the quality control return, reference BS/U/3/10157/JP, pertaining to the third year Issues in Human Resource Management module he had taught in the previous semester. The form should have been completed in April, but he had forgotten it – and now Brush, at the behest of some functionary in the dean's office, was throwing his professorial weight around and demanding the paperwork. Pendegrass racked his brains for anything he could include on the form. All he could remember was the wondrous Lucinda Trott-Knightly, heavily into saving whales and undernourished Africans, who punched a classmate for suggesting, not unreasonably, that slaughtered whale would fill starving stomachs; then there was the luscious Melanie Crabbe, may the Nazareth and Ewesbottom Repentant Sinners forgive such thoughts, who always sat at the front, and whose essays were as skimpy as her skirts. Pendegrass shook himself, and tried to bring himself back to reality: none of this, he realised, was suitable for the university Monitoring, Evaluation and Statistical Services unit, disdainfully referred to throughout the institution by its acronym.

Pendegrass was especially taxed by the demand on page four of the return to assess the modality of the application of value-added to the on-going student

72

experiential discourse, having particular regard to the teaching and learning strategies adopted in the light of stated student outcomes. Lynne Truss would doubtless have something to say about such abuse of language: he would have to see what the great lady had to say when he got home. For the moment, though, and to Pendegrass's chagrin, his customary response in such circumstances of 'not applicable' was, sadly, not applicable. Something more in the spirit of the question was required, something equally meaningless to keep the MESS-mates happy. Americans like that sort of psychobabble, he reminded himself. After all, they invented it. So there must be phrases on the internet he could borrow and drop into the report. Hoping the computer would be more responsive than it had been to the Chinese girl's demands – what was her name? Something ridiculously dated... Emmeline, or some such nonsense – he opened up Google and tapped in 'academic gobbledegook'. He frowned, and wondered if he had spelled it correctly. On a whim he altered it to 'gobbledygook', and pressed search.

The first thing he discovered was that his hesitation over the spelling was entirely reasonable: no-one else could spell it either. Or at least they could, but in six different ways. 'Gobbledegook' vied with 'gobbledygook', 'gobblygook', 'gobbldygook', 'gobbldegook' and finally 'gobldygook', all of which seemed to have, in greater or lesser measure, their own adepts and adherents. Pendegrass was astonished: if every word in the language boasted six spellings, no-one would ever pass GCSE English. Come to think of it, few did, at least in any meaningful way: an A grade, even A*, was no guarantee a student could spell.

Pendegrass peered at the screen. What caught his eye was – and he noted the words precisely, including the typo and exclamation mark – a 'hilarious academic

73

postmoderm [sic] gobbledegook random generator!'. The random generator had produced, it seemed, a learned treatise on the semioticist paradigm of expression – whatever that might mean – in the works of some character called Gibson. Pendegrass read the treatise with mounting incomprehension and, at the same time, mounting wonder. Had a machine, a gobbledegook random generator, really produced such apparent wisdom? At the bottom of the page was a disclaimer that the content was pure gobbledegook, but Pendegrass wasn't sure. The text was convincing, not that he understood it, and he wondered if it wasn't a case of double bluff. In other words the text, while claiming to be nonsense, was in fact sense. An attempt, perhaps, to trick the reader into grappling with intellectually demanding theory, believing it to be twaddle, whereas in fact the premise was sound, or as sound as anything to do with semiotics was likely to be.

There was no time, however, to dwell on bluff and double bluff, for soon Pendegrass realised he had stumbled into a powerhouse of gobbledegook generators: if electricity, and not gobbledegook, were so generated, the energy problems of the world would be solved at the click of a mouse. His favourite was a site – tongue-in-cheek from the Plain English Society – that allowed him to generate his own gobbledegook. Click the so-called generator bar and, in a pop-up box, appeared a succession of splendidly vacuous phrases. It was just what Pendegrass wanted. With a whoop of joy, he jotted down the choicest circumlocutions and started to compose his response to the question of modality and value-added and on-going student experiential discourse. He began: 'The administrative matrix approach adopted for this module offered a window of parallel reciprocal mobility facilitating an experiential asset time phase to...' and was congratulating himself

74

on an auspicious start when he realised there was a suitcase, on its end, standing before him.

'Haaar,' the suitcase intoned.

Pendegrass stared. He knew what it was: magnetic levitation. The force fields and whatnot whizzing around in the basement of Wole Soyinka had escaped, permeated the building, as he feared, and entered his skull. That was the only explanation. After all, the suitcase had a head, arms and legs; it was jigging up and down, emitting strange sounds. His mind was frazzled. This was it, the end; this was what happened when trust was placed in science, not scripture. This was...

A hand, previously clasping the case, shot out in the direction of Pendegrass, who recoiled.

'Haaar,' said the suitcase – or rather, as Pendegrass noted, a pale, rotund face peering over the top. 'We meet.'

Pendegrass looked hard at the apparition before him. His fear about magnetic levitation was beginning to recede: here was a young man clutching a suitcase to his chest and, by his gesture, offering friendship. Nevertheless, caution was required.

'I'm sorry,' he countered, 'but I don't think...'

'Wang Ti,' the face said, lowering the case slightly. 'Tutee.'

'I don't want tea,' Pendegrass said slowly, wondering if the university had introduced a refreshment trolley to the corridors of Wole Soyinka. He looked round in vain for an appropriate conveyance, until it crossed his mind the suitcase could well be some kind of servery. It was possibly a descendant of those cases, remembered from childhood, which lugubrious salesmen in gabardine macs dragged from door to door, and from which spilled polishes, bootlaces and brushes of varied breadth and bristle that

75

no-one wanted to buy. Like now.

'No tea,' he repeated firmly and, fearing his visitor might wish to stay, added: 'And certainly not two teas.'

The case, which had already fallen slightly, fell even more, as did the face.

'No tea,' it repeated, looking puzzled.

'Ah, well... that's alright, then,' said Pendegrass, sensing a means of getting rid of both case and carrier. 'If you've no tea, then I suggest you go and get some. I mean... there might be others who want tea. Not everyone drinks coffee, you know. Though how you manage not to spill anything in that case... the way you're holding it... is a mystery.'

'Haaar... case,' said the face. 'You want see...?'

'No,' said Pendegrass, standing up, and moving towards the door. 'I don't want see. Please... take it away. There's no custom here.'

'No custom. Excuse me... I not understand. A minute.'

So saying, the face put the case carefully down beside him and, fishing in its pocket, pulled out what looked like an electronic organiser. It tapped with a forefinger at the keypad.

'Please... you spell. Custom...'

'What?'

'You spell. Please. K-a-... '

'No, no. Custom, with a c. C-u-s-t-o-m. But why...?'

'Haaar,' said the face, interrogating the keypad. There was a pause as it looked down, then up at Pendegrass, and down again at the gadget in its hand. 'Haaar,' it repeated, with less certainty.

It struck Pendegrass that if this was a tea-man, albeit with no tea, it was an odd way to behave. He became aware that the tea-man's face, like his language, was damaged: the mouth was bruised and the skin around a

76

strange, darkish hue. There also appeared to be a slight swelling on the forehead. It looked as if the man had been fighting, and Pendegrass suddenly felt afraid.

'If you don't leave,' Pendegrass said, searching deep for an authority and gravitas as alien to him as touch-typing to a gorilla, 'I shall have to call security.'

The face looked at him. 'Security,' it intoned. 'Please... you spell.'

'For pity's sake,' Pendegrass spluttered. 'I'm not going through that rigmarole again. Look. I don't want your tea. Coffee... whatever. And I'm not standing here all day while you test me on spelling. I've... um... things to do. Meetings... students to see...'

'Students. I student. You see me.'

'I've no wish to see you. You're not one of my...' Pendegrass began, and stopped. Mists, swirling in the baser regions of his mind, began to lift. 'Just a moment,' he said. 'What did you say your name was?'

The face gave him a blank stare.

'Your name,' urged Pendegrass, and then, more quietly, 'Your name.'

'Haaar. Wang Ti. You... professor. My professor. Professor Pendegrass.'

For a second time, a hand shot out in the direction of Pendegrass. This time, Pendegrass took it.

'I'm not a professor,' he mumbled, freeing himself and moving to his desk, where he rummaged through a pile of papers and eventually found what he was looking for: a print-out of the names of the incoming MBA cohort. There it was: Wang Ti. A note next to the name indicated the student had been delayed and would arrive later than expected. Pendegrass had no recollection of writing the note, though it was in his handwriting.

He told Wang to sit and went to a filing cabinet from which he took a student welcome pack. This, because

77

of its bulk, was anything but welcome, and probably useless. According to a survey, students read their welcome packs only at the end of their course, coming across them as they were clearing their rooms. All the carefully collated information on student support and services, clubs and societies, town and gown, study guides, banking, health and safe sex, was wasted. Students, the survey concluded, preferred to drift through university as they would through life, relying on chance rather than choice. After all, life itself came with no welcome pack: why, therefore, should a degree programme?

Pendegrass handed the document to Wang, who accepted it with a reverential bow of the head, as if receiving an award from a high-ranking party official.

'And this,' said Pendegrass, suddenly coming across an A4 sheet on his desk he had been looking for earlier, and handing it to Wang, 'is the induction week programme. Essential if...'

'Please... induction?' ventured Wang.

'Induction... orientation,' said Pendegrass, instantly regretting the connotations, given Wang's provenance, of the second word.

'Please...?' queried his visitor, about to attack what Pendegrass now realised was an electronic dictionary.

'Forget it,' he said, hastily. 'Induction... it's an introduction...'

'Introduction... but you say induction. Please... how to say this word.'

Pendegrass wiped a bead of perspiration from his forehead and wanted to open a window, but remembered the frames had warped or were gunged with paint, or both, and hadn't opened for years.

'It's two words,' Pendegrass said weakly. 'Just think of it as... as...'

'Getting-to-know-you week,' chimed Wang, looking

up from his translator, which at long last seemed to have rendered sense out of nonsense.

'Ah,' said Pendegrass. 'Getting-to-know-you week. I must remember that. Anyway, this is crucial. Particularly the study skills session and the English diagnostic testing.'

Wang's faced creased in puzzlement.

Pendegrass explained. 'An English test. A test. In English. To make sure that you...'

'Haaar. English. Cambridge proficiency. English... super spiffing.'

'Yes, I'm sure it is,' Pendegrass heard himself say, not believing a word of it. 'But we still like to test. Know where we stand, and all that.'

A shadow passed across Wang's countenance. He was sitting, the professor was standing; what was there to know about that? Perhaps, though, he should stand. Possibly the professor had issued an invitation to stand, even a command, and to remain seated would be either impolite or insubordinate. Wang rose to his feet and, examining the professor, thought he detected stress or strain, probably because of all the great works he had produced and was surely about to produce once more. He decided to capitalise on this realisation.

'You... very good man. Great professor.'

'I'm not a...' Pendegrass began.

'Great honour for me... Wang Ti... be student at famous Cram Vale University. Very great honour. Now I pay. Pay honour. Pay good money. Pay bill. Yes.'

Flushed with pride at his speech, and bowing, this time from the waist down, Wang picked up his case and laid it on top of the papers and books on Pendegrass's desk. The student, thought Pendegrass, looked somehow defenceless – motherless came to mind – now the case was no longer clasped to his person as it had been when he first saw him.

79

'For you,' said Wang, twiddling with the clasps, which seemed reluctant to yield.

Pendegrass was about to say that he didn't want a case, that he had a perfectly good briefcase, several suitcases, numerous hold-alls, backpacks, rucksacks, knapsacks and black sacks – and that anyway British university teachers were not in the habit of accepting gifts, for the good reason no-one ever gave them any – when the case flew open.

'Haaar,' said Wang.

'Ah,' echoed Pendegrass, as banknotes, loose, unbound, spilled from the case onto the desk. Some fluttered to the floor and fell at his feet. Fives, tens, twenties and even – though Pendegrass couldn't be sure, never having handled any – fifties. Films, pensioned off to the retirement home of the television early afternoon slot, raced through his mind: villains stuffing cases full of used notes to spirit glamorous and ultimately perfidious countesses across cold war borders, or to hire assassins to dispose of wealthy young heiresses whose dowries had been squandered on gambling. Perhaps, thought Pendegrass, with a frisson of excitement, he had been selected for such a task. He felt he could manage a winsome, weeping heiress, and lead her back on the path of righteousness. A countess, probably horsy and domineering, was a less certain prospect. Better, therefore, to leave the loot where it was and stick to teaching: dull but predictable.

Pendegrass realised that Wang, fired by the success of his first speech, was indulging in another.

'British pound sterling... very good money. Good money. Pay MBA... pay teacher... pay room... pay food. You take, professor, sir, my pound sterling... your pound sterling. Great honour...'

Something clicked in Pendegrass's mind. This money, this cash, which presumably the fellow had hauled halfway round the world... unless he had just committed a robbery, which might account for the facial injuries... was to pay his tuition fees, his accommodation... whatever. Good grief: didn't they have banks in China? Or did they think everyone in Britain kept their money under the bed, like French farmers? At any rate, this was ridiculous. The money couldn't stay. It would have to be handed over to... to whom? Pendegrass had no idea. He'd never been faced with this before. Suddenly he felt very tired, and sat down.

Wang, in the meantime, was in full flow, drawing on eloquence neither he nor even the most sympathetic of Cambridge proficiency examiners dreamed he possessed.

'Uncle... good man. He help. He say: MBA good. MBA make good money. In new China. Uncle ride. In village, town. Here, there, all where. Uncle ride quick. Ride good. Collect good money...'

So, the lad's uncle was a jockey. That would explain the cash. Picked up from punters at various race courses. Although why English money... perhaps there were package tours to China catering for race-goers seeking something more exotic than Cheltenham or Ascot. After all, you never knew what riffraff you might meet at places like that. Probably the Earl of Cramcaster.

'Look,' said Pendegrass, waving a hand to silence Wang. 'This is all very well, but because of security... no, not security,' he added hastily, not wishing to be quizzed again on spelling, 'because of... er... we need to get this money somewhere safe. Like... the finance office,' he added in a moment of inspiration, without knowing where this might be found or, indeed, if this was its name.

Puzzlement greeted Pendegrass's proposal.

81

'The finance office. Where fees are paid. Fees. You pay your fees to the finance office. Not to me,' Pendegrass struggled gamely on. 'Fees... it's like... like a sort of bill. You know... bill. You pay your bill...'

'Haaar... bill. Pay bill. Pay good money,' said Wang, visibly relieved there was a word he recognised.

Pendegrass seized the moment and, with it, his visitor. Stuffing errant notes back into the case, and indicating that Wang should close then carry it, he bundled his visitor from the room. Outside, in the corridor, he locked the door and, gesturing for Wang to follow, set off to find the finance office.

Or any office. Pendegrass didn't much care. Anywhere that would take the money and, ideally, the student. Get rid of them both. Then he could go back to his desk for a well-earned nap.

13

'I think there's a problem with some of this dosh. Funny money, you might say.'

Wang chuckled. 'Haaar... funny money,' he repeated, delighting in the rhyme and the sound of the words. He looked at Pendegrass, to share the pleasure with his professor, but the great man was not smiling. Nor, indeed, was the finance officer trawling through the contents of the case, and to whom Pendegrass had taken an instant dislike on account of his head of hair that would grace a yak: no man, whose locks are thinning like Pendegrass's, feels anything but revulsion towards a male of similar age without the decency to allow his hair to fall out.

'I mean... what's this?' said the shaggy one, extracting a five pound note and waving it under Wang's nose. 'You taking the piss?'

'Please... piss. What mean...?'

'Crap... that's what it is.'

'Haaar... crap. Piss mean crap.'

'No,' said Pendegrass. 'I don't think so. What the man means is the money. He's saying it's not right.'

'Haaar... good English pound. Pound... more good than dollar.'

'More good for nothing,' the hirsute one snorted. 'Monopoly money, that's what it is. Monopoly money.'

Wang frowned. He knew about monopolies. Monopolies were those curious constructs which, in the past, in private hands, were bad; in state hands, however, good. Now they were just bad, for no-one else could get a look in. Perhaps this was what was meant: he had no right to have all this money. Perhaps the money should be opened up to competition, shared, but wasn't that what he was doing by paying his fees? Surely... but his professor was speaking.

'I haven't seen one of these for ages,' Pendegrass was saying, holding up the offending note between finger and thumb as if it were infected with SARS or swine flu. 'Probably worth a bob or two now.'

'Could be,' the yak said, narrowing its eyes so they were barely visible beneath a scrub of overhanging eyebrow, and snatching the note from Pendegrass. 'Could well be.'

Wang was conscious that the morning, which had started so auspiciously, was beginning to pale. He had met his estimable professor and made, he felt, an indelible impression; he had enjoyed his impromptu campus tour as his mentor, after much detour and asking of directions, tracked down the finance office. En route he had practised his English by asking the professor at every opportunity 'Please... you say me what building is this?', so much so that he felt now he knew the campus better than Pendegrass who, Wang thought, had little idea where they were or where they were going; and, once at their destination, they had laughed over his confusion when a hairy man introduced himself as Bill, which Wang thought was something, rather than someone, to be paid. But now this self-same Bill, at first jovial and friendly, had turned cold and hostile, and Wang was unsettled.

'Excuse,' he said. 'My money...'

'See here, sunshine,' Bill began, as Wang looked round for a ray of light and hope, 'most of this isn't worth jackshit.'

'Jackshit,' repeated Wang, vaguely.

'I mean,' Bill said, taking the five pound note he had shown Pendegrass and waving it in Wang's face, 'it's no good. Out of date. Not legal tender.'

Wang's eyes and brain were beginning to glaze. 'Not legal tender,' he mumbled.

'What he means,' Pendegrass cut in, 'is we don't

use money like this any more.'

'Haaar... England use euro?' Wang queried, furrowing his brow.

'Over my dead body...' Bill snorted.

Wang had no idea what dead bodies had to do with anything, but watched as Pendegrass pulled a wallet from his pocket and extracted a five pound note. He motioned to Bill to pass him the old-fashioned currency he was holding, and then held the two notes next to each other to show Wang.

'Look,' he said. 'This one... it's bigger and bluer. And it's got this funny picture of a woman with a helmet...'

'The majesty... the queen,' Wang ventured.

'Mrs Thatcher, more like,' Bill countered, flicking dandruff onto his collar, which Pendegrass noted with guilty glee.

'No, not the queen. And this was before Thatcher. Anyway this one... the one we use today... it's a different colour. And smaller.'

'Both five pounds. Note say five pounds.'

'Yes... but we don't use this one. And I expect that applies to most of the notes in your case.'

'Too right,' said Bill. 'Obviously, we'll have to go through it. Find out exactly what's what. But what I want to know is... where's it all come from?'

Pendegrass explained that a relative, a jockey, had won the money through racing. Quite why he should have got hold of notes no longer in circulation, though, was a bit of a mystery. Bill said he wasn't surprised: they were offered all manner of payment in the finance office. An African had once proposed his sister in lieu of fees and, when they declined, suggested a camel and two goats instead.

Wang said if Bill wanted two coats he would write to his uncle because Chinese coats were very good and

85

very warm in winter. Bill, barely able to conceal his mirth, said that would be useful because they had given out a bad winter on the radio. Wang poked furiously at his electronic dictionary. 'Teacher give out book,' he said. 'Radio give out winter. Please... I not understand. How...?'

'Please,' said Pendegrass, feeling reality was slipping from him, 'this is getting us nowhere. All we can do now is wait until we find out how much money is in the case.'

'Much money...'

'I don't think so, cock,' said Bill. 'Anyway... we'll count it up and take it from there.'

Wang pricked up his ears. His face, earnest, solemn, creased with a grin. 'Take it from there,' he beamed. 'Take money from suitcase. Good. Now... no problem. All fee paid.'

Bill guffawed. Pendegrass glared at him, and gazed at his tutee in despair. 'It's not quite that simple,' he began.

'Oh, yes, it is,' said Bill, closing the case. 'Perfectly simple to me.' Then, putting the case under his arm and turning away into the interior of the office, he bade Pendegrass a cheery 'Good luck.'

I need it, thought Pendegrass. This is only the start. And teaching hasn't even begun. Talking of teaching... and he looked round to see Wang's radiant face staring up at him, full of hope, full of expectation. Pendegrass groaned inwardly.

'Please... now you take me find accommodation. You very kind man.'

Pendegrass shut his eyes.

'You know how find accommodation?'

Pendegrass was silent.

'Haaar... we find together. I practise English. I ask... where find accommodation.'

'You don't need me to come with you and...'

Wang's crestfallen countenance indicated the contrary.

'Fine,' said Pendegrass wearily, as thoughts of a mid-morning nap receded. 'You ask where find accommodation. Lead on. I follow.'

14

It was the work of seconds. A reminder on a notice-board to users of university audio-visual equipment that 'due to Considerations of a health and safety nature no Cables is to be stretched across the isles of teaching rooms by order Marcus Dunlittle Director Of Physical Plant'. Swift strokes of a marker pen to correct the spelling. Ditto the superfluous capitals. Three out of ten and a note to 'See me'.

The saintly Lynne Truss would be proud, and Pendegrass felt better at once. Gone, at the flick of a pen – the frustration, the irritation, steadily increasing as he escorted his tutee from finance to accommodation, hall of residence to international centre, refectory to library. And the interminable questions. Where's this? What's that? You please tell, you please show... questing, querying, until Pendegrass felt himself reeling, weak at the knees, punch-drunk, on the ropes. Much more and he would be out for the count. He had finally given the student the slip by dodging behind a stack of periodicals in the library and dashing like a dervish to the exit. The Nazareth and Ewesbottom Repentant Sinners would surely disapprove of such an uncharitable deed but, as Pendegrass told himself, there was only so much a repentant sinner could take. Besides, the deception would offer the chance at chapel for a show of repentance: he had repented of nothing of late, and the sinners might think him unworthy. Perhaps he was. Perhaps his adulation of Lynne Truss was evil. Thou shalt have no other gods before me apart from the Truss... no, that was wrong, wicked. But at least the opportunity to do her will, and correct poor English, had revived his flagging spirits.

When Pendegrass returned to his office, he found an

email waiting. It was from Bill Lukras, senior accounts administrator. The cash had been counted and came to just £1255 in useable notes. All the rest – several thousand pounds – was worthless. Finance was prepared to accept the £1255 as an instalment on fees, but a direct debit or some such arrangement would be needed to pay the rest.

Pendegrass leaned back in his chair, and sighed. He would need to summon the student, whom he had just escaped, back into his presence and tell him the bad news. Or, rather, try and tell him. There was as much chance of him taking it in, at least in one go, as there was of Noah's Ark sailing up the Cram. It was all very well, Pendegrass reminded himself, for the university to accept overseas students and the fees they brought with them, but it was never the planners and accountants who had to deal with them. It was mugs like him who would have to tell the student – attempt to tell the student – that unless he could stump up the outstanding fees he would be out. No classes, no exams, no degree. Pendegrass groaned.

He turned to the keyboard in front of him and, with some difficulty, accessed student contact details. Wang, fortunately, and rather to the surprise of Pendegrass, was already allocated an email account. The tutor tapped out a terse message requesting the student come to his office at his earliest convenience. No, not 'earliest convenience', Pendegrass thought, striking the delete key: the gadget, the translating machine, would tell the student he wished to meet in the gents' toilets. Then he'd be accused of lavatorial liaisons with male students and next thing he'd be out on his ear, no job, no pension, and probably up in court. No, 'earliest convenience' was an inconvenience to be avoided at all cost. 'As soon as possible' would do just as well, and was probably more in line with the student's

89

understanding, despite that certificate he went on about. Cambridge proficiency, or whatever. Inefficiency, more like.

Pendegrass sighed, pressed the send key, and shut down the computer. At the same time, he could feel himself shutting down. Slumber, sleep, too long that day denied, were crowding, clouding his brain, blanketing it like mountain mist, blotting everything out. Resistance was futile: Pendegrass knew the symptoms, and welcomed them as friends, as allies. Moments later he was fast asleep, soothed in his somnolence, and lulled by his own gentle snoring.

**

'Haaar... but banknote say...'

'I know perfectly well what it says. You've told me at least ten times in as many minutes.'

'Banknote promise to pay bearer on demand sum of five pound. I bear note... you pay sum... I pay fee.'

Pendegrass shut his eyes. As he feared, the interview, a few days after the email, was not going well. The student still hadn't grasped that the money, the clearly rotten fruits of the race-course, was useless. The Nazareth and Ewesbottom Repentant Sinners disapproved – as they did of most things – of gaming and gambling, and Pendegrass wondered if this was God moving in another of his mysterious ways. Possibly the Almighty was trying to teach the student that betting was bad, and so make him renounce his wicked ways and tread the path of righteousness. The flaw in this argument, as Pendegrass realised, was that the wicked ways were those of the uncle, the jockey, rather than the nephew. Perhaps this meant the sins of uncles were visited on nephews in the same way fathers' peccadilloes were passed to sons. If so, this

90

seemed unfair, and Pendegrass thought at chapel on Sunday he might venture a prayerful word with the Almighty to intercede on the student's behalf. Or possibly – those mysterious ways again – it was not the student but Pendegrass who was being tested. For whatever reason, God had chosen Pendegrass to lead the student to grace and fiscal salvation. Pendegrass the shepherd, Pendegrass the light. Yet he had already tried, at any rate, as far as fiscal salvation was concerned, and failed: the university hardship fund, for which he thought the student might be eligible, was hopelessly over-subscribed and, besides, it was too late to submit the paperwork. There was nothing for it. Path of righteousness or not, the student would have to stumble along it as best he could, without assistance. And he needed to be told.

Pendegrass opened his eyes, to see Wang staring at him.

'Look,' he said, 'there's no point beating about the bush. Either you get in touch with this uncle of yours, the jockey, and ask for more money... proper money... or else, and this would probably be quicker, you start to put your own house in order.'

'No house. Room in Martin Luther King hall of residence. Very comforting.'

'Comfortable. Not comforting,' snapped Pendegrass, immediately regretting his impatience as Wang, nodding his gratitude, and repeating the word 'comfortable', produced his electronic dictionary.

'Don't bother with that thing now,' Pendegrass said. 'No time. What I'm saying is that you need to do something to get the money to pay the university. Get a job, for instance. I know with your university work it won't be easy, but...'

'Bicycle. I know all about bicycle. Uncle... good teacher. Like you, sir, professor. I repair bicycle...

91

make good money. Uncle wise... uncle give universal repair tool... see, in pocket, Uncle say very useful, always have...'

Pendegrass wondered what a jockey might be doing with a universal repair tool. True, the universe needed repair – there was much wrong with it, as the Nazareth and Ewesbottom Repentant Sinners were constantly reminding themselves – but whether this young man was the person to fix it was debatable. On inspection, when Wang proudly produced the universal bicycle repair tool from his pocket, it turned out to be a sort of Swiss army knife, with spanners and screwdrivers and a couple of evil-looking prongs. Perhaps these were for getting stones out of horses' hooves, Pendegrass thought. He told Wang to put it away, adding there was probably not much of a market in Cramcaster for repairing bicycles.

Recalling that Qi had said at the airport much the same, that bicycles in Britain were – what? some sort of therapy for the insane, something like that – Wang's face fell. Pendegrass, noting the student's disappointment, saw his opportunity.

'A proper job. That's what you need. Perhaps... a restaurant. Lots of them in Chinatown. Two a penny... but all very good,' Pendegrass added quickly.

'Haaar... restaurant,' Wang said. 'Work in hotel in Beijing. Very fine. Work in room service, reception, kitchen, restaurant. Very good waiter.'

'There,' said Pendegrass triumphantly. 'Problem solved. Get yourself a job and you're sorted. Because if you don't... if you end up owing the university money... then no MBA. Simple. No fee... no degree.'

Wang's face began to pucker. 'No fee... no degree,' he mumbled.

'Got it in one,' boomed Pendegrass, relieved that, finally, his tutee appeared to have grasped the seriousness of his situation. 'That's it. Finish. Curtains. Over.'

Wang looked towards the window, but saw no curtains. All he registered was grey: grey grime, grey sky, and grey realisation that, without money, his hopes, his dreams, would be dashed.

'Haaar,' he began. And paused. Then, his features contorting in anguished determination, and from between clenched teeth, he said: 'No. Wang Ti not over. Wang Ti... get MBA. You see... get MBA. This... start. Wang Ti... start here.'

It was the turn of Pendegrass to stare at the student. It sounded as if Wang had been infected by the Monopoly money he had brought with him, and was about to embark on a variation of the game. Start, pass go and collect £200, get out of jail free, just visiting; but all the same this was a different Wang from the pathetic creature that rambled about jockeys and certificates and bicycles. This was... but in the blink of an eye, Wang had gone.

'Good heavens,' said Pendegrass, staring at an empty chair. And then again, to convince himself the student was really no longer there, 'Good heavens.'

15

Professor Arthur Brush, stifling a contented belch, placed his knife and fork on the empty plate and pushed it from him. Just what he needed to put him on until evening. Then, with a bit of luck, if his wife was dashing off to one of her innumerable council meetings, he could dump whatever she had dug from the freezer into next door's bin and slip out for a takeaway from the Bay of Bengal. Better still, enjoy a sit-down meal among the welcoming aromas of the restaurant.

All the same, the professor had to admit that the bangers and mash he had just consumed at the College Arms ran the offerings at the Bay of Bengal a close second. A very close second for, when washed down with a pint of cool and nutty ale from a local micro-brewery, there was no tastier or better value pub lunch for miles around. In fact the College Arms, situated opposite the Cram Vale campus but separated from it by one of the main roads leading out of Cramcaster, was noted for its bangers and mash, and each lunchtime attracted a discerning, if not eclectic, clientele.

Indeed, as Brush reminded himself, wondering if he dared risk another half pint and if anyone would smell it when he went back to the university, within the College Arms could be found a cross-section of society as classless and as harmonious as any utopian might desire. Academics rubbed shoulders with school failures, tax-office clerks with benefit-fiddlers, and bank cashiers with burglars. All met on equal and, in winter, sweaty ground – a result of the roaring coal fires stoked like furnaces in the main front room and the smaller snug at the rear. Undoubtedly the coal fires were responsible for the grime that seemed to coat every surface in the College Arms, including the ancient playbills for long-forgotten melodramas and the saucy pictures of music hall artistes, displaying shapely ankles and rather less shapely bloomers, which adorned the smoke-stained walls. Everyone admitted the College Arms, proudly and obstinately devoid of muzak and fruit-machine, was an anachronism. But, because of this it was cherished – not only by the lunchtime bangers and mash brigade but also by the Cramcaster clubs and societies which met there in the evenings. These included the Esperanto Society on the first Monday in the month, the Coin and Stamp Collectors' Colloquium on alternate Tuesdays, the Labour Party – fiercely Old Labour – whenever its secretary remembered to contact the comrades, and Women for Kosovo which, as everyone knew, was a convenient cover for a girls' night out.

Brush glanced at his watch and decided another half pint was in order. Besides, if he stuck around for another quarter of an hour, that woman from languages might drop in. Brush fancied her: still nice-looking, probably a real stunner in her heyday. Perhaps her greatest asset though, apart from the fact that she was not his wife, not Councillor Rosalind Brush, was that in the College Arms she was always alone, never with anyone else, still less any man, and she wore no ring. This augured well and, when Brush discovered she had been drafted in to teach English to foreign students in the management school, he realised he had a chat-up line. Not the most enticing, perhaps, but, at least to someone as out of practice in the chat-up stakes as Arthur Brush, highly convenient.

All the same, Brush recalled, standing at the bar as his half-pint was pulled, the woman seemed to spend most of her time in the College Arms sitting on a stool and chatting to the landlord, Ed. She seemed to share the publican's enthusiasm for single malts, and took delight in sampling whatever he had on offer. Brush did

95

not care much for the landlord, and took his freshly poured beer from him with a scowl and a grunt. The problem was, as Brush knew too well, that the publican was considerably more learned than he was: altogether more erudite, sharper, better-read, better-travelled, and altogether wiser.

Quite what the man was doing in a pub was a mystery. He ought at the very least to be running a university department, probably an entire university, for his learning and knowledge gave him a breadth of understanding which was phenomenal. It was rumoured that Ed was a Brain of Britain or Mastermind winner, which was not the case, but this did not prevent the curious coming from far and wide to test him on various abstruse topics. Brush had sat back in astonishment to hear the man respond at length to barbed questions on silver mining in the Andes, Newtonian physics, Smithsonian economics, the symphonies of Louis Spohr, Occitan troubadour poetry, the construction of the Suez Canal and the life and times of Hermitules Grunge. The fellow was a polymath, Renaissance man, and Brush was acutely jealous. His own theory was that Ed was a defrocked priest, a disbarred lawyer, a doctor struck off. Brush had asked around, made enquires, but no-one knew anything. It was all a bit of a mystery.

The lunchtime customers in the College Arms were thinning out. Brush knew most of them, at least by sight: they rarely spoke but exchanged the furtive glances of people who knew that a lunchtime tipple was no longer socially acceptable. Brush looked round the bar, in case the woman had been hiding in a corner, talking to others. There was no sign of her. The only person who showed no indication of moving was a youngster, not much more than a student, whom Brush recognised as a reporter from the local rag. Jason

Hackley – that was his name. Hackley had spent a morning with Brush interviewing him about the effect of rising oil prices, or something vaguely in the news. When the interview was printed, Brush was livid: the report made him out to be a cretin by completely misrepresenting his views. Brush had rung the Cramcaster Evening Herald to complain and was told Hackley was a trainee who might be forgiven the odd mistake but who, nevertheless, had all the makings of an superb reporter. Brush had not been convinced. He scowled in the direction of Hackley, and gulped his beer.

Clearly, the woman from languages was not coming. Probably got a class, Brush thought. Quite likely at this very moment she was standing, for her sins, in front of overseas students in his own management school. Brush wondered if the woman had any sins. He rather hoped she had. If not, he could think of a few he wouldn't mind sharing with her. He chuckled to himself and drained his glass, banging it down on the bar. Then, bunching his coat round him, he stepped outside into the damp and drizzle of a Cramcaster October. Scanning the passers-by, in a forlorn hope that the object of his desire had been delayed and was in fact about to materialise on the threshold of the College Arms, he failed to spot a small, scantily-clad figure, hunched against an inhospitable British climate as it scurried past the pub.

Wang was on a mission. The student had an aim, a goal, far more focussed than the professor's wishful, wistful yearnings. Quite simply, he was about to put things right. To put things right with a little help – or rather a lot – from friends.

16

The mansion in Compton Park was as Wang remembered it. Huge, rambling, slightly dilapidated, slightly mournful – but then so was pretty much everything else in Britain including, Wang felt, the people. It took him some time to master the entry-phone, and even then there was a further delay before it was answered. Eventually the familiar tones of home, of Mr Wu, greeted Wang's ear. After establishing that Wang was not the delivery driver from a food emporium in Chinatown, that he was Qi's friend who had turned up one night unexpectedly a couple of weeks ago, he was finally admitted. Not, Wang thought, without some surprise, even hostility, and not before Mr Wu had ascertained he was alone and had not, like last time, brought the police with him.

'No police,' Wang assured Mr Wu, recalling the panic the word 'police' had caused when he arrived the first time at Compton Park.

'In that case I suppose you'd better come in,' said Mr Wu, releasing the gate and admitting the visitor.

Some moments later Wang was sitting in the kitchen surrounded, as before, by all the signs of a repast in preparation. He suddenly felt hungry, and realised he hadn't eaten properly for days. He wondered if Mr Wu might offer him something to eat, at least to drink. Tea would be welcome: hot, black, as only the Chinese knew how to make it. But Mr Wu was not accommodating. In fact, he was scowling.

'Mr Qi was not pleased,' he said. 'In fact, I think you've got quite a nerve coming back here. After all Mr Qi did for you.'

Wang gulped. 'Haaar,' he began.

'Pretty disgusting, I call it. And that vase was expensive. Unique, you might say. In more ways than one. And then there was the floor...'

Wang shut his eyes. He suddenly recalled his first night in Qi's house, the voices, the need to relieve himself, the vase and its contents. All this had been pushed to the back of his mind. In his confusion over his own financial worries, over Uncle Peng's useless banknotes and the prospect of leaving the university without a degree, the events of his first full day in England had become a blur. And yet now, here they were, coming sharply into focus, dispelling any thoughts of a cosy chat with Mr Wu to sound him out about casual work in Qi's organisation to help pay the fees. It was all going wrong, hopelessly wrong, and not for the first time in the past few weeks he felt his eyes watering.

'Anyway,' Mr Wu was saying, 'at least you've done the honourable thing and come to apologise.'

He paused, waiting for Wang's confirmation. The student nodded, bleakly, sensing this was the required response.

'Good,' said Mr Wu, and Wang felt his spirits lift. Perhaps the apology would clear the air, let bygones be bygones; perhaps now he could raise the question of part-time work. He cleared his throat.

'Of course, there's the matter of compensation,' Mr Wu continued, crossing to a cabinet on the far side of the kitchen and extracting a sheet of paper. 'In conjunction with Mr Qi, I've drawn up an inventory of the damage. Let's see. The floor. Professional cleaning job: Mr Qi was quite adamant. Then there's the vase. Luckily for you, it was repairable. We had the bits pieced together so now only an expert would spot the blemish. Of course, skills like that don't come cheap.'

Wang moved his lips, but no sound came forth.

'As for the contents of the vase... regrettably, owing to their somewhat delicate nature, these were not

99

recoverable. A great pity. Of course we tried but, alas, we were too late. So, all in all...'

Mr Wu handed Wang the sheet. The student ran a watery eye over its carefully enumerated findings, until he alighted on a figure in British pounds.

'What?' he managed to croak. 'But that's impossible. It can't be...'

'You're lucky. It could have been considerably more than £1,887. Fortunately for you, at the time, the vase was not being used to capacity. After Mr Qi's visit...'

'I can't pay that,' Wang gasped. 'I haven't got that all that money. No way. In actual fact...'

'Of course you haven't got that sort of money,' Mr Wu soothed. 'Mr Qi knows that. I know that. And that's why Mr Qi is offering you the chance to repay the debt you owe him.'

'Repay...?' Wang blinked.

'Mr Qi is happy that, if you work for him for a certain period of time, he will consider the debt repaid.'

'But...' began Wang.

'Mr Qi fully understands about your studies. He has no wish to cause undue interruption to them or interfere in any way. But, somehow, this debt must be settled. Of course, if you don't wish to avail yourself of Mr Qi's most generous offer...' at this point Mr Wu's eyes narrowed '... I should perhaps remind you he has certain friends. Friends who get impatient when debts are outstanding. Friends not only here, but also back home. And we don't want any accidents.'

'Haaar,' Wang gulped.

'Excellent,' said Mr Wu, taking the paper from Wang's trembling hand. 'All agreed. So, may I suggest that next Monday morning, early, six sharp, you're in the bus shelter across the road from the main university building. In front of the College Arms. What the British call a public house. You can't miss it.'

100

'But...'

'Make sure you're there. A bus will arrive and take you where you're going. In the meantime... I think that's all you need to know.'

A look on Mr Wu's face told Wang this was indeed all he needed to know. Further questioning would lead nowhere – except, perhaps, Wang thought, to acquaintance with Mr Qi's impatient friends.

'Monday,' Wang mumbled. 'Six sharp.'

'Good,' said Mr Wu. 'And now... I think we'll see you out. You ought to get some studying done. Next week you might be a little busy.'

At the front door, where Mr Wu punched a code into the keypad to open the outside security gate, he turned to Wang and said, 'You're a very lucky young man. Mr Qi is not always so indulgent towards those who offend him. You just remember that when you're waiting for that bus.'

The weather had turned colder as Wang set off back to the university. A chill north wind swept down from the hills, a harbinger of a harsh and sorrowful winter. But Wang was not concerned with climatic conditions. His own winter had already arrived.

17

The girl was looking at him. At first, Wang thought he was mistaken. Her face was partly concealed behind glasses which, catching the fading sun that leached apologetically into the classroom, flashed impatiently in his direction. There was, however, no doubt that Wang was the object of her attention. He tried to look away, to concentrate on what the teacher was saying, but his gaze was drawn inexorably back to the girl. Moreover, every time he looked at her he believed she was smiling: just a small, shy movement of the mouth, accompanied by a slight inclination of the head. It could be his imagination, Wang told himself, a trick of the light, of the dust particles swirling in the room and distorting his vision. But no – the girl was definitely giving him the eye. It was unnerving, unsettling, and Wang felt hot and clammy. He wished someone would open a window or, indeed, that he had the courage to ask for a window to be opened, but that would only draw attention to himself, and one way or another he was under enough scrutiny as it was.

Wang knew the girl, at least by sight, though he had never spoken to her. She lived in the same student residence, but on a different floor. He thought her name was Lana... Lina, something like that. Wang remembered that, in the getting-to-know-you week, she had organised an outing to Cramcaster. She said it was so the Chinese students, far and away the largest in the Martin Luther King residence, could learn about the buses, explore the shops, and visit Chinatown. Safety in numbers, she told them. Wang thought her a little bossy: his uncle had warned him about women like that who, he said, were taking over the world. For that reason Wang had not gone on the Cramcaster trip – that, and the fact that, given the parlous state of his finances, even a bus fare was out of the question.

He had also seen the girl in the library, hunched over books and dictionaries. Not that this was unusual, as Wang well knew. All Chinese students worked hard, partly to repay the privilege of studying abroad and partly through necessity, to master the jargon particular to the MBA modules and written in a language that would tax even native speakers. Even so, the girl seemed just that bit more determined, just that bit more studious. There was something about her which seemed to single her out and make her special. Wang stole a furtive glance in her direction to try and discover what that was, and was disconcerted to find she was still looking at him. He squirmed and in panic looked up at the ceiling, then down at the text in front of him. The words danced before him, writhing, cavorting, mocking him, defying sense and meaning. He must concentrate, listen to the teacher, try and impress. If he could get good grades, prove his skills, then perhaps he could get a fee-waiver. At least a loan or credit. That way he could pay off Qi and Mr Wu and then later, when he applied all his new learning and taken his uncle's cycle repair business and turned it into something fit for the 21st century – battery or solar-powered bikes, perhaps – he could repay the university. This, after all, was the foundation of Western capitalism and, increasingly, the way business was conducted in his own country. Who, these days, paid for anything, whether goods or service, outright, up-front? Why should education be different? Didn't British students, on precisely that principle, have loans? So why shouldn't...?

Stirring, shifting, stifled giggles returned Wang to reality. He looked up to see the girl still staring at him, this time with disapproval and, he thought, disappointment. At the same time a voice, English, registered its presence.

103

'William. It is William, isn't it?' the voice enquired. 'I mean... your English name.'

'Haaar,' said Wang, by way of reply, as around him hands fluttered to faces to conceal unseemly mirth.

'According to my seating plan,' persisted the voice, which Wang realised belonged to the teacher, 'I have you down as William. Though I suspect one or two of you have moved.'

'Moved,' Wang repeated, as giggles, thus far contained, turned into chuckles.

'Okay. Well... if you've moved... then who are you? I mean... your name is what, exactly?'

'William. My name... William.'

'Right,' the teacher said, with an ill-concealed sigh. 'William it is. So, William... we've discussed what we mean by the dole. Perhaps, therefore, you could express the sentence in a different way. That is... using different words.'

Wang looked at the teacher, looked at the sheet in front of him, and felt his eyes filling.

'Haaar,' he ventured. His neighbour, a gangly youth with acne whose name Wang did not know, pointed a bony finger at a line of text. Through the mist that filmed his gaze, Wang made out: 'Over 2000 workers were thrown on the dole.'

'Haaar,' he began again. 'Worker... bad. Boss punish worker. Boss throw worker... like garbage... in hole.'

Wang was aware of a murmur, a muttering, rising, welling round him. He paused, blinked furiously to clear his eyes, and immediately saw across the room the spectacles, pitying, despairing, gazing on him. At that moment he wished the floor would open, swallow him, whoosh him through the earth and deposit him on the other side, back home with Uncle Peng.

The teacher was talking. 'No holes,' she was saying.

'Though I suppose if you lose your job you end up in a hole. As it were. But...'

'Haaar. Hole,' said Wang, seizing on the implication, and stretching his arms wide. 'Hole. Wang Ti in hole. Wang Ti in big hole.'

Silence. Everyone was looking at him: he knew it, he could sense it, but he ignored it. What did it matter? They all knew about his weird and wacky cash, teased him that his uncle didn't trust banks; soon, no doubt, if he didn't turn up for class, they would find out he was working to pay off further debts. This wasn't just a hole. It was a pit, an abyss, and one with no way out.

The teacher, startled by Wang's behaviour and by the ensuing silence, saw her chance to get the lesson back on track. 'Come on,' she said. 'Can anyone help Mr... er... William... out of his hole? I mean... can anyone explain...?'

Someone could. The spectacles could explain. The spectacles could explain volubly, enthusiastically, in flowing English, albeit largely incomprehensible to the teacher and the class. In fact the only thing Wang could make out was the girl's name, at any rate her English name, which the teacher used. Emmeline. Wang could taste the syllables. They reminded him of wild berries, plump and lush, popped into the mouth, rolled on the tongue, their shape and texture savoured, before bursting on the back of the throat in a lusciousness of juices and joy. There was a fullness, a wholeness in this name which Wang had never before encountered. Suddenly, he wanted more. More of this fruit aching with succulence and promise. More, more of Emmeline. Yet, as the spectacles bobbed before him, fluent, confident in their explanation, Wang felt ashamed. He had let himself down, in front of the teacher and the class; above all, in front of her. There was no way she would look at him now. He had lost

105

her, even before he found her. In despair he spread his arms on the desk, in an inverted V, and slowly let his head sink onto them. Here, so cradled, he shut his eyes. Tight. Keep out the world, its miseries, its iniquities. Keep it out... and it might just go away.

**

Christine Reeve, teacher of English as a foreign language, steadied herself against the corridor wall outside the classroom. Ahead of her the last of the Chinese students, chattering in their own language, moved away to their next class. She looked back into the room to make sure she had left nothing behind. Some classroom, she told herself: a redundant chemistry lab, still equipped with stained wooden benches nippled with gas taps – surely a health and safety hazard – where she was supposed to teach English to 48 Chinese postgraduates. Poor kids: not a clue about English, let alone business English, and these were MBA students. What was it today? The dole. Okay, perhaps not an everyday word... though in this recessionary age... but, compared with the books on human resource management, finance, or business administration the Chinese were required to study, a word like 'dole' should have been a walk in the park. Except it wasn't. Fancy that lad, the scared, skinny one, William, whatever his name was, thinking the dole was a bigger and deeper hole. Though understandable, after a fashion. English was a pig of a language. It would have been kinder to butcher it at birth, instead of these days having it butchered every time it was spoken or written. Especially written. And not just by Chinese students.

And those names, Christine continued to herself, summoning the energy to relinquish the support of the

106

wall and to propel herself down the corridor. William. Emmeline. To say nothing of the Mabels and Idas, Edwins and Reginalds: you could chorus an entire Gilbert and Sullivan opera with names like that. But why? Why did the Chinese adopt English names when learning the language? There was a time when Christine taught German; indeed, that was her speciality, but a collapse in foreign language learning, particularly German, forced a choice between early retirement and woeful pension, or retraining to teach English. As Christine knew from her German-teaching days, there was no question of calling her students Hans or Hannelore. So why should the Chinese adopt English names culled, in the main, from a bygone, probably colonial, age?

It seemed that, in donning an English mantle, it was as if identity were suspended. As if another person – appropriately, perhaps, a foreigner – were involved in the learning. A cipher, an amanuensis; an alter ego in whom this alien language, alien culture could be vested without approaching, still less challenging or damaging, the real self. Look, the person seemed to be saying. This isn't really me wrestling with language and culture far removed from my own. It's someone else, a fiction, an imaginary friend. This way I preserve my integrity, retain my dignity, safe in my bunker, while powerful enemy forces lay siege to my very being. And so, in fact…

Oh, stop it, Christine told herself crossly. That's stupid. The poor buggers probably give themselves English names because they think they're doing us a favour. Think we'll never get our minds or our tongues round Chinese names. I wonder if they're patronising us. It might be interesting to do some research, write a paper. But no. Who'd be interested? Besides, Cram Vale is hardly a top-flight research institution. More a

107

continuation of school. If key stage five is sixth form, then university – now characterised less by the code of the lecture theatre than the classroom, with background wittering, insolent familiarity and adolescent petulance – is key stage six. At least the Chinese students are well-behaved and quiet, eager to learn. That's more than can be said about many of the English students.

Damp, cool air struck her face as she pushed open the double doors leading from the former chemistry building onto the path coiling along the River Cram. For a moment she paused, gazing out across the sluggish waters of the river, beyond the playing fields on the opposite bank, and towards the College Arms, dominating that part of the campus. Christine glanced at her watch. There was no point going back to her office before the next class: everything she needed was in her bag. There was, however, time to visit the College Arms – less for a drink, she told herself sternly, more for research. Research for the spy thriller with which she was wrestling for her creative writing class, and in which the central character was based on Ed, the landlord. The publican had been a spook, a secret agent, Christine had convinced herself: his air of mystery, his knowledge, his worldliness, suggested an undercover, cloak-and-dagger past, and the more she could get to know him, the more credibly she could write. Such insight might also get the thriller back on track. The book was a struggle, and many times Christine felt she should abandon it.

But Ed would provide inspiration. He would also know why Chinese students gave themselves English names; he would discourse on the malaise of the modern university; he would provide sympathy and understanding. Ed was wise, learned, almost a university in himself, an entire body of knowledge. A body in a body. Ed's body... and a shiver ran through

108

her own.

She set off towards the College Arms.

**

Entering the pub, Christine adjusted her eyes to the gloom. She cast a hasty glance round to see if Professor Twat – as she dubbed him – was sitting in his customary seat. She didn't know him, didn't want to know him, but was aware that the oaf who was in effect her boss while she was teaching business students couldn't keep his leery eyes off her. Fortunately, there was no sign of him.

The only person she recognised in the pub was Greg Chattermole, from performing arts, who had played someone's cousin in a single episode of a soap opera and never tired of reminding people about it. Chattermole, as usual, was talking loudly, telling his companion – and, it seemed, most of Cramcaster – about his summer vacation in Mauritius.

'But the most incredible thing,' Chattermole boomed, as Christine, giving him a vague smile, flitted past, 'was who we saw getting out of this taxi. And, I might tell you, who she was with. Talk about a small world.'

Mauritius, thought Christine. Okay for some.

'Of course, she never saw me. Probably doesn't know me from Adam. Just as well, or I might not have a job,' and Chattermole roared with laughter. 'But talk about coincidence...'

I don't how Ed puts up with it, Christine reflected. Pub talk. Gossip. The bragging of failures, windbags like Chattermole. All day long. It takes someone special to ride above it, not let it get to you. And she sidled up to Ed at the bar.

'Saluton,' she said, in her one word of Esperanto.

109

Ed, however, was in no mood to reply in a tongue he cherished, and which he had picked up with ease after a couple of sessions with the Esperanto Society. Instead, he greeted her with a scowl.

'Look at this,' he said, pushing a letter at Christine. 'It's your lot. The university. And it's not on.'

Christine took the letter from Ed and began reading. 'Good grief,' she said. 'This is ridiculous.'

'Isn't it just? I mean… a planning application. An arts and media centre. On the site of the College Arms. Over my dead body.'

'I didn't think they had the funding for any new development…'

'They won't have a penny by the time I've finished with them. I'll fight them every inch of the way. I've got contacts. Contacts. And it's time to pull in a few favours.'

Christine had no idea what contacts Ed was talking about. Again, she realised how little she knew him, what an enigma he was. Before she had time to probe, Ed had turned to a shelf behind him, taken down a bottle and tumblers, and poured two generous measures.

'A Speyside,' he said. 'Arrived today. Just in time to confound our enemies. Go on… drink up. So, slainte mhor… the College Arms! And eternal damnation to those who would forge the future by pissing on the past.'

**

Wang had been the first to leave the classroom at the end of the English lesson. Despite his inclination to remain semi-recumbent, resting on his arms with his eyes shut, he knew if he did so he would attract if not the ribaldry then the curiosity of his classmates, and

110

Wang was in no mood for banter. Instead, as soon as he was aware the teacher was concluding the lesson, reminding the students of the grammar they had covered, he tensed, ready to dart from the classroom.

Having taken the corridor at a run and left the building, he was crossing the green towards the safety of Martin Luther King, before he began to slow his step. Almost immediately, he heard footsteps behind him. Even before he turned, in some irritation, he knew whose footsteps they were. They could only belong to the girl. To the spectacles.

'Wait,' she said, panting slightly. 'Hold on.'

Wang stared. She was pretty. Big round eyes framed, perhaps enlarged, by the glasses. Smooth black hair, shoulder length. Silk. And smiling. Oh, that smile. Like the first rays of morning, golden, glowing, reflecting from the dew-damp tiles on the rooftops in his uncle's village. Heralding another day, heralding hope. And yet… she was so tiny. Smaller than he was, and at best he would be deemed slight. A few moments ago in the classroom she had seemed huge, her presence everywhere, her volubility filling space; but now, this tiny figure, bundled in a minuscule jacket and short, pleated skirt, seemed so vulnerable. Wang wanted to reach out, envelop her, protect her.

'Haaar,' he said.

The girl blinked. 'I've been wanting to talk,' she began. 'Look. I'm Lina…'

'Haaar,' Wang said; then, remembering his manners, added: 'Wang Ti.'

'I know who you are. I've been… watching.'

It was on the tip of Wang's tongue to say that he knew, that during the lesson he'd watched her watching, but thought it might be rude.

'You seem… a bit out of it. Not quite settled in. I mean, I know, it must be difficult with the money. Or,

111

rather, without it. But I'm sure things will sort themselves out. Anyway, that's why...'

She paused. Trying to gauge his reaction. Wondering if she was getting through. But not knowing.

'That's why I want to ask if you'll come on our trip at the weekend. Saturday. A place called Blackpool. By the sea. This time of year, it's all lit up. Lots of lanterns, I imagine. A sort of festival of light. It's very important in the English calendar and people make a pilgrimage to the lights. And it's easy to get there. We can go by train.'

She fell silent, looking up at him, awaiting a reply. Wang felt he should speak, but didn't know where to begin. Someone, a girl, appeared to be asking him out, a sort of date, with something to do with lanterns and lights and pilgrimages.

'Haaar,' he said.

The girl frowned slightly. She'll think me a half-wit, Wang thought, panic-stricken. A cretin, an imbecile, especially after my performance just now in class.

'It's... I...' he began. Then: 'I can't. I... too much work. And there's the money.'

'It's okay,' Lina said, gently. 'We understand. We know how awkward that must be. So... we'll pay. And you...'

'No,' said Wang. 'Please... no charity. I mean...'

'You pay us back later. When you've got your money. When things have sorted themselves out.'

Wang gulped. His mind was in racing, trying to make sense of what he was hearing. The other students had ribbed him, made fun of him, when they discovered he had tried to pay his fees with ancient imperialist currency his peasant of an uncle had been fool enough to buy. But now they were supportive, understanding. Extending friendship's hand. Perhaps trying to make

112

amends. Suddenly it became clear. The girl, Lina… she was behind it, she was behind this reconciliation. Wang was grateful.

'Thank you,' he said. 'You're very kind. I mean, really. I appreciate it. But… I don't think I can.'

The girl's face, which had begun to brighten, suddenly clouded, and her bottom lip began to quiver. Wang was instantly sorry he had spoken.

'Look,' he said, quickly. 'You don't understand. It's complicated. I… I have to work.'

The girl looked at him, expecting more.

'It's… I… I need to spend time in the library. The internet.'

'We all do,' she said. 'It's tough. So much to get through. And the language. But… everyone needs a break. And while we're in Britain we ought to try and get around a bit. Take in the culture. I mean… it's not as if we're ever coming back.'

Wang was torn. On the one hand, Lina was right. It would be good to have a day away from his books. Moreover, if on Monday he was to start working for Mr Wu, then it would be sensible to have a trip to the sea, breathe in fresh air and gather strength for whatever lay ahead. On the other hand, there was the expense… even a simple day's outing would have to be paid for, eventually. And, with working for Mr Wu, he would have less time for reading, making notes. The more he could get done before Monday, the better.

'I'd love to,' Wang began.

Lina's face lit like the lanterns she was promising.

'But I can't.'

The girl's head jerked back and the spectacles, catching the light, glinted.

'What do you mean… you can't? Why not? Something wrong with you? Some disease, or something? Something you want to keep quiet? Or is it

113

like everyone says? You're a wuss. Just a pathetic wuss. Honestly... you're useless.'

Pushing past him, Lina set off in the direction of Martin Luther King. Wang stared at her retreating form as she pulled her jacket more tightly round her, as if to block him out, and her skirt swished defiantly, angrily at him.

'Wait,' he called.

Head high, she increased her pace.

'Please,' he called again. 'Wait. I can explain. Lina.'

The girl stopped abruptly, without turning to face him. Wang broke into a brief run to catch her up. When he reached her, drew level with where she was standing, he noticed two tears roll down her cheeks.

'I'm sorry,' he said. 'But... you don't understand. I mean... when I said work... I meant work. Proper work. Not university stuff. Work to get money. To pay the university. To pay what I owe Mr Wu. And Qi. To pay...'

'Who's Mr Wu?' Lina demanded, sharply. 'And this Qi fellow? What have they got to do with anything? I don't get it.'

Wang paused. Then, suddenly, out it poured; a torrent of words, unstoppable, floods, as if a dam had given way. Uncle Peng, dodgy banknotes, unpaid fees, Qi, the airport, the house in Compton Park, voices in the night, bunk beds, Mr Wu, the kitchen, cooking pots and laundry, and finally Qi's offer of work, starting Monday.

'And there was a vase,' Wang concluded. 'It got... a bit damaged. Also... what was in it. That's why I owe Qi. But as soon as I've paid him back, doing this work, then I can start paying the university. So, see, it'll be fine in the end.'

Lina looked at him, a faint frown fanning across her features.

'It will,' Wang said, earnestly. 'I know it will.'

While they were talking the wind had risen, and the sky turned drear and overcast. It was not a day for standing round in conversation.

'Come,' Lina said. 'Back to hall. What we need is tea. And more talk. Lots more talk.'

18

The youth was at prayer, kneeling in an act of piety and devotion, his rear end towards anyone entering the room, uttering imprecations in an unknown tongue to an unknown god, which appeared to reside in a desktop computer. The deity, Arthur Brush recalled with distaste, moves in mysterious ways: it must do if it needed the clot Pendegrass and his wacko sect of repenting weirdoes to do its work on earth. Therefore divine occupation of a computer, though strange, would not constitute a theological impossibility. In fact, the professor told himself, many people worship their computers. They spend more time in electronic or virtual devotion than to their nearest and supposedly dearest. He ought to know. He was one of them.

As it was, Brush was not surprised to stumble on mid-morning worship at Cram Vale University. In compliance with some politically-correct act of parliament, most of the rooms in the university, or so it appeared to the professor, were now designated faith zones for exclusive use by this or that religious group. In fact, it seemed remarkable there were any rooms left at all for anything as secular, as satanical, as teaching. Signs on every wall, internal or external, pointed to mosques or synagogues or chapels – and probably, Brush thought, if one could read Arabic, madrasses, and similar places of enlightenment and tolerance.

The only mildly puzzling feature of the youth's adoration, though, was that it was conducted in the outer office of the vice chancellor's suite, or what Brush assumed to be the VC's suite, and for a moment he thought he had walked into the wrong room.

'Sorry,' he said, backing off; at which point the youth, realising he was not alone, twisted to face the visitor and, waving a screwdriver at him, stood up.

'Well, now,' he said. 'And what might I be doing for you?'

Brush was nonplussed. The screwdriver might, under other circumstances, have been threatening. He had read that children carry screwdrivers into schools, probably to protect themselves against intellectual exertion, and he counted himself fortunate not to be a schoolteacher. On the other hand the youth's manner, despite his scruffy appearance and the ring dangling piratically from an earlobe, betrayed no menace.

Moreover, Brush's assumption – that the youth or, as he now realised, young man, had been at prayer – was in retreat. It was more likely he was a technician, a repairman, called in to service Cram Vale's creaking computer network, without which the university would collapse. Yet the voice, mellow and quietly confident, was not that of a computer technician – at least not the voice that Brush, in his limited dealings with computer technicians, would associate with them. But how did such people speak? Loudly, of course. All tradesmen... builders, plumbers, garagemen... shout. To make themselves heard over cement mixers, blow-lamps, car engines. Or that most vital of kit, the ghetto blaster. Except... but the young man was looking at him. Awaiting a response. Brush cleared his throat.

'I was looking for Pat,' he said. 'But she's not here.'

'Now, to be sure, those are true words indeed,' the young man grinned. 'She's not.'

Brush frowned. Was it Irish he could detect in the intonation? He continued: 'You've no idea, I suppose, when she might be back? Where I could find her?'

'Well, there's a thing,' the man paused. 'That's very difficult. Very. You see... this Pat you keep on about... I'm bound to tell you she's a figment of your imagination.'

'What? That's ridiculous.'

117

'No more ridiculous than saying Shakespeare was an Arab... an Arab sheikh... Sheikh Spear, if you get my meaning.'

'I've got an email... look...'

'Well, well,' the man said, laconically. 'An email.'

'An email. With a signature. Pat Kerry... PA to the VC. The vice chancellor's personal assistant. Hardly a figment of my imagination.'

'I wouldn't be so sure. You see, you could look at this in different ways.'

'I don't want to look at it in different ways. I want to speak to the VC. Or, as it says here, in this email, she wants to speak to me. Arthur Brush. Professor. It's very important. It's probably about my deanship. At last.'

'A deanship. Well, well... who knows. All the same... the VC won't be speaking to you today.'

'But it says here...'

'Not today. She can't. She's not here. You'll have to make an appointment.'

'This is ludicrous...'

'Let's not be getting all worked up, now. Think of your liver. Tell you what we'll do. I'll make you an appointment. If I can just find my little book. It's here somewhere...'

'What do you mean? You'll...?'

'Ah, to be sure, that's me all over. Begging your pardon, but I don't think we got properly acquainted. Off on the wrong foot, if you like. Pat Kerry, at your service. Personal assistant...'

'Pat Kerry? Why didn't you say so?'

The young man gave Brush a look of great sadness, the sort reserved for an animal in distress or a child about to be told baby crocodiles make poor pets.

'To be sure... you were so certain it was a lady you were seeking. And I think you'll agree I'm no lady.'

Brush felt an urge to sink a fist into the grinning

countenance before him. Figment of the imagination, indeed: there'd be no figment of the imagination by the time he'd done with him. On the other hand, it wouldn't do to duff up the VC's PA. Not the best way to get things done. Brush ground his teeth in fury.

'Okay,' he snarled. 'Just get me this appointment. What about later today? Tomorrow?'

Kerry, having recovered an appointments diary from beneath computer parts strewn across the desk, and opened it, shook his head. 'You'll be lucky. The VC's in a meeting all day with people from physics...'

Brush frowned. 'I thought physics had gone. Shut down.'

Kerry looked up from the diary. 'Just so. A meeting, they tell me, on the strategic possibilities of the physical sciences in the postmodern non-physics university. Cutting-edge, apparently. Now... tomorrow... no, afraid not. The big city. Three day conference of vice chancellors and principals on learning leadership... pushing the envelope of innovation and enterprise.'

'Okay. Next week.'

'Next week... next week. That would be... oh, quite out of the question. San Francisco. Fourth international colloquium on the implications of global warming and the greening of the higher education curriculum. Flying in from all over, for that, they are. After that... no, that's no good... nor that. But I could give you a ten-minute slot on the 18th...'

'The 18th... that's two weeks away. That's hopeless. I mean...'

'Please, no point in getting all agitated. Again, think of your liver.'

'I couldn't give a damn about my...'

'Well, now, I can see that. A crying shame, to be sure. But there we are. If you can't abuse your own

119

liver, then who's can you? But listen. I'll tell the VC you were here...'

'Good.'

'And I'm sure she'll be in touch. Or I will. One way or another. So, if that's all we can be doing for you...'

Kerry shot an impish grin at Brush and, picking up his screwdriver, turned to continue his interrupted devotions to the great god-computer.

Crying out loud, thought Brush, stalking from the office and banging the door behind him. What a waste. I could have been spending the time in spider solitaire... in research, he corrected himself. No wonder this place is the state it is. But give me that deanship, and I'll show them. Shake things up. Including that little bogshite Kerry.

19

'I'm telling you,' the man said. 'It's what gave the Frogs the idea.'

The gaggle of students, sheltering from the rain in a café on Blackpool promenade, trying to make their milky English tea last as long as possible, smiled and nodded in polite agreement at their new friend who had latched onto them at the railway station. One or two looked to another friend, their electronic dictionary, to fathom what he was saying. In the café, dictionaries were vital. The booming litany of 'legs eleven,' and 'two little ducks,' from the adjacent bingo parlour, as well as accompanying whistles and quacks, plus the clickety-click of slot machine tokens from the arcade on the other side, rendered comprehension difficult.

'I mean,' their self-appointed guide continued, 'it stands to reason. That Eiffel fellow comes to Blackpool on his hols... dirty weekend, more like, they're like that, the Frogs... sees our tower, not that he can miss it, says set mannyfeek, like they do, then goes back to Frogland and builds his own. Proper cheek, if you ask me, but, it's what I say, that's what they do, the Frogs.'

Muted muttering among the Chinese, and stabbing at dictionaries. Then a small voice, timidly raised in question.

'Haaar. You say frog. Dictionary say frog small animal. How small animal make tower...?'

An amplified 'Kelly's eye', and a raucous roar of 'Number one,' drowned the rest of the sentence.

'You'll have to speak up, laddie,' the man said, cupping a none-too-salubrious hand against a rubicund ear, which suggested a life spent beneath piers or huddled in promenade shelters. 'These walls are paper thin. Rice-paper thin,' and he guffawed at his joke. 'Rice-paper. You lot'll know about that.'

121

The Chinese students did not know about that, having barely understood a word. As usual, though, they grinned politely at what was evidently a great witticism. Wang, for his part, was not inclined to press his question. The moment had passed: the man was more intent on extracting something from his ear than engaging in conversation; though it struck Wang that because of the dirt under his nails he would be more likely to add rather than remove anything.

Wang had been persuaded to join the Blackpool trip somewhat against his inclination. Lina had been insistent, even forceful, and refused to take 'no' for an answer. She said a day by the seaside would take his mind off his financial worries, that the fresh air would do him good. Wang told himself it would be churlish not to go, especially since the other students were happy to pay his fare and have him tag along. Besides, he thought, if he didn't go, he risked losing Lina. Not that she was his to lose, he reminded himself. He didn't own her, they weren't going out, and nothing had been said. But sometimes nothing needs to be said: you just know. There was obviously something between them, some chemistry, but quite what sort Wang was not sure. Or was not sure he wanted to be sure. It excited him, fascinated him, but frightened him.

All the same, when the dozen or so students met outside Martin Luther King that morning to walk to the station, Wang thought Lina was ignoring him. She gave him a cursory greeting, barely looked at him, and then strode off at the head of the group, chatting gaily to the gangly youth with acne who had sat next to Wang in the English lesson. His name, Wang now knew, was Lu Jingen. They made an odd pair, Wang thought: she slender as a water-reed, he tall and willowy, twice her height.

Again, on the train, Lina made no effort to ensure

122

Wang sat next to her or even near her. Wang, bringing up the rear, had boarded the train last and, by the time he entered, the seats around Lina were taken. As they left Cramcaster she was engrossed in conversation with Jingen and others about China's place in the world, whether it was ready to play the role of a superpower, and what in practice this meant. Wang sat morosely across the aisle and, having exchanged pleasantries about villages and families with a plump girl whose name he failed to catch, he stared out of the window at jaded fields and jaundiced towns at which the train hooted, almost with derision, as it clattered its way to the coast.

The next thing he knew, someone was shaking him. 'Come on,' Lina's voice was saying. 'Wake up. We're there.'

Wang stirred himself, and peered out of the window. He saw nothing: the rain, sheeting down, rendered the glass a niagara of opacity. He stood up and followed Lina to the door of the train.

'Quick,' she said, setting off at a sprint along a platform long since shorn of its canopy. 'Run.'

Wang followed and found the others, damp and steaming, huddled in the shelter of the station concourse. Someone produced a phone and took a picture of the bedraggled group; meanwhile Jingen, Wang observed, had produced an umbrella and was asking Lina if she would like to share it. Wang cursed that he had no umbrella. Why couldn't his uncle have put something useful like that into his case instead of a stupid bicycle repair kit? Immediately, almost by way of reproach, Wang felt the universal repair tool he carried with him – why? Habit? Loyalty to his uncle? – turn in his pocket. He frowned. At the same time the plump girl, as if reading his thoughts, sidled up to him, brandishing a brolly, and said if he would hold it she

123

would be happy for him to come under it. Glancing across at Lina, who was smiling at Jingen, Wang nodded a reluctant acceptance.

The students were still debating whether to wait at the station for the rain to ease or to make a dash for a shop, where at least there would be something to look at, when the man appeared. He told them there was a place round the corner where they could get good quality umbrellas cheap. He knew the owner and said he could get a discount. When this information had been duly dictionaried and digested, the students who were without rain protection – most of them – thought this a good idea.

'Right you are,' the man said. 'Follow me.'

Pulling around him his coat, which had seen better days, and erecting a cock-eyed umbrella missing a spoke, the man launched himself into the rain. The students followed in his wake, splashing through puddles swollen to ponds and leaping the surging waters that churned the gutters to a foaming frenzy. After a minute or two it was obvious the umbrella shop was anywhere but around the corner. Several corners, perhaps, certainly not one; but just as the students, despair-drenched, dispirited, were ready to abandon their quest, the man brought them to what Wang believed for a moment was the edge of the world. A road, railings, then beyond a nothingness of grey, from which the rain, horizontal, lashed and slashed, driven by a fury fit to blast him whence he came. As Wang struggled to stay upright, he realised he was clinging to the plump girl, and she to him, their anchor in the storm. He tried to free himself but his efforts were arrested by an apparition; an apparition drifting, floating before him, a vision of brilliance against the gloom beyond. A tramcar, serene, stately, lit with more bulbs, more neon, than existed surely in the whole of his uncle's rural province. As Wang gazed in wonder at such radiance, he saw from the corner of his eye the man's umbrella blow inside out, and his lips move in muted imprecation. He gestured for the students to follow, at the same time pointing at a small sea-front shop, which he approached and, pushing open the door, entered. The students, grateful that here at last was shelter, crowded behind him.

The shop was narrow, but appeared to go back some distance. The students seemed to fill the space between the displays: china ornaments, picture postcards, buckets, spades, dolls, hats, pictures – much, Wang thought, with his limited experience, tawdry, tacky. Someone, apparently the owner, emerged from the rear of the shop: he bore a resemblance, Wang saw, to their guide. There was a brief conversation between the two men, whereupon the owner, grinning hugely, disappeared, to return clutching an armful of stock.

'Umbrellas. You like…? You want…?' he said, in best pidgin-English, pitching his patter to his clients. 'Good umbrellas. Very good umbrellas. Made in China. Ten quid. Each.'

The students, though, were now in no mood to buy umbrellas. They had seen the effect of the wind on their guide's umbrella, folded their own away, realising that, in this weather, an umbrella was no protection. Besides, they were wet and cold. All they wanted was a hot drink.

The man saw their hesitation. 'Tell you what,' he said. 'Specially for you. 'Cos we're friends. Amigos. For you… seven quid. Can't say fairer than that.'

The students were starting to grow restless. The man sensed his oratory was not meeting with its usual success. 'Okay,' he said. 'Last offer. Five quid. Five. You'll not find better anywhere. That's a promise.'

One or two of the students had begun to move to the

door. Wang, to his irritation with the plump girl in tow, began investigating a tray of Blackpool rock, wondering what it was. It was too heavy for a firework, and there was no touch-paper. The girl thought it might be something to be planted and grown, then perhaps harvested. 'Or else it's for self-defence,' she said.

Meanwhile the shopkeeper realised he was getting nowhere. 'Right,' he said. 'Two quid... at this rate I'm giving them away. But hurry. Can't hold that price for ever.'

The students who were still listening began a brisk discussion, in hushed tones, pointing at the umbrellas. A confident, knowing look passed over the man's face: the old magic never failed; he could feel a sale, several sales, coming on. The chatter stopped, and one of the girls turned to face him. The girl – it was Lina, who had been elected spokesperson – began talking.

'Umbrella... too much,' she said, mustering as much dignity as possible, given her bedraggled state. 'Too much. In China, where we make umbrella, we buy umbrella 20 pence. See...' and she pointed at Jingen's furled brolly '... good Chinese umbrella. 20 pence. No more.'

The man's lip curled. 'If that's your attitude, fine. Take it or leave it. But you're not in China now. And if you're not going to buy anything,' he added, addressing Wang and the plump girl, now surveying a monstrous porcelain buddha, 'you can get out now. It's all the same with you foreigners. Yeah, go on, the lot of you. Scram.'

Sensing hostility, the students edged towards the door, but not before one of them had politely thanked the shopkeeper and another told him, 'Very nice shop.'

'Piss off,' the man said.

The students spilled onto the rain-swept promenade, wondering what to do next. Someone suggested a group photo; a phone was produced and a quick snap taken, which, on examination, showed the tower growing out of Jingen's head. Wang allowed himself a smirk: the protuberance suited him. Meanwhile the plump girl, still clutching at Wang and trying to shelter behind him, although his lean frame offered sparse protection, spotted a café a couple of doors away. The students made a dash towards it. Here was a chance to sit down, dry off, and get a hot drink.

Once in the café, and having ordered tea – or what passed as tea in England – they discovered their guide had followed them. He squeezed onto a bench at the table where Lina was sitting, and appeared much offended when no-one bought him a coffee. All the same, he proceeded to regale them about the wonders of Blackpool: the piers, the theatres, the entertainers, the ballroom, the pleasure-beach and, of course, the tower.

The students – at least those close enough to catch his gist – were little inclined to believe the yarn about the tower. Everyone had heard of the Eiffel tower, no-one of the Blackpool tower. The idea that the Eiffel tower was a copy was highly improbable, and the students said so. The man shrugged. He seemed unconcerned that his story had fallen on doubting ears.

'Of course,' he continued, 'you're here for the illuminations. A bit blown about, perhaps, but they'll be okay. We're used to a spot of wind round here. Anyway, take it from me, the best way to see the lights is from a tram. So when it goes dark... that's what you do. A tram. Mind you,' he added, leering at Lina, 'I could help out. No trouble. I've got my car, see. So... a couple of you... perhaps one or two of the little ladies... I could take on a drive around. See the sights... see the lights. If you get my meaning.'

The students did not got his meaning. At least, not

without much prodding at dictionaries, at each other, and not without muttering and whispering. Meanwhile, the man was still talking.

'The car'll be more comfortable than the tram. Cosier. Warmer. And we could stop off for a drink. You'd like that, wouldn't you?' the man said, reaching over to Lina and putting his hand on hers. 'Come on. The car's just out here...'

An anguished howl from an adjacent table stopped the man in his tracks and, for what seemed an age, silenced the bingo calls from next door. At the same time something small and wiry, like a spring uncoiled, shot from its seat – spilling tea into the copious lap of the plump girl, who screamed – and with one bound reached the table where the man was still clutching Lina's hand.

'Haaar,' it raged, raining blows onto the man's back. 'You not touch. You take hand... off. Off friend. Off girlfriend. Off Lina.'

Jingen, now on his feet, grabbed Wang by his jacket collar and began to drag him away.

'You not nice man. You wicked man...' Wang addressed his victim.

Other students seized his flailing arms and, together, they hauled him back to his seat.

'Here,' the man said, standing up, little the worse for wear, 'you saw that. That's assault, that is. GBH. I've a good mind to call the police. That little turd wants locking up.'

Jingen, standing guard over Wang, a hand clapped on his shoulder, glared at his captive. 'What did you do that for?' he hissed. 'That was pretty stupid.'

'That man,' Wang said. 'He's evil. A pervert. He wanted to take Lina off...'

Jingen tightened his grip on Wang's shoulder, giving it a sudden twist. 'Don't you worry about Lina. Just

128

you remember she's spoken for.'

'Yes,' Wang said, staring up at Jingen with a decisiveness he had not seen before. 'You're right. She's spoken for. She's mine.'

Jingen, taken aback, released his grip, and as he did so Wang sprang to his feet. For a second, Jingen thought Wang would hit him. He was relieved, though, to see the café owner bearing down on them, brandishing a mop to wipe the floor where the tea had spilled, and looking as if he would lay into both of them if there was any more fighting. Waving the mop handle at them, he said he wanted nothing to do with the police or illegals, and told them to pay up and get out. The students obliged, apologising for the disturbance. Wang in particular, now much calmer, was at pains to make amends, offering to clean the floor, but the café owner wanted rid of them. Of their self-appointed guide, and would-be chauffeur, there was no trace.

Outside, where the rain was still coming at them at right angles, there was no appetite to linger. The lights, they felt, would be a wash-out. No lantern could survive in that wind. The girls were complaining of the cold; the plump one said she thought she had pneumonia. Someone pointed out that, if the man rang the police, they might be arrested any minute. There was unanimous agreement to return to the railway station at once.

They set off. As they did so, Wang felt a hand pressed into his own.

'Thank you,' Lina said, peering up at him over misted spectacles. 'You saved me.'

From the bingo parlour reverberated the caller's voice. 'Young and keen,' it intoned. 'Young and...'

'Bingo,' someone cried. 'Bingo.'

129

20

In the warmth of Cramcaster Central Police Station, PC Gruff – laboriously compiling a report on yet another driving with no insurance, and trying to remember whether 'proceeding' had one e or two – was relieved to be interrupted by an email from the press office at Cramcaster United football club.

'Here,' he said, calling across the room to Dutton, who was making good use of police equipment to search the internet for a Morris Minor boot lid. 'At last. Cop a load of this.'

For a copper, Dutton had no particular wish to cop anything, unless associated with the automotive magic of Cowley. Out of deference though to his colleague, and knowing Gruff would have him cop whatever was to be copped whether he liked it or not, he paused in his quest and assumed an air of expectant interest.

'It's what I thought,' Gruff said. 'No-one by the name of Queer at Cramcaster United. Not in the first team, not in the reserves. And no-one on the staff. No parking attendant, no bog attendant, nothing. Never heard of him. I tell you... we've a mystery on our hands.'

The only mystery Dutton had on his hands was sourcing a boot lid at a reasonable price. He had no idea what Gruff was on about.

'I bet if you looked hard enough you'd find a few queers in the squad. I mean, statistically there's bound to be a couple,' he said, turning back to his computer.

'That Chinky chappie,' Gruff said. 'You remember. The one we fished out of the gutter and then gave a lift to that posh place in Compton Park. The one with all the security. Said he'd had his car nicked.'

The word 'car' caught Dutton's attention. 'With you,' he said. 'The footballer fellow.'

130

'That's what I'm saying. He's not a footballer.'

'What is he, then?'

'How do I know?'

'Okay, okay. Thought you'd got it sussed.'

'I haven't. Not yet. But I don't like it. Fishy, if you ask me.'

Dutton frowned. 'It seemed a bit odd at the time. That business with the car, I mean. I wonder if he ever reported it nicked?'

'Good one,' said Gruff. 'I'll check. Missing vehicles from Compton Park. You know... I reckon there's more to this than meets the eye.'

'Perhaps,' said Dutton, whose eye was back on the computer screen. 'Can't do anything, though, if he doesn't report it.'

'We'll see about that. You don't have to report a crime to solve one. Initiative... that's what it takes. Which some of us have... and others don't.'

But Dutton wasn't listening. Sleuthing skills that might have been employed to round up stray dogs, stray children and other irksome malefactors were concentrated on the apprehension and subsequent custody of a boot lid. Keeping a Minor was, as Dutton would tell anyone foolish enough to listen, a major task.

21

The campus was quiet, veiled in early morning mist that wreathed the playing fields and hung like shrouds in the branches of the blackened trees. Damp dripped clammy cold from limpid air: shapes and shadows formed and reformed beneath the fleeting glow of lights along the path from the student residences. A fox, its dull coat matted, slunk lean and low across the path and disappeared into scrub above the river bank.

Another creature, lean and low, a flimsy jacket bunched around it, scurried along that path. A creature with a debt to pay, heading for a bus stop and a 6am rendezvous with its employer.

Wang knew he could not be late. There was too much at stake. The previous day, following his return from Blackpool, and with Lina's help, he had found the bus-stop, worked out the quickest route from the hall of residence, and timed himself on the walk. He needed just six minutes. He had set his alarm for 5.30 to give himself time to wash, dress, gulp down some tea and set off. In the event he was awake an hour earlier, listening to the clonk of distant pipes and the creaking of a building adjusting to the seasonal damp. On the floor above someone flushed a toilet and from beyond, on the main road by the bus stop, wailed a passing siren.

The next thing he heard was a hammering outside his room. He rose unsteadily from his bed, his head heavy, solid with sleep, and, pulling open the door, blinked into the brash light of the corridor. A torrent of admonishment, of reproach, knocked him back into the room. Fingers, hands, clawed at his pyjamas; a voice, shrill and concerned, urged him to change, get dressed, it was gone quarter to six and there was no time to lose.

Lina had come to see Wang off, wish him well on

132

his first day with Mr Wu. However, instead of being able to offer encouragement and reassure him she would take notes in class and share them with him that evening, she found the door to his room tightly shut and no sign of movement. She guessed at once what had happened. As soon as she managed to rouse him she swept into the room, already plucking at his pyjamas, exhorting him to remove them. Then, elbowing him aside, she crossed to the wardrobe, extracted jeans and a shirt and flung them at him. She found a pullover on the back of a chair, underpants and socks on the floor – never mind if they were dirty – and trainers under the bed. Within a minute Wang was dressed, save for his jacket, which Lina snatched from a hook on the back of the door and thrust at him. She glanced at his bedside clock.

'You've not eaten,' she said.

Wang shook his head. 'No time,' he mumbled.

'Two minutes. Wait here... no, get to the main door. I'll see you there.'

So saying, she darted from the room. Wang, in a daze, unable to think, followed instructions and shambled into the corridor to head for the stairs and the exit. When he got there Lina, as if by magic, was waiting.

'Here,' she said. 'I got it in Blackpool. Best I can do.'

Wang stared at the proffered gift, similar to the tubular object he and the plump girl had puzzled over in the shop. A firework that wasn't, a weapon of self-defence, a truncheon, perhaps, or else something to be stuck in the ground to grow? He pulled a puzzled face.

'It's fine,' Lina said. 'You suck it. Now... you've got six and a half minutes. Go.'

Wang looked as if he was about to say something. Lina put her finger to her lips and, with her free hand,

133

tugged at the door.

'See you tonight,' she said and, without further ado, bundled Wang into the chill of a Cramcaster morning.

Precisely six minutes later Wang was standing at the bus stop, panting, watching his breath vaporise, merging with the mists rolling off the university playing fields. Wang could already feel the damp rising from the pavement, permeating his trainers, his feet, and starting to work its way up his legs. He stamped his feet to keep his circulation going, to maintain some sort of feeling in his toes, but already he sensed he was fighting a losing battle. Perhaps the food-stick Lina had given him, and on which he had to suck, would help. Cold fingers scrabbled at cellophane, which at first refused to budge and then, when it did came away only partly, in strips, with the rest clinging obstinately to the stick. No matter: he was hungry. Wang had seen nothing like the food-stick but, if Lina said it was okay, then surely it must be. As he put the stick to his mouth, he noticed there was writing curling round the inside edge. He paused to try and make it out, but in vain. All the same, this was encouraging. Perhaps the food-stick was a sort of fortune cookie which, along with a prognosis for the future, would provide nourishment and energy for whatever lay ahead. Wang put the stick into his mouth, and sucked hard. Nausea swept over him as something sweet and sickly clogged his taste-buds. At the same time a strip of cellophane came away into his mouth, and wrapped itself round his teeth. As he began to cough and choke, he realised that out of the mist and murk of the Cramcaster morning a minibus was bearing down upon him. Wang flung himself into the road, spluttering and gasping, and, clutching his food-stick and waving it at the driver, indicated the bus should stop. Brakes squealed and the vehicle slewed to a halt as Wang, just in time, leaped out of the way. The door hissed open and the driver stood framed on the step.

'You stupid bastard. What do you think you're playing at?'

'Haaar. You Mr Wu friend?'

'You what?'

'You. Mr Wu friend.'

'Mr Who?'

'Haaar... yes. You Mr Wu friend. So... you take in bus...'

'Bugger off. And get away from my vehicle. It's not in service. Can't you read? It says at the front: Not In Service. The first one along here's not for half an hour.'

'Half an hour...'

'You got it, sonny. And stop waving that magic wand thing in my face. Who do you think you are? Fucking Harry Potter?'

So saying, and muttering about bloody students and late-night parties, the driver stepped back into his bus and, as the door sliced shut, roared off along the road, leaving Wang with a lungful of diesel.

This was all very strange. Mr Wu had been quite particular about the time. Six o'clock sharp, that's what he'd said. And Mr Wu did not strike Wang as being in any way vague or inefficient. But now it must have gone six, a good few minutes after, and the bus had come and gone without picking him up. Wang placed his hand on his sleeve, pushed it back, check his watch; but the watch was not there. Clearly, in his haste to leave his room, he had forgotten to put it on. However, if the bus was not due for another half hour then he could go back, pick up his watch, grab something more savoury than Lina's food-stick, and still be back for the new pick-up time. So thinking, he trotted across the dual carriageway, heading back towards Martin Luther King. He had reached the other side of the road when behind him, where he had been waiting, he realised another bus was stopping. Wang peered through the still-swirling mists and thought he made out Mr Wu sitting at the wheel, scanning the pavement. In a trice he dashed back across the road – at that hour, traffic was light – and arrived, panting, beneath the windscreen behind which Mr Wu was perched. His employer frowned as he saw Wang approach from the wrong direction, but opened the door for him.

'You're late,' he said. 'You were told to be here at six.'

It was on the tip of Wang's tongue to explain, but something in Mr Wu's face made him think better of it.

'You're lucky I didn't drive off. Make sure it doesn't happen again. Otherwise, no second chances. Got it?'

Wang nodded sadly. He got it only too well.

22

A left-click brought Brush no nearer to solving the enigma of the queen of hearts and the seven of spades. Their significance in achieving a low-move, high-score win remained as elusive as ever: he was sure they were the key to success, but proving it was a different matter. However, the last 78 games indicated the ace of spades might be a factor. Play the ace in the second round, ideally placing it on a card in the third column from the right, and the statistical probability of a win in less than 130 moves appeared in the region of 47%. That was comparable with any combination involving the queen of hearts and the seven of spades. Brush frowned. Thoughts of the best-seller stocking filler, Improve Your Spider Solitaire – to be published under a pseudonym, lest his university standing be damaged but which, unlike scholarly publication, would attract serious money – were fast receding.

A 'have-a-good-day' American voice broke in on the professorial musings to tell him he had new mail. Brush was piqued. Generally, when engaged in high-level, pioneering research of this nature, he switched off the sound to his computer. Now his concentration was broken. He might never know whether the ace held the key to solitaire success: at any rate the breakthrough, if such it was, would have to wait.

Annoyed, Brush prodded the keyboard to bring up his mail. He saw at once he had a message from the vice chancellor. At least, on examination, from the VC's PA, which was the next best thing. Brush straightened himself in his chair and read:

Dear Arthur. I have been conscious for some time of the need to strengthen the Senior Management Team, and accordingly I would like to appoint you forthwith as Assistant Vice Chancellor (Acting) (External /

Internal Relations). You will be aware...

'Yeah,' roared Brush, punching the air with his fist. 'Yeah. Result!'

Fearing the professor was being attacked by insects or, worse, students, Michelle, his secretary, poked her head round the door from the outer office. 'You okay?' she asked warily.

'This is it,' Brush babbled. 'At last. Oh, eat your heart out...'

It crossed Michelle's mind to ring for a doctor; universities did strange things to people.

'Eat you heart out, Rosalind Brush. You and your tin-pot council... poxy committees... this is Assistant Vice Chancellor Arthur Brush. Assistant Vice Chancellor. That'll show you...'

Clearly, thought Michelle, the man was hallucinating. He might be in charge of a university department, but assistant vice chancellor... that was ridiculous. There was no way anyone in their right mind would promote Brush to senior management. On the other hand, the number of right minds in any university hierarchy was probably a minus figure, and so therefore... Michelle wondered whether she should call, if not a doctor, then security.

'I just need to...' she began, backing away to the safety of her office.

'Look,' said Brush, gesticulating at the computer screen, and reading. 'Get this. Key Role... serve with Distinction... Public Face of this University. That's me. The public face. Oh, there'll be changes round here. Changes, I tell you...'

The man wasn't drunk, Michelle told herself. At least, not on whatever the College Arms might have on tap. It was too early. But if he wasn't high on booze, then he was high on something else. Himself, most likely. There were a lot like that, Michelle reflected, at

138

Cram Vale, all high on themselves – and Brush was a prime example.

'Here,' the professor said. 'See for yourself.'

Something wild, unbridled, in Brush's demeanour told her it would be foolish to refuse. All the same, she was reluctant to approach: in his present state he might do anything.

'Read it,' he said. 'Out loud. So I know I'm not dreaming.'

With some trepidation Michelle approached the desk where Brush was sitting, and positioned herself as far from him as she could manage.

'Dear Arthur…' she began.

'Yes, yes… we know that,' Brush said impatiently. 'Here… the rest of it.'

'Er… Assistant Vice Chancellor (Acting) (External / Internal Relations). You will be aware this is a new Post and, due to its Experimental Nature, will be provisional in the first instance…'

'Humph,' grunted Brush.

'I therefore see no need to enter at this stage into a Formal Appointments Procedure…'

'Proper thing too. Just get on with it. That's my motto.'

'This is a Key Role and all the more important due to my many Commitments at home and abroad in the service of Higher Education. This means I am unable to represent the University as much as I might like both on and off Campus. I am sure you will serve with Distinction as the Public Face of this University…'

'Distinction. Hear that?'

'I understand you will need to reassess your own Role as Head of School. It will also mean your valued Research is put on Hold, but I am sure you will galvanise Members of your School to Up Their Game to maintain Standards…'

139

'You bet. Bunch of skivers. That idiot Pendegrass, for instance.'

'Indeed, Research is the Name of the Game. And it's signed by the VC, Professor Barbara Redwell-Nope BSc (Hons) MSc DSc DipGD, but actually sent by someone called Kerry.'

'Arsehole. Kerry, that is. Not the VC. I'll be working with her on a daily basis. And now, get my wife on her mobile. She needs to be told... pronto.'

Michelle made a welcome escape to her own office and looked up Councillor Rosalind Brush's number. Why the professor couldn't make the call directly was beyond her. Already too grand for anything as humdrum as making a phone call.

When the phone rang on Brush's desk, the professor was ready.

'Councillor Brush, I believe?' the professor asked, putting as much scorn into the word 'councillor' as he could muster. 'This is Assistant Vice Chancellor...'

'What do you want?' his wife snapped. 'I'm busy. Site visit. Architects, planners, the lot. Also, the portfolio holder for...'

'I was about to tell you...'

'Don't. It'll wait. And get some loo rolls on your way home. We're out.'

'But...'

The phone went dead.

Typical, thought Brush. The woman couldn't give a monkey's if it wasn't to do with the council. But she'd be sorry. When I'm wining and dining with government ministers... secretaries of state...

The phone rang again. Brush grabbed the receiver and bellowed into it.

'Yeah... thanks a bunch. Very supportive. And you know where you can stuff your loo rolls.'

Silence.

140

Emboldened, Brush continued. 'Of course, whenever you do something, it's different. Get elected, go on some committee, get your name in the paper, all we hear is "who's a clever girl, then?" But when I…'

'I thought we'd established I'm not a girl.'

'What?' said Brush.

'You still seem to be labouring under the misapprehension that I'm female. I suppose it's a reasonable mistake to make, but under the circumstances…'

'Shit. It's you. It's…'

'Quite. Pat… or perhaps I should start calling myself Patrick… Kerry.'

'I knew that. I mean… bollocks. I thought… when the phone went…'

'I was someone else. The story of my life. But never mind. Listen. I've sent an email…'

Brush flinched. It was a mistake. A cock-up. The fool had sent the email in error, wanted to retract, apologise. There was no vice-chancellorship. The little turd. He'd get him shifted to student appeals, have him hunting disputed exam papers for the rest of his pathetic days. Except the papers wouldn't exist. Brush would personally remove them, shred them, toss them in the Cram. He'd…

'You still there, Professor Brush?' Kerry was asking.

'Yes,' Brush growled.

'The VC would like a response as soon as possible. Of course, before you accept, you might want time to consider.'

'Consider?' Brush snapped. 'Is a turd shit? Of course I accept.'

'Excellent, Professor Brush. Excellent. I… that is, we… knew you were the man for the job.'

The phone clicked dead in Brush's ear.

141

23

It was impossible to concentrate. The words flowed past like scraps of washed-out lives, like the clothing, books, furniture and corpses which, when she was a child, had swirled past her uncomprehending gaze after the river upstream burst its banks, inundating the villages that bordered it. Everything was dislocated, nothing in its place. There was no sense or meaning; nothing to hold to, cling to, latch on to. Lina felt she was drowning.

The module – Global Marketing in the Global Economy – was sufficiently abstruse without the lecturer making it more so. The man was affable enough, the students decided, and appeared to speak knowledgeably about his subject, though this could not be confirmed because what he said was largely incomprehensible. He had puzzled the students at the start of the semester by introducing himself as A. Jordy, not that this was the name on their timetable, and said he came from a place called Newcastleman. The students had diligently written this down, believing it to be a vital part of the module, one on which they might be examined, but those who searched for Newcastleman on the web found no trace of it. Several Newcastles, both in Britain and beyond, and variations on it, such as Newcastle-under-Lyme – which suggested the place had been buried and thus, strictly, had no right to exist – but certainly no Newcastleman. It was a puzzle, compounded by the fact that the lecturer began each class with the enthusiastic question whether the students had watched the match-man. The Chinese nodded politely: an appropriate response, they felt, and probably expected of them, which seemed to encourage the lecturer to broaden their minds on the subject of you-ni-ed and gaw-als and leeg tay-bles. All

142

this they scribbled down, or as much as possible, grateful for the opportunities postgraduate study in Britain afforded them; but when, after the class they checked their notes against the textbooks, to discover how their new-found knowledge fitted into Global Marketing in the Global Economy, they were invariably disappointed.

Lina stared out of the window into a bleak and dreary Cramcaster morning. If she expected the Jordyman's words to be written, as if by magic, in the sky, she was disappointed. As indeed happened when she and Wang spent a fruitless afternoon traipsing the corridors of Wole Soyinka, examining names on office doors in an attempt to track down Mr Jordy. Lina wanted to confront him, to ask him to explain all the puzzling terms he had introduced but which she was unable to find in her books. The man, however, was as enigmatic as his utterances, for there was no door bearing the name A. Jordy. When she and Wang told the other students, they said Lina worried too much. Jingen told her no-one failed the exams because the university couldn't afford to send any of the Chinese students home on account of the fees they brought with them – at least, some did, Jingen said pointedly, looking in Wang's direction.

Then he said they didn't need fret even about the dissertation. 'The tutors write it for you,' he told them. 'The English tutors. At least, if not exactly write it, they check the language and polish it. They do it for next to nothing because most of them only work part-time. That means they need the money. Good, or what?'

Lina frowned, and tried to wrest her mind back to the present and to what the mysterious Mr Jordy was saying. She would earn her MBA on her own merits. No scraping through exams because nobody ever failed them; no getting some struggling, underpaid teacher to

143

write her dissertation. Nor would Wang. He, too, would pass this course on his own endeavours, even though – as she reminded herself – he was dependant, while toiling for Mr Wu, on the notes she was struggling to jot down. Oh, it was so hard, and rendered harder still by Wang's absence. What was he doing? Where was he? Somewhere out in the global economy, that selfsame global economy which, in theory, was the subject of Mr Jordy's class. Lina felt better after this realisation; Wang seemed somehow closer, even part of the lecture. But if only she could understand what was being said. That would make her feel better still.

**

If Wang was indeed out in the global economy, then it was an economy which modernity appeared to have missed. At any rate, this was Wang's impression of the place into which he had been ejected – along with three other Chinese – from Mr Wu's minibus, which had promptly turned and lurched away down the rutted track on which it arrived, taking the remaining passengers with it.

The journey from Cramcaster had passed in silence. Mr Wu had said nothing, concentrating on steering the minibus which, Wang noted, seemed inclined to drift to the middle of the road, which required the driver to haul hard on the steering wheel to bring the bus back into line. Then, when the houses in the still-sleeping suburbs of Cramcaster gave way to more open spaces, and metalled roads became lanes and then little more than cart tracks, Mr Wu needed all his strength to wrestle with the wheel to prevent the bus slewing into ditch or hedge.

Like the driver, the passengers were quiet. Most were asleep, apparently unconcerned at the perils

144

facing them with every twist of the wheel. Or perhaps, Wang thought, they were used to it, had seen it before, accepted it as a necessary prelude to the working day. Wang, though, could no more shut his eyes than – had he been asked – recall the month in which the lunar year had begun. He was too keen to see where he was going, to try and learn what lay in store. This was no time for sleep.

Rubbing with his sleeve at a steamed-up window, he peered out onto fields; open, empty, and laced with long straight ditches or channels, which appeared to stretch to the horizon. At first he thought these waterways must be for irrigation, but this struck him as odd, since all it seemed to do in Britain was rain. Then he realised. The ditches were for drainage, to take the water away, quite the opposite of what he was used to at home. He peered with renewed interest at the channels, and tried to count them as the minibus bounced over flimsy bridges with no parapets; but then they ran alongside one of the larger channels and Wang, concerned lest the bus slither from the dyke into the water below, lost interest in counting. Instead, he tried to make out what was in the fields. Many appeared to be fallow and, where there were crops, it was impossible in the timid light of morning to recognise them. There were no cattle, no sheep: this was clearly arable, rather than grazing land. From time to time the tedium of the landscape was broken by a straggling hedge, or tree, or even a copse. Periodically a farmhouse loomed into view, tired, run-down, and surrounded by ancient, rusting farm implements.

The spot where Wang was now standing, already up to his ankles in mud, was no different. A two-storey dwelling built of red brick, presumably a farmhouse, which appeared not to have seen paint since it was constructed. One of the upstairs windows was broken,

145

and a piece of faded curtain flapped lamely from it. Nevertheless the place appeared to be inhabited: smoke rose from a chimney and, behind a grimy downstairs window, a light bulb, dangling from a flex and unshaded, was glowing. A figure moved in front of the light and, as Wang watched, a door opened and a portly man, with a florid face and huge ruddy hands like the hams Wang recalled from the hotel where he worked, stepped out. The man glanced at the new arrivals standing forlornly in the yard, scowled, and grunted something Wang did not catch. Then he strode past them into an adjacent barn.

'What's going on?' Wang turned to one of his countrymen. 'What do we do now?'

'We wait,' came the reply. 'We wait for...'

The rest of the response was rendered incomprehensible as machinery of some sort, an engine, exploded into life. At the same time thick blue smoke billowed from the barn and the air was filled with the stench of diesel. Wang began to cough, and he felt his eyes watering. Blinking, he realised something was emerging from the barn. The roar of the engine increased and, through the fumes, appeared a tractor towing what looked like an overgrown chariot. The portly man was astride the tractor, pushing and prodding at levers, which seemed to affect neither the noise nor the fumes which it produced in abundance; indeed, quite the contrary. And no wonder, thought Wang, who, while no expert on farm machinery, realised at once that this particular specimen, which had now jolted to a halt before them, would be more at home in a museum than on the land. For a start, it had no cab, and its two front wheels were tiny, with barely any tread. The tractors Wang remembered from the fields around his village were monstrous machines, with huge gnarled tyres and cabs equipped, it was said,

146

with air-conditioning and radios and other luxuries. As for that carousel thing or whatever it was it was pulling…

'Hey!' Wang felt a dig in the ribs. 'Get a move on.'

He turned to see one of the other workers, who had been on Mr Wu's bus, gesture at the contraption before them. Wang looked at him, puzzled.

'Don't tell me. First day. And no idea why you're here. Never mind, you'll find out soon enough. Come on. Up you get.'

So saying, the man climbed on the trailer and beckoned to Wang to follow.

'Welcome aboard,' he said. 'And hold tight.'

**

Something was happening in Mr Jordy's classroom. Something that drew Lina's thoughts away from Wang and back to the global economy. Or, rather, to Mr Jordy's explanation of it. The lecturer, instead of standing before the class mumbling in his largely incomprehensible way, had become animated, excited. He was pacing up and down, making great sweeping movements with his arms, and talking in rapid, urgent tones. It crossed Lina's mind he might be ill – a fit, perhaps, even a heart attack – and, never having witnessed such crises, she gazed in anguished anticipation on the would-be victim. However, Mr Jordy was still upright, displayed no signs of keeling over, and the sweat he flicked from his forehead could be a result of the stuffy and airless room. Moreover his behaviour, in particular his voice, usually muted but now shrill and almost strangulated, suggested that what he was attempting to convey was of particular significance. Lina, roused from her reveries, strained to unpick the meaning in the professor's words, which she

147

felt she should note and pass on that evening to the absent Wang.

If Lina understood correctly, someone called Thatcherman – a name with which Lina was unfamiliar – had liberated markets by disposing of state assets to private enterprise. There was nothing remarkable about this, Lina felt, since it was happening in China, which made it somehow alright. Mr Jordy, however, appeared to take a different view. Privatisation, he squeaked, was an abomination, a travesty – what was that? Lina wondered, fingering her electronic dictionary – inflicted on the British people in the name of efficiency. 'Efficiency,' Mr Jordy piped, eyes bulging, sweat bouncing from his brow onto surrounding students. 'Efficiency... not in a month of Sundays, man. Think of all those people coming up your street delivering parcels and packages. In the old days just the postman, man, but now, why, any number of Mickey Mouse outfits... one man and a dog... all doing the same thing. Duplication of effort, man, like Communist East Germany...'

Lina scribbled furiously. How a mouse and dog fitted into the global economy was unclear, but Lina was sure the professor would explain. Or would he? The Thatcherman, he declared – was it a trick of the light, or was he foaming at the mouth? – set up competing private companies simply to create jobs. Not proper jobs, manufacturing jobs, man, but non-productive, bureaucratic, Mickey Mouse jobs. Ah... the mouse again. Lina underscored 'mouse' twice for good measure and resolved after the class to visit the library to find out more.

'And the result?' Mr Jordy spluttered. 'The result, man, is all we do today is send each other emails. Emails to co-ordinate hole-diggers and fence-erectors, cable-layers and cable-testers, hole-fillers and tarmac-rollers, and temporary traffic-light installers with the lot of them. At the same time gas companies sell electricity and water companies broadband, while here-today gone-tomorrow railway companies paint and repaint their hired trains to drive on someone else's track. Bonkers, man, and grossly inefficient. And serviced by armies of people in dead-end jobs. A treadmill... and Thatcher, Thatcherman, the evil behind it all. I mean,' Mr Jordy continued, 'take the health service...'

But Lina was in no mood to take anything. Her head was spinning with dogs and mice, holes and temporary traffic lights. How was she to explain any of this to Wang when she couldn't explain it to herself? She hoped the expensive textbook she had bought might offer explanation, but she rather doubted it. Nothing in Professor Jordy's lecture seemed to accord with anything she had found in the book. She sighed. Suddenly she was overcome with envy for Wang. He was spared this. He was working, doing an honest day's labour, helping a fellow countryman; he was travelling, broadening his mind, even if only in Mr Wu's minibus. A shiver of excitement ran down Lina's spine. She was looking forward to seeing him, to hearing what he would have to say. As far as Lina was concerned, the evening could not come soon enough.

24

Green wellington boots. Caked in mud and, Wang thought, this being a farm, probably much else. A hint of corduroy trouser and, level with this, a hand – hairy, clutching a curious conical canister suspended from a metal handle with a wooden grip. The canister might have begun life, several decades ago, bridal white, but now its surface was pitted, metallic, Monday-morning grey. Behind, beyond, a vista of damp and dripping field. The view from beneath a farm-cart is by necessity restricted, Wang reflected, but at least the vehicle offered shelter from the relentless rain during what seemed to be a mid-morning break.

A dislocated voice called out, belonging, probably, to the boots – though from beneath the cart, it was difficult to tell. ''Ere. It's yer baggin'. Take it. I'm gettin' fair drenched.' As if to urge acceptance, the canister jigged and jerked on its handle, and drops of dark liquid, making a bid for freedom from beneath the ill-fitting lid, rolled down the canister's cracked and once-enamelled surface, running with the rain.

'Yer want yer baggin' or not?' the voice was slightly raised. 'Fer God's sake... take it.' So saying, the boots creased slightly, as if whatever was inside were about to bend, lower itself, thrust the billy-can beneath the cart; even perhaps stoop to peer at the dispirited souls huddling together out of the wet.

'Tea,' one of Wang's compatriots said. 'It'll warm us up. You'd better take it.'

'It's all we get for the next few hours,' the other said. 'Make the most of it.'

The billy-can launched into a furious fandango, and more tea spilled out. Wang, last beneath the cart and closest to the boots, extended an arm to take it. Its reception was acknowledged with a grunt, from beyond

150

his range of vision, and was followed with a growl: 'Five minutes. That's all yer got. All this rain an' we get behind.' The boots turned, easily, on the mud, and squelched away in the direction of the tractor and harvester.

Wang passed the billy-can to the elder of the two other workers squatting beneath the cart, who accepted it as if it were his right. The man removed the lid and, to Wang's surprise, turned it upside down and began to pour tea into it. The second man, waiting his turn, seemed to read Wang's thoughts and said: 'One cup between three. What do you expect?'

Wang had no idea what to expect. Instead, to make conversation, he said the first thing that came into his head, and asked the man how long he had been working for Qi, or Mr Wu, and how long he had been coming to the farm. The man looked sadly at Wang and his eyes, the student thought – though it might have been moisture in the air – clouded over.

'A year,' he said. 'Maybe two. I don't really know.'

Wang was about to ask more – where the man came from, how long he was going to stay, what he did in China before he left – but the first man, having finished slurping his share of the tea, passed the billy-can and cup to the second one. Wang watched as he, in turn, poured the still-steaming liquid into the crazed cup and drank in long, satisfying draughts. These slipped down his throat with a gurgle and reminded Wang of the plumbing at the hotel where he had worked.

Having finished, and having wiped his mouth with the back of his hand, the man handed the billy-can to Wang. At first he thought it empty: the can was lighter than when he accepted it and took it under the cart. Peering into the stained and murky interior, however, he was relieved to find more than enough liquid remained. It crossed his mind perhaps the can was magic and never ran out but this, he told himself sternly, only happened in children's stories: certainly not in a field on a farm in rain-rinsed, blustery Britain. He poured the tea into the cup as his colleagues had done, put the cup to his lips and, noting the others were watching, took a cautious sip.

He spat it out at once. It was vile: sickly sweet, teeth-tingling thick. As much sugar as tea, Wang guessed, gazing with distaste at the remainder of the concoction. The other two men roared with laughter, nudging each other, pointing at Wang.

'You'll get used to it,' one said. 'It's what they drink round here.'

'Sugar,' the other said. 'For energy. Keep you going until they bring the food at midday. Or what passes for food.'

The two men exchanged a knowing glance and, again, laughed.

'Go on,' the younger man said. 'Get it down you. Seriously, you need it to keep up your strength. It won't kill you.'

Wang wasn't so sure. However, he could see sense in building his energy and getting something warm inside him. With a grimace he drained the contents of the cup. As he was replacing it on top of the can, he spotted approaching wellington boots.

'That's it,' a voice said. 'You've 'ad yer baggin', an' now it's time t'get some work done. Come on, you lazy sods. Look lively.'

The three Chinese crawled out from underneath the cart into the driving rain, pulling up the collars of their jackets, and splashed across to the waiting potato harvester. Wang, handing the billy-can to the farmer, and emboldened by its contents slopping in his stomach, ventured a question.

'Haaar,' he said. 'Please... bag in. What mean bag

in? Potato from field... go in bag. Now you want me say... potato from field go bag in. But this no bag,' Wang added, indicating the billy-can. 'Bag... paper. This... metal.'

The farmer stopped in this tracks and stared at Wang. 'Baggin'. It's yer tea. Yer drink. What yer think it is, yer numbskull? Fish an' ruddy chips? Yer stop wastin' my time with tomfool questions an' get yerself up on yon 'arvester. 'Ar-ves-ter. Comprendo?'

There was little comprendo. Puzzlement, yes; despair, frustration, but little comprendo. Very little of that. All the same, as Wang scrambled aboard the harvester, hoping its tarpaulins would offer protection from the elements, an idea was forming. As yet ragged, remote, but nevertheless an idea. If he could just... but at that moment the tractor belched into life, enveloping any idea in a puff of angry diesel.

'Haaar,' he said, to no-one in particular. And again, more brightly: 'Haaar.'

**

Dozy Pendegrass sat at his computer and stared with a sense of mounting shame – no, guilt – at the message displayed on its screen. He had indeed been out of order. Perhaps he should have confessed to the Nazareth and Ewesbottom Repentant Sinners. On the other hand, it had nothing to do with them. But now his misdeed had come to haunt him. The message was a circular from Marcus Dunlittle, director of physical plant and resources, complaining that official university notices were being defaced, which gave a poor impression of the institution. The message finished: 'Any One Caught Defaming University Notice's Will Be Delt With Severally'.

Pendegrass frowned. There was no suggestion that

153

perhaps grocers' apostrophes, self-important capitals or orthographical horror might create an even poorer impression. But then, why should it? No-one, apart from Lynne Truss and he (ought that to be him? himself?) was in the least bit bothered about grammatical nicety. No-one these days would recognise a solecism even it smacked them (him? her?) over the head with Partridge's Usage and Abusage. No-one, except the suggestively named Truss. Wasn't that some sort of medical device? Perhaps, but it also evoked ropes, shackles, handcuffs and what Pendegrass thought might loosely be termed bondage. Smoky images – from furtive misuse of the university internet – of pink-draped beds and slinky, leather-clad females slowly divesting themselves in sleazy rooms above launderettes pervaded Pendegrass's mind. He wondered if Lynne Truss wore leather. Or wielded a whip. Or visited launderettes. He felt a fascination stir in his crotch and his hand moved to offer solace. A woman with such feel for the erogenous zones of language... ah... would be able to manipulate her partner... ah... explore the sensuality of syntax... sin... Lynne... ah... ah...

A crackle from the computer caused Pendegrass to open his eyes. Damn that screen-saver, he thought savagely, vowing to replace at the earliest opportunity the picture of the repentant sinners' chapel with Lynne Truss, preferably nude, or sporting the skimpiest of racy underwear. Damn it. Elation yielded, as always, to deflation, and Pendegrass returned his errant hand to the desk where it flicked the keyboard to restore Dunlittle's message.

A rectangle in the lower right-hand corner of the screen told him he had new mail. The sender: Professor Arthur Brush, head of school. Pendegrass groaned, and clicked the icon.

154

The message was – for Brush – succinct. As you might or might not be aware, Pendegrass read, I have been promoted to the post of Assistant Vice Chancellor. This will have an effect on my ability to continue my pioneering research into spiders, probability theory and the effect on individual cash-flow. The VC, quite rightly, insists the school's research, particularly the funding it generates, however slight, must be maintained. Your own research must therefore make up the shortfall my promotion will inevitably produce. I look forward to receiving by the end of the week a breakdown of your current and proposed research. You will, of course, realise this is critical not only to the school but also your own personal and professional development. Signed: Professor Arthur Brush, Assistant Vice Chancellor (Acting).

Pendegrass sank back in his chair. He did not do research, had never done research, did not intend to start now. The master's dissertation, all those years ago, was quite enough research – if a so-called literature search could be classed as such – for any reasonable person. Or unreasonable, come to that. On the other hand, was there not a veiled threat in Brush's message? No research and... what? Out? Packed off with a pitiful pension, a set of suitcases and an oversize farewell card signed with low wit and insincerity? Was that to be his fate?

Pendegrass pursed his lips. He felt hot, bothered, clammy... and not just his face, his forehead, but the area of his person where his hand had been so recently engaged. Bugger, thought Pendegrass, immediately regretting this most unrepentantly sinful of profanities. And then – bugger again, as his thoughts veered from his own person to that of the sainted Truss. Now there, he thought, would be a figure worthy of research at the highest level. Or perhaps the lowest... His hand sank

155

once more beneath the desk.

**

'You what?' the man frowned, deftly flicking a mud-caked potato into the centre of the carousel. 'You'll have to speak up.'

Conversation on the potato harvester, as it bounced over the bleak and blasted field, was all but impossible. The rain, drumming against the tarpaulin flapping and flailing in a forlorn attempt to protect from the elements, was bad enough. But then there was the clonking of the carousel itself, scooping up huge clods from the field below and depositing them on a circular conveyor. Freezing fingers, yet surprisingly nimble, extracted the potatoes and, knocking away as much earth as possible, tossed them onto a central chute. From this, they tumbled out at the back of the carousel into a waiting sack which, when full, was sealed and dropped back onto the field whence it would be collected later.

Dirt and noise, noise and dirt: every orifice, every pore, clogged, choked, blackened, blocked. Wang felt sullied, thought he would never be clean again; longed almost to leap from the harvester and, casting off his clothes, cavort in the savagery of the storm, feel the rain scourge his skin, flail the filth from him. But he knew this was not to be. His task was to learn from his two countrymen, whom he now knew as Shu-jun, the younger of the pair, and Peiliang; acquire their dexterity in plucking potatoes from the damp and intractable earth cast onto the conveyer, discover how to operate the hand-held twist that sealed the bags with a metal tie – as Peiliang was now doing – without slicing off a finger. So much to learn, so much to understand... which was why Wang was determined to

156

persist in his dialogue with Shu-jun.

'I said,' Wang raised his voice over the howling wind, the clanking machinery, 'I said... why are they using something like this... this clapped-out old thing... when back home they've got the latest stuff?'

'You might just as well ask why they're using us. Exactly the same reason.'

'I don't understand.'

'Because we're cheap. This stupid so-called harvester. And us. We're cheap.'

Peiliang, on the back of the carousel, straightened up, having just dropped another bag of potatoes onto the field. 'You shouldn't be talking like this,' he growled. 'Get on with your work.'

'It's okay,' Shu-jan roared at him, into the wind. 'Just friendly chat. Anyway,' he added, jerking a thumb in the direction of the farmer astride the tractor towing them, 'he's no idea what we're on about.'

Peiliang looked sour and bent down once more to his bags.

'I don't think this can be very efficient,' Wang said. 'I mean, at home it's state-of-the-art. I've seen it.'

'Oh, they've got the stuff,' Shu-jan said. 'Latest self-propelled harvesters, loaders, balers. You name it, they've got it. Barns full of them. At any rate, the larger farms. Except they never use it. At least, not if they can hire it out at ridiculous rates to the smaller farms. And that's where we come in... here, watch what you're doing. That's at least two big ones you've let past.'

'It was just earth...'

'It wasn't. I saw something. Definitely. It's because the ground's so wet... waterlogged... it's all clinging. But if he...' Shu-jan motioned again towards the farmer '...if he finds any of his precious crop lying on the field when he comes to collect the bags, we'll be for it. Half a day's pay... up in smoke. Just like that.'

157

'I still don't see...' Wang began.

'Give it a rest, you two,' Peiliang ordered, from the back of the harvester. 'Too much talk. You save your questions, young man,' he said, addressing Wang, 'for that university. That's the place for talk. I tell you... this is the last place for talk.'

Wang shivered. It was turning even colder, and the wind had developed an edge that drove the rain harder. Perhaps Peiliang was right. This was not the place for questions. Yet they remained, gyrating in his brain like the clods on the carousel before him. At some time those thoughts, like the potato crop, would need harvesting.

25

It was strange, Lina thought, that Wang had not turned up to the Friday English class. Strange and worrying. He had told her he would be there: English was important, he said, he needed to improve; and while Lina could take him through the classes he had missed earlier in the week – which she had done, on two evenings, struggling to make sense of the notes she had scribbled – she could not, as Wang pointed out, learn English for him.

So it was all the more surprising in the English class, when the lady professor, Mrs Christine, taking the register, called out: 'William? Where's William? Anyone know where William is?'

No-one knew. In fact no-one, apart from Lina, was interested in knowing. Wang was an oddball, a butt of jibe and joke – after all, he was the one whose stupid peasant uncle had sent him to England with a suitcase full of worthless money. Lina sighed. She should have gone back to Martin Luther King to find him, but she had been busy in the library, or information resources hub or whatever it was called, attempting, in the aftermath of Professor Jordy's class, to ascertain the relevance of mice to the global economy.

As soon as the class was over Lina crossed the campus to look for Wang at their hall of residence. It was funny to call a place Martin Luther King, she thought, as she braced herself against the wind that blasted her round every corner. After all, the hall was populated neither by Americans, nor church reformers – Lina had looked Luther up on the internet – nor royalty: as far as she knew there were no members of the British monarchy, no eligible young princes, at Cram Vale. Too interested in dressing as Nazis, someone had said, than reading books. No, the name

159

was curious, because Martin Luther King was populated almost exclusively by Chinese postgraduates. True, it was rumoured a Polish girl occupied a room on the second floor, and an African on the fourth. No-one, however, claimed to have met them, still less spoken to them, and a counter-rumour began that the two 'foreigners', if they existed, were not students but cleaners. This, the Chinese felt, would account for the grime that bedecked Martin Luther King, since neither Poles nor Africans could be trusted. Poles were a shifty bunch whose so-called solidarity movement created anything but solidarity in central European Communism, while Africans were feckless and workshy and spent all their time in tribal butchery financed from plundered Chinese development funds. Clearly, neither could be relied on to make a decent job of cleaning.

Entering the hall of residence, Lina went immediately to Wang's corridor and knocked shyly on the door of his room. There was no reply. Lina frowned, and knocked harder.

'Go away,' a faint voice said.

'It's me. I was just wanting to know...'

'Please. Go away. Just leave me.'

Placing her hand on the handle, and depressing it, Lina nudged the door and, to her relief, found it would open. An odour of opposite sex, of masculinity and young male, assailed her nostrils, which she found faintly and briefly thrilling; yet the pervading stench was of sweat, of reeking, unwashed bedclothes, of temperature, sickness and fever.

'What...?' she said, seeing Wang, shivering, among a tangle of sheets and blankets on his bed.

'Please. Leave me alone. I'll be okay...'

'You will not be okay,' Lina said firmly, her spectacles flashing their concern at Wang. 'At least, not without help... someone to look after you. How long have you been like this?'

Wang mumbled something Lina did not catch.

'It's that farm,' Lina said. 'I knew it. You've been out in all weathers... caught a chill... why, it might be pneumonia... double pneumonia...'

Wang cleared his throat and, twisting in his bed, pulled the covers up to his face. 'No fuss,' he croaked. 'Don't want any fuss...'

'Fuss be blowed,' Lina said. 'The first thing I'm going to do is get you a hot drink. Then... then I'm going to find the student health centre. Get someone to come and look at you...'

'I don't want anyone...'

'You'll do as I say. I'm going to fetch someone, and there's an end to it. In the meantime... we'll sort this bed. It's all over the place...'

So saying, Lina bent over the stricken Wang, who sank back on his sweat-stained pillow, and, seizing ends of errant sheet and blanket, gathered them up and tucked them in some semblance of order under the mattress. As she worked her way from the foot of the bed towards Wang's small, trusting countenance, Lina was seized with a desire to kiss him – even in his present, hardly salubrious state – but she checked herself. It would be wrong, terribly wrong to take unfair advantage. All the same...

'That'll do for a start,' she said, primly, straightening herself up. 'Now... that drink. I'll not be long. You stay there... and rest,' she finished lamely.

Wang blinked up at her.

'Thank you, Lina,' he gurgled, managing a wan smile. 'You're very... you're very kind.'

**

161

The student health centre was busy – it was the season for coughs and colds – and Lina, growing increasingly anxious about Wang, had to wait almost an hour before she was seen. The nurse spent the first few minutes trying to ascertain from Lina what was wrong with her and seemed disappointed, indeed annoyed, when she discovered Lina was as right as rain and had come on someone else's behalf.

'This friend of yours will have to come and see us in person,' the nurse told Lina. 'This is a drop-in, not a drop-out centre. We haven't the resources to go gallivanting round the campus chasing every Tom, Dick and Harry who can't make it to classes.'

'My friend not Tom, Dick, Harry. My friend William. William sick. Very sick. William work hard...' – the nurse snorted – '...now William in bed. Perhaps... dead.'

'I don't think that's very likely...' the nurse said, a note of nervousness sounding in her voice. 'At this time of year the incidence of campus death is low. Exam time is different, of course...'

'You come to William... to Wang Ti,' Lina flared up, thrusting her spectacles into the face of the startled nurse. 'You not come... I go to embassy... yes, Chinese embassy. Chinese government not like if Chinese student die in English university. Very bad. No more Chinese student come...'

The nurse gulped, reached for a telephone, and muttered something into the receiver. Replacing it, she said sweetly to Lina: 'If you'd just give me the name of the patient and the room number in the hall...'

162

26

It had been surprisingly easy to collect Wang's medicine. Lina expected there would be form-filling, production of identity cards or passports, verification, more forms, but she had walked into the campus pharmacy, shown the prescription the doctor had written, put a cross on the back of the form and signed her name, and a few moments later a neat white bag containing something that rattled was passed over the counter to her. It was too easy, Lina thought, and she half expected to feel the hand of authority on her shoulder as she crossed the campus for what seemed the umpteenth time that day to return to Martin Luther King.

Wang, it seemed, was not at death's door, and the young medic – Lina wondered if he was a student and not a proper doctor – sent from the health centre seemed disappointed to diagnose a chest infection rather than discover a corpse. He took Wang's temperature, listened to his chest, told him to say 'Aaaah' – the patient, sensing common cause, responded with a spirited 'Haaar', which rather took the doctor aback – and suggested the student eat more.

'You're the opposite of what we usually get,' he enthused at Wang. 'I mean... most of them round here are built like buses. Too much junk food. Cheeseburger and fries would do you a power of good.'

'You give William cheeseburger...?' Lina scowled, advancing on the doctor. 'William need medicine, not cheeseburger...'

The doctor, pen poised over prescription pad, took a step back. 'No, I mean, I don't mean... I mean, obviously, he needs medicine. Look,' he said, waving the pad at Lina as if for protection, 'it's an antibiotic. I mean, I merely said about burgers because... no, forget it,' he added hastily, as Lina's features began to harden. 'It's okay. I mean... what he needs is medicine, rest, fluids, and keeping warm. In fact, just take it easy.'

'But... what about Mr Wu...?' rasped a voice from the bed, its owner attempting to pull itself up before falling back in a fit of choking and coughing.

'Yeah... and no visitors. I mean... all those germs flying round. Very nasty,' the doctor said, thrusting the prescription at Lina and beating a rapid retreat.

So, an hour or so later, Lina found herself scurrying across the campus, holding the small white bag and its precious contents safely to her person. After everything she'd been through that day, she told herself, it would hardly do to lose it. It would help Wang get better, put him on his feet... but she knew as soon as he was well enough he would be back in the fields, working in all weathers for that Mr Wu, and make himself ill again. Lina shook her head. Wang wasn't made for that. Wang was... delicate, a flower to be tended, nurtured, before it would bloom in all its wonder and... well... beauty. Take a grip on yourself, Lina told herself sternly. This will never do. But, all the same, Wang... poor Wang... he couldn't go on like that. He'd make himself seriously ill... hospital, then where would he be with his work? And his studies. He'd have to...

From a building in front of her emerged a figure, slightly bowed, that Lina recognised as the English professor, Mrs Christine. Wang had missed her class that morning: the professor should be told why. Lina quickened her pace and caught up with her teacher.

'Excuse me,' Lina began.

'Good heavens,' said Christine Reeve, startled, her thoughts already on the College Arms – or rather, Ed. She wanted to know how the campaign to save the pub was going. If the pub went, Ed with it, something would slip from her. She wasn't sure what.

Companionship, yes. A touch of humanity. Perhaps even hope. She frowned, and turned to face the voice that had addressed her. 'You gave me quite a shock,' she said.

The girl was familiar. It was the spectacles that did it. She was in that awful English class, the one with too many students to make any progress, and all squashed into a redundant chemistry laboratory. Christine sighed: there were things she liked to forget when leaving work. She walked on.

'Excuse me, many apologies, William not in class this morning. Very good class. Very good teacher. But today... William ill. Very hot. Cough...' Lina cleared her throat, twice, to illustrate her point. 'Doctor see William say very ill I get medicine. Here...' and Lina thrust the bag into Christine's face.

'I see,' Christine said. 'That's very interesting. That is... I'm sorry your friend's ill. Perhaps... er... I mean, perhaps you'd remind me in class when I've got the register, and I could make a note.'

'Make note... yes. But... perhaps William not come to class.'

'Oh,' said Christine, cheered that the loss of a student would make her job that little bit easier. 'Is he leaving?' she enquired brightly.

'Wang... William... William work. Work very hard.'

'That's good,' said Christine cautiously. 'I mean... that's what we like to hear. But, if he's working hard, why's he leaving?'

'William work in field. Long hours... very long hours. And in rain... wind... storm... then he become ill. Very ill. Go to hospital. Might die. Please, professor Christine... you do something. You help my friend Wang. Please.'

Christine was aware of a hand tugging on her arm.

165

She stopped, looked down, and immediately saw two upturned eyes or spectacles, tearful, and gazing imploringly, beseechingly, up at her. Clearly, something was troubling the girl. It was moments like this she found herself lacking as a teacher, a mentor or even a human being. She wished she had taken the counselling course offered before the summer.

'Look,' she said, feeling very inadequate and very British. 'I don't think this is quite the time or the place. I... er...' A thought struck her. 'You're business studies people, aren't you? I mean... it's Mr Pendegrass... he's your course tutor, isn't he? Perhaps... if there's a problem... then I think Mr Pendegrass should know.'

'Mr Pendegrass... very nice man...'

'Very nice. Look... if I email Mr Pendegrass... then I'm sure he'll... you know... be in touch. If I tell him... what's your friend called?'

'William...'

'William. That's right. From the English class...'

'William. Wang Ti. Mr Pendegrass nice man. He help Wang Ti a lot. Wang Ti like Mr Pendegrass...'

'Good. That's settled,' said Christine, feeling she had redeemed herself, at least partially. Then, as an afterthought, she added, 'Sorry. I didn't quite catch your name...'

'Emmeline. My name Emmeline. In China...'

Of course. Emmeline. How could she forget? The bright one, always had something to say, unlike the rest of them. She should try and remember the name. There was really no excuse. All the same, the older she got, the more difficult it was to remember. Or summon the enthusiasm to do so. Especially all those crazy Victorian or Edwardian names the Chinese adopted. She groaned inwardly. She could certainly do with that drink.

**

As luck would have it, Christine was crossing the car park on the way to the College Arms, having disengaged herself from Lina by reminding her the patient needed his medicine, when she spotted the familiar form of Dozy Pendegrass.

To a casual observer it might have appeared that Pendegrass was attempting to supplement his university pay with theft. Car theft, to be precise. He was fumbling at the lock of an elderly Ford with a cluster of keys of which any safe-breaker would be proud. The only thing lacking was the hood which, Christine supposed, was essential for the well-dressed petty criminal of today. That, and the fact that Pendegrass was probably a good 30 years older than the average car-cracker.

'Hello,' said Christine, approaching. 'I was going to send you an email.'

Pendegrass jumped, and dropped the keys.

'Good job there's no drain,' Christine said. 'Might have lost them. You'd be stuck then.'

Pendegrass leered at Christine as if she were the spirit of deans past, present and future.

'I'm sorry,' Christine said briskly. 'I startled you. Look…' and she bent down to retrieve the keys.

'I was just trying to get into my car,' Pendegrass mumbled, taking the keys. 'Lock's stuck. It always happens this damp weather.'

'WD40,' said Christine. 'Got any WD40?'

'Yes,' said Pendegrass, momentarily brightening, only to add: 'But it's in the car.'

'Oh,' said Christine. 'But why don't you try the passenger door?'

'Now, there's an idea,' said Pendegrass. 'Why didn't I think of that?'

167

Christine didn't answer, though several replies sprang to mind. She had known Pendegrass for years; not well, but they had served together on examination boards, in the days when business studies students took foreign languages. She recalled his propensity even then to nod off, and she was faintly surprised he hadn't been fired years ago. If he'd been working anywhere but a university...

'I was going to email you,' she said, 'about one of your tutees. He doesn't seem to be very well, seems to have some sort of problem...'

'Don't they all?' said Pendegrass, tugging at the passenger door.

'Yes, but this one...'

'At last!' cried Pendegrass, as the door flew open, knocking him for the moment off-balance. 'I say... all these months I've been battling with that wretched door. Needs a new lock, I suppose, but I was waiting to get it done when it goes for its MOT. But the passenger door. I must remember that.'

Christine doubted he would. Pendegrass, she recalled, was incapable of remembering anything much at all. She continued: 'This student... he's missed at least one of my sessions. One of the other students is worried about him. I think you ought to have him in... find out what's going on.'

'Right,' said Pendegrass. 'Right. Very important. Can't have people missing class.' Then, looking intently at Christine, he said: 'I didn't think any of our students were doing languages. I mean...'

'It's not German. It's English as a foreign language. With the MBAs... the Chinese...'

'Oh, the Chinese...' said Pendegrass, flapping an arm, as if to ward off evil, and at the same time lowering himself into the passenger seat. 'Don't get me wrong. Decent enough people. But they don't half

168

make work. Do you know... one of them brought his fees in cash. Old pound notes, in a suitcase. Of course, no-one would accept them. Totally worthless. Dreadful business. Caused a few headaches, you might imagine.'

Christine tut-tutted, partly in sympathy, partly in amusement.

'I tell you, though,' Pendegrass lowered his voice, 'it's got to the stage that if I see one coming, I hide. Anywhere. Gents. Ladies. Cleaners' cupboard. The library used to be okay... but it's colonised by Chinese. Library today, world tomorrow, I suppose.'

Such eloquence from Pendegrass was a rarity. It was obvious Christine had touched a nerve. She began to back off. 'I just thought I'd let you know,' she said, as Pendegrass began to contort himself from passenger to driver side. 'I think it's just this one student. The others aren't a problem. But if you could have a word with him... William, it is. Wang Ti...'

Pendegrass, his body suspended between the two seats, his legs skewed beneath him, twitched violently, and collapsed with a howl of pain or rage – Christine couldn't be sure which – onto the gearstick. 'No,' he shrieked. 'No. Not Wang Ti. He was the one... with the suitcase... the money. And now... no. It's too much...'

Christine, worried, tugged at the driver's door which, surprisingly, opened at once: why it had not responded to Pendegrass's earlier attentions was a mystery. She leaned into the vehicle and put her hand on Pendegrass's flailing arm, causing him to flinch, again bringing him down onto the gearstick.

'Go away,' he winced. 'Please...leave me. I'll be all right. Just go.'

Christine hesitated. Pendegrass looked anything but all right. 'I think you need to calm down,' she said. 'Why don't you... why don't we... perhaps a drink. The College Arms...'

'No,' said Pendegrass firmly, extricating himself with a grimace from the gearstick and, leaning over to the passenger door, pulling it shut. 'No way. Nazareth and Ewesbottom Repentant Sinners. Repentant Sinners, don't you know.'

Christine didn't know. Even if she had wanted to know there would have been no time to find out, for Pendegrass slammed the driver's door and, somehow finding the correct key, stuck it in the ignition and fired up the Ford. It lurched backwards, rattling its exhaust on the car park curb, and stalled.

'It must have been in gear,' Christine said. 'You probably hit the gearstick when...'

Pendegrass glared at her from behind grubby glass and restarted the engine.

'I still think it would be better...' Christine began.

Pendegrass wound down the window. 'Nazareth and Ewesbottom Repentant Sinners. No alcohol. Work of the devil. Like magnetic levitation... all those electrons flying around in that building. They get to you. And now it's the Chinese. It all adds up. Think about it... repent... before it's too late.' So saying, and flinging Christine a look of despair and pity, he crunched the gear into first and the Ford jolted down the car park, sparks flying from a dangling exhaust.

As she watched the retreating pyrotechnics, Christine wondered if she could work Pendegrass into her spy thriller. The novel was losing its way, not – Christine was now realising – that it had much direction in the first place, and it needed fresh impetus. Perhaps Pendegrass could become a spy? Better still, a spy-master. Beneath that bumbling exterior lurked a razor-sharp mind: the man was a computer whizz, a martial arts expert, fluent in Russian, Arabic and Chinese, expert in... but no. Not Pendegrass. It was altogether too ridiculous. Put Pendegrass into a book and no-one

170

would believe her. No. The novel, if it were to get anywhere, would have to do so without Pendegrass.

**

The first person Christine spotted as she entered the College Arms was the performing arts lecturer, Chattermole, sitting by himself but ostentatiously perusing The Stage.

'He's been on the same page for the last three quarters of an hour,' Ed told Christine as she settled herself at the bar. 'Don't know why he bothers. With a conk like that, they wouldn't even have him on radio.'

Christine giggled. 'At least he's quiet when he's not got company. No-one to sound off to about fancy holidays in Morocco or wherever.'

'Mauritius,' Ed said. 'Quite definitely, Mauritius. And, as it happens, thanks to Mr Chattermole over there, I've been making one or two enquiries. And come up with something.'

Christine waited for Ed to continue, but the landlord was saying nothing. There was a twinkle in his eye though, and Christine thought him more relaxed, more confident, than in the past few weeks. All the same, she couldn't be sure. Understanding Ed was like watching a film in another language: American, for example, when you catch only so much before hillbilly drawl or low-life gangsterese render understanding opaque. So with Ed: you think you are following, when all the time the meaning is passing you by. Not for the first time she told herself how little she knew him. She wondered if anyone did. And thought she would like to know him better.

'Early days yet,' he winked. 'But I don't think we can write off the College Arms just yet. Dum spiro, spero, and all that. Anyway... what's it to be? I kept a

171

drop of that Speyside specially for you. And while we're about it, I think young Mr Hackley over there might enjoy a snifter, too.'

Hearing his name, the reporter looked up. Ed motioned towards the bottle, and Hackley's face lit up. He slipped his notebook into his pocket and, draining his pint, stood up.

'Bright lad, that,' Ed told Christine, as Hackley strode towards them. 'I've great hopes for him.'

27

It was as Lina feared. As soon as Wang's medicine began to take effect, the patient talked of returning to work.

They were sitting together one evening in the communal kitchen on Wang's corridor in Martin Luther King, drinking tea, when he told Lina – shyly thanking her for looking after him – that he was feeling better and would go back to work in the next day or two. He said Mr Wu had been understanding, had kept his place open for him, but wanted him back as soon as possible. Moreover, the days missed through illness would have to be made up, Mr Wu had said.

'Therefore,' Wang concluded, 'the sooner I get back, the better.'

Lina frowned. She said the work would have a detrimental effect on his health as well as his studies. Then she asked how much Mr Wu was paying him. Wang said it wasn't any of her business, and he was coping. When Lina pressed him, offering to help him work out his finances – how much he owed the university, how much he owed Mr Wu, or the mysterious Qi – Wang became evasive.

'Not now,' he said. 'I'm not up to sorting money at the moment.'

'A minute ago you were saying how much better you felt and it was time you went back to work. You can't have it both ways.'

'It's okay. Everything's under control.'

Lina removed her glasses and, taking a tissue from a box on the table, began polishing the lenses. 'I don't think you've any idea how much you're getting... or supposed to be getting,' Lina reproached him. 'I daresay nothing's been said... and I bet you've no contract, nothing on paper. In fact, I bet you've never

173

actually been paid.'

'It's not about pay,' Wang retorted. 'It's this debt. Once that's settled then I'll get my money. I mean... Mr Qi's been very kind...'

'Kind... I think you're being ripped off. You need to find out exactly where you stand... ask Mr Wu... and if you don't get any sense then you should pack it in and concentrate on your work.'

'I am concentrating on my work.'

'Not that work, stupid. Your studies.'

'I am. Concentrating on my studies.'

'How? I don't see that grubbing up potatoes all day is going to get you your MBA.'

'I've got it worked out...'

Lina threw up her hands in despair. Truly, Wang could be so irritating. Why did she bother – why did she run around after him as if she were his mother? This was nothing to do with her. She had quite enough on her plate with the reading, the studying, without piling Wang on top of it. And yet... she had to admire him. Admire him for his pluck, his tenacity, his sheer determination. And not just admire. There was something else. Ever since that incident in the café, when Wang had sprung to her defence, Lina knew there was a bond, a tie, between them. He had been so noble, gallant: no-one had ever done anything like that for her before. They hadn't spoken about it again, but Lina felt they didn't have to. Sometimes words aren't necessary.

'Okay,' she said warily, replacing her glasses. 'How've you worked it out?'

'It's to do with the dissertation. I know what I'm going to do it on.'

Lina looked at Wang in astonishment. No-one was giving any thought to the dissertation. Not at the moment, at least. The dissertation was for later, the following semester, the summer.

'Go on,' she said.

'Research,' Wang said firmly. 'I'm going to do research. Research into human resources. The labour market...'

'It's too big. You haven't time. Besides, where are you going to get the information?'

'Easy. Mr Wu's bus. Also...'

'Mr Wu's bus...?'

'Listen. All those people... from all over China. How did they get here? Why are they here? What are they doing? When are they going back? There's so much to find out... it's perfect...'

'I don't like it. It's... I think it's best you don't ask.'

'What do you mean... don't ask?'

Lina was about to reach across the table, to take Wang's hand and squeeze it, but thought better of it.

'Sometimes... you hear things. Read things. I know people back home... I mean... think about it. What you've said... all those people in that big house... Mr Wu... Qi...it's not right.'

Wang gave a huge grin. 'Of course it's not right. And I mean to find out.'

'You've got to speak to Professor Pendegrass. He'll...'

'I shall. But what do you think? Perfect, isn't it?'

So saying, Wang leaned across the table and planted a tea-tinged kiss on Lina's astonished lips.

28

Away from the kitchen in Martin Luther King where, after Wang's unexpected passion had given way to surprised and embarrassed silence, emotions of a different kind filled the air of a meeting room at Cramcaster City Council. The monthly session of the neighbourhood regeneration review and scrutiny committee was in full flow – or as Jason Hackley, hunched over his notebook at the press table, told himself, full trickle. Hackley was covering the meeting as part of his training and so far had enough material for a 30-word filler. The editor of the Cramcaster Evening Herald would not be pleased. Hackley stole a glance at his watch: still too soon to leave. He stifled a yawn. The committee, it seemed to Hackley, was speaking a foreign language: something about rolling out a pathfinder toolkit to implant statutory and non-statutory consultation in the context of the strategic guidance framework of performance monitoring and evaluation. Hackley was wondering about the toolkit, and how it might be rolled out, and whether it had wheels, when he realised the debate had taken a different direction.

'I have to remind the member,' Councillor Mrs Rosalind Brush was saying, 'that the question of foreign workers is hardly the concern of this committee.'

'Rubbish,' said a wispy, sallow man, whom Hackley recognised as the British National Party victor in a by-election (turnout 14%) and whose name he couldn't remember: Buzzcock, something like that. 'I tell you... these people are flooding in, stealing jobs from honest, hard-working British people...'

'I repeat,' said Councillor Mrs Brush, 'this does not fall under the remit of this committee...'

'Regeneration. That's what this committee's about. That's what I'm saying. Regeneration of jobs. British jobs for British people. And these illegals…'

'May I refer to standing orders…' began Mrs Brush, as Councillor Angus McGorgon, assistant executive member for neighbourhood regeneration, rose to his feet and her rescue.

'The chairman is perfectly correct to say this is beyond the remit of this scrutiny committee. I would remind Councillor Buscombe…'

Gotcha, thought Hackley. Buscombe… that's the bugger.

'I would remind Councillor Buscombe this council has robust and rigorous policies regarding employment of foreign nationals and will act with the police and immigration service to root out illegals…'

'That's crap, and you know it,' sneered Buscombe, rising from his seat.

'May we please have some respect,' said Mrs Brush. 'As chair of this committee…'

'It's out of control. This council hasn't a clue how many are here. Where they are… what they're doing. Except sponging off society… benefit scroungers…'

McGorgon fixed Buscombe in his sights, and pulled the trigger. 'And what would your employment be?' he enquired.

'Registered disabled. Which means…'

'I know what that means. You don't work.'

'But I'm legit. Not like these blighters. Smuggled in, smuggled out. And this council turns a blind eye. We've got Ukrainians in the parks department…'

'Graduates from an agricultural college in the Crimea,' said McGorgon. 'Outstanding young people making an enormous contribution to our Cramcaster in Bloom initiative. As for foreigners in general, I can assure the councillor the situation is carefully

177

monitored. This council works hand-in-hand with the police... officers on the street trained to deal with illegals. I repeat: the situation is firmly under control. And now, Madam Chairman, I think we might proceed.'

Yes, thought Hackley, tee-lining himself to a frenzied finish and flicking shut his notebook. Result. A page lead, at least. He could see it now: 'Clueless' Council In Scrounger Rap. That would keep the news editor off his back. This called for a celebration. A beer at the College Arms, where he could write up his story and send it over to the newsdesk.

Slipping his notebook into his pocket, Hackley rose from the table and sidled from the room. At the door he turned, giving a brief nod in the direction of Councillor Mrs Brush. An unnecessary gesture, for the chairman was oblivious to anything other than agenda item four and the report to be received on the regenerative incentivisation impact of Cram Vale University's new arts and media centre. Councillor McGorgon raised a hand, and said he would like a few moments to talk to the report.

Bloody hell, thought Hackley. They lock people away for talking to inanimate objects. Though not, apparently, councillors. I'm out of it.

Half an hour later, while McGorgon was still talking to the report, Hackley was sitting in front of a pint of Cramcaster Brewery Old Stinkle in the snug at the College Arms. He pulled out his notebook, peered in some distaste at his tee-line shorthand, and began writing. Cramcaster City Council is 'clueless' about foreign workers, a councillor claimed last night. He frowned, put a line through what he had written, and began again. A councillor has condemned as clueless council policies on foreign workers. At a meeting last night... He paused, and took a sip of beer. Slippery

178

things, words. Like people – slippery. Only more so.

**

Rosalind Brush was not best pleased when she arrived home later that evening. Her meeting had been hijacked; firstly by the BNP thug Buscombe, then by McGorgon, who at least had tried to make it up to her in the pub afterwards. All this talk of immigrants. It wasn't East European immigrants, but Scots immigrants who were the problem. It wouldn't be so bad, she thought, jolting her car to a halt behind her husband's, if the Scots were to keep out of sight, like the Poles or Lithuanians, who spend all their thankless days plucking chickens or picking vegetables miles away from anywhere. And anyone. But, no. That wasn't good enough. The Scots had invaded the corridors of power. Suddenly she understood the fuss about Brussels and the European Union. It was a red herring, an Aberdeen herring, to divert attention from the fact that England, one of the most ruthless colonisers the world had known, had itself been colonised from within by the Scots. It was all the fault of the Act of Union, a political Trojan horse wheeled behind the walls of Westminster. In fact, thought Rosalind Brush, we are de facto Scottish but without the advantages: scenery, subsidised care homes for the old, free universities for the young. The only small mercy, Rosalind Brush told herself, banging the car door and marching to the back of the house, was that bagpipes, with their funereal flatulence, were heard south of the border only on those ghastly Hogmanay television shows without which no year could begin. All fake bonhomie with old father time, tartanned bimbos and plastic heather thrown in for bad measure. And pre-recorded. Yes, New Year: like government,

179

something else the Scots had hijacked. On the other hand, Rosalind Brush asked herself, who are we English to wax superior about Hogmanay or bagpipes? Morris dancing and cricket... say no more.

Wondering if her comments were politically correct, and if the word Muslim were substituted for Scots – do Muslims play bagpipes? – she could be done for incitement to racial or religious hatred, she flung open the back door. She found her husband seated at the kitchen table with an open laptop before him, playing a card game. He looked up, startled, and snapped the computer shut.

'Caught you red-handed,' said Mrs Brush. 'Computer games. You always tell me you're working.'

'I am... was,' mumbled Brush, gathering the papers scattered on the table and sliding them under the laptop. There was no point trying to explain to Mrs Brush the research into spider solitaire and how it would confirm his reputation as a scholar of renown and repute. 'I've been working... see, notes. I was just taking a quick break.'

'Huh,' said Mrs Brush. 'All right for some. Some of us have been working. Properly working. Creating a Cramcaster fit for the 21st century. A city fit for work and play. And for study. We were hearing about the new media centre... the one on the site of that eyesore... what's it called?... College Arms, or something...'

'Nothing wrong with the College Arms...' began Brush.

'College Arse more like. It's a slum. Surprised it hasn't fallen down years ago. But I tell you... it comes to something when I find out more about this media centre from a council planning report than I do from a member of senate... and assistant vice chancellor, no less. Talking of which...'

Brush groaned inwardly. He knew what was

coming. It had been a recurrent theme in the Brush household ever since he had revealed his elevation. The subsequent reiterations of Mrs Brush about his assistant-vice-chancellordom were as inevitable as the shipping forecast, but without the mellifluous musicality of Viking, North Utsire, South Utsire, Forties, Cromarty and Forth. It was obvious that in sea area Rosalind Brush it was north to northeast, six to gale eight; very rough or high; squally showers; good. But not for Brush. The professor battened hatches, and braced himself.

'I see from your last payslip there's been no adjustment to your salary. Surely it's about time someone pulled their finger out and got this sorted. I mean, if this were the council, we'd be hauled over the coals. Reported...'

'Yes, dear,' muttered Brush, scudding before the squall which, experience taught, was the best way to weather it.

'Anyway... what are they supposed to be paying you? Have they told you? And why didn't you ask? Surely anyone with half a brain would have said: What does this mean financially? But you... oh no...'

'It's only assistant vice chancellor acting...' Brush began, attempting a lubberly and short-lived tack into the eye of the storm.

'Acting, my foot. You're still doing it, aren't you? Acting or not... you have to be paid. You need to take this up right away with the vice chancellor...'

'Yes, dear...'

'Get this sorted at once. You can't go on like this...'

'No, dear...'

'You go in there tomorrow and say...'

'Yes, dear...'

'Don't "yes, dear" me in that tone of voice, Arthur Brush...'

181

'No, dear…'

'I mean it.'

'Yes, dear…'

'You'll be a laughing stock…'

'Yes, dear. Or should that be: No, dear?'

For a second it looked as if the squall might develop into something more furious: a gale, perhaps, or a storm. But the squall abated as quickly as it had risen. It was spent, satisfied; it had made waves and sent them crashing over the useless hulk it had been her misfortune to marry. There was no point swamping it, sinking it. Every wifely squall, Mrs Brush intuitively realised, needs a husbandly hulk to toss around from time to time, else what was the point of marriage? The surging waters in sea area Rosalind Brush receded, as smoother, calmer currents replaced them.

'I'm off to bed,' the sea area said.

'I'll stay down here,' the wind-whipped hulk replied.

Minutes later, he could hear Mrs Brush moving around upstairs: a creak of the floorboard on the landing outside the bathroom, a whirr of an electric toothbrush, a click as a wardrobe opened and closed. Brush did not move. He had been humiliated. But he would show her. Tomorrow he would go to the VC, haul her from whatever meeting she was at, insist on his rights. He wouldn't let that little twerp Kerry stand in his way. Why, anyone would think Kerry ran the place… always there, never the VC. But Brush would change things. He'd go right to the top, sort things once and for all. Oh, yes. Things were about to change. Big time.

29

Wang was troubled. His impetuosity in the Martin Luther King kitchen, when he cast aside all decency and, in a moment of folly, kissed Lina, disturbed him. He had never kissed anyone before, let alone a girl. Moreover, and more significantly, he knew, despite what he saw around him in the decadent West, that respectable people did not kiss. In China kissing was frowned on. People might offer a brief hug, even touch – he could still feel Lina's grateful hand in his at the end of the day in that awful, windswept seaside town – but a kiss, even one, was unforgivable. So unforgivable, in fact, that he recalled with a shudder there was even a university in China which employed students to patrol the campus and separate kissing couples. Simply, kissing was unclean. Saliva sticking, they called it. Germs could be transferred from mouth to mouth: what if he had infected the girl now marching beside him on their way to Professor Pendegrass?

Wang stole a glance at Lina. She had made no reference to the kiss, either then or later. She had been as surprised as he was, he was sure of that, fluttering her eyelashes at him from behind her spectacles. What did that mean? Was she angry? Probably not, Wang reflected, after he fled to the safety of his own room and flung himself on his bed, where he twisted and turned through an anguished, sleepless night. She couldn't be angry, for surely she would have said something. But suppose she never spoke to him again; suppose she started spending time with that Jingen… what then? And yet…. By the early hours of the morning Wang had convinced himself, as far as a fuzzy head and aching limbs would permit, that something had changed. He was unsure what. He was too exhausted to articulate it, but it was as if, through that kiss, he had somehow taken a lead, asserted himself, or at any rate readjusted their relationship. And Lina didn't appear to mind. She might have hit him on account of his temerity; she might have screamed, called for assistance, but no. She simply sat there, at the table, motionless. Apart from those eyelashes, which were long, and silky: why had he never noticed them before? The spectacles, that was why. What else were they hiding?

The following morning Wang was less certain of his thesis. Perhaps it was a dream; perhaps he had imagined it. There was no kiss, no shift, however imperceptible, in their relationship. All the same, when he tentatively asked Lina to come with him to see Pendegrass, because her English was better, she agreed. Readily. That was a good sign. And, furthermore, it occurred to Wang that for the first time they were doing something together that he had initiated. It wasn't her inviting him, it was the other way round. That's what it was. A balance had been struck: she could take a lead, and now so could he. That felt good. Good not only to him but also, Wang believed, casting another glance at the creature beside him, bunched in her tiny jacket against the cold, it felt good to her, too. It was as if they were meeting as equals.

Wang allowed himself a small sigh of relief, which vaporised before him in the brisk autumnal air. It reminded him of dragon-breath: after all, there was fire in his belly. He wondered if he should take her hand but decided, after the tribulations of the previous evening, this might be a little rash. At least, for the moment.

**

Pendegrass had enjoyed his mid-morning nap but was peeved to be woken prematurely by an email pinging into his computer. It was from Brush, still head of school, but signing himself Assistant Vice Chancellor. The email was a reminder that, if jobs were to be retained, scholarship was imperative. However, neither of the two research proposals received, the email continued, was suitable. A six month sabbatical in Tenerife to examine the hotel industry or a study of the recession on Hamburg brothels would not attract funding. This last proposal, the email assumed, was a joke. Pendegrass was not sure.

At any rate, this second communication from Brush about research emphasised its importance. Pendegrass took the view that initial emails could be ignored. If the matter had some urgency, however, a second email would arrive which would suggest action of some kind – at the very least an acknowledgment – was required. Pendegrass sighed. It was all getting a bit much.

Besides, there was the more pressing matter of the Nazareth and Ewesbottom Repentant Sinners' accounts. Not the accounts they would give of themselves when it would be their everlasting fortune to be called to the Pearly Gates – for some, this could not come soon enough, while for others it would come soon – but accounts of a more mundane nature. It was Pendegrass's duty to present to the elders a half-yearly balance sheet – a task on which he had been engaged before sleep had assailed him. For a group that scorned unearned wealth the sinners were extremely – indeed, obscenely – well endowed, thanks in the main to substantial bequests from founding sinners in the late 19th century. The funds had been prudently invested in railway stock and government bonds, both at home and abroad, and owing to cunning reinvestment over the years still provided an income which would satisfy the most venal of third world dictators. Of course no-one, least of all Pendegrass, had any real grasp of how the money was generated. Statements appeared at regular intervals from solicitors in London saying they had moved £150,000 into low-risk ethical bonds or high yield growth funds. Pendegrass felt he ought to understand this world of high finance, which beckoned to him in this way, or at least make the effort to understand, but he had little enthusiasm and even less aptitude. Besides, the elders – of which he was by far the youngest, and who boasted a collective average age, including his, of 84 – were not interested in detail. 'Tell me, young man,' one of them would say, when Pendegrass came to present his approximation of the accounts, 'are we in the red?' When he assured them that, quite the contrary, they were anything but in the red, there was an approving nodding of heads, followed by a call for quiet contemplation to reflect on the bounteous gifts bestowed upon undeserving sinners by a merciful and munificent Lord. Moments later, the room would resonate to the gentle rumble of grateful, and thankful, snoring.

The problem was, as Pendegrass realised, that the sinners had nothing on which to spend their wealth, which daily grew larger and larger. Any suggestion that the rotten window frames of the chapel give way to double glazing, or the leaking roof be fixed, or the Victorian heating replaced, was met with horror: suffering was as innate to the sinners as fleas to a monkey. It was permitted to send an occasional hamper of food to a sick sinner, possibly meet a small bill for a sinner in financial distress, but no more; and since the Grim Reaper had savaged their ranks, and it was now rare for attendance at Sunday chapel to reach double figures, the opportunities for even these small generosities were limited.

It crossed Pendegrass's mind that some of this money could be redirected for charitable use beyond

186

the meagre needs of the sinners. No-one would know if a couple of hundred – indeed, a couple of thousand – were to find their way to a cash-strapped worthy cause of which, if the newspapers could be believed, there were any number. It was not a question of lining his own pocket: whatever his faults, he was not dishonest. On the other hand the money had been given the sinners presumably for good works, whatever those might be, and Pendegrass felt it somehow his duty to see that a least a portion of the money was used in accordance with the spirit in which it was obtained.

He wondered if Lynne Truss ran a charity for the preservation of the apostrophe, or the adverb, or for the extermination of the self-important capital. Causes like these, he felt, would go hand in hand with sin and repentance: ye sinners in syntax repent, seek salvation in the sainted Truss. Appropriation of money in this way would surely prove inoffensive to the chapel elders, should they ever discover how their wealth was serving syntax. The idea, thought Pendegrass, was inspirational, perhaps even divinely inspired, and the prospect of writing to Lynne Truss, placing funds – and himself – at her disposal sent a tingle of forbidden pleasure through his body.

Placing fingers on keyboard, about to compose his missive, he became aware of scrabbling outside his office door. His first thought was mice, which was unlikely since, listening more closely, he was able to distinguish snippets of conversation. To the best of his knowledge mice were not given to verbal exchange, except in children's fiction or television cartoons. He listened again. Too late he realised that what he was hearing was not English and, as a knock came at the door, which immediately opened, he jerked back his chair and dived for safety under his desk. As he went down his head struck the edge of the table-top, causing

187

everything to shudder, and displacing a pot-plant which crashed to the floor, cascading earth and foliage.

'Ouch,' he said.

'Haaar,' came a response.

And then: 'Professor sir fall from chair. Professor sir not right. We help.'

Pendegrass, twisted beneath his desk, and with a head beginning to buzz like a Sunday afternoon of strimmers and mowers, shut his eyes to await his fate.

**

By the time Brush reached the vice chancellor's office he was more or less word-perfect. He had slept little, turning over in his mind the phrases he might use on Professor Redwell-Nope to help her decide the remuneration appropriate to his new responsibilities. He envisaged countless scenarios in which he emerged triumphant, and with promise of immediate removal to a state-of-the-art office peopled by short-skirted assistants adept at spider solitaire, partial to curry, and generally as antithetical to Mrs Brush as the average football fan to women referees. Each take began the same way:

Scene: Interior. Vice chancellor's office. Morning. A door opens. Brush enters.

Brush: Ah, vice chancellor. I hope I'm not disturbing...

Redwell-Nope: Arthur... how lovely to see you. You're looking well... despite your harridan of a wife. What can I do for you?

Brush: It's like this, vice chancellor. I was...

Redwell-Nope: Please... call me Barbara. We don't stand on ceremony at Cram Vale. Now... you were saying...

At this point the scene faded as Brush tried

188

desperately to recall the vice chancellor's features. Professor Barbara Redwell-Nope BSc (Hons) MSc DSc DipGD was nothing if not elusive. Indeed, Brush reflected, invisibility – a characteristic of chief executives and senior managers – was her defining quality.

As Brush strode confidently into the outer office of the vice chancellor's suite, he saw that cocky little so-and-so, Kerry whatever his name was, swing round in his chair to face him and, Brush thought, grab a phone and talk into it. Brush blinked: he might have imagined it, or it might have been a trick of the light, but he could have sworn the man was not on the phone went he went in. But there he was, in full flow, saying the VC had left that morning for a meeting in Brussels before moving on to Berlin, Vienna and Prague. She did not want to be bothered with university business, Kerry said, and would not be back until the end of the following week.

'I suppose you got that,' he said, putting down the phone.

'Who were you talking to?' demanded Brush.

'Oh... UCAS... wanting the VC to give a talk on admissions. Don't know when I'm going to fit it in. Busy schedule.'

'Busy schedule be blowed. I need to speak to her. But I suppose, as usual, it'll have to wait.'

'All in good time,' said Kerry. 'But I'm glad you're here. I need to bring you up to speed about the new arts and media centre.'

'Arts and... oh, yes. My wife... on the council, you know... said it came up at a meeting. I must say, I have a soft spot for the College Arms...'

'So we hear.'

'Hate to see it go.'

'Progress, professor. Progress. That's why the VC thinks it's got to the stage where we need to go public.

189

Bring in some sponsorship... get industry on board...'

'What industry? There's none left round here. Unless you count charity shops.'

'Very droll, Professor Brush. But no... it doesn't have to be large employers. A lot of sponsorship comes from small firms... accountants, lawyers. And it would be your role to head up our sponsorship drive...'

'Head up...?'

'The very person. The public face of the university, I think we said. So you need to get out... get talking. Make some contacts.'

'I don't think... wait a moment. What about restaurants?'

'I'm sorry?'

'Restaurants. They're small firms. I could... er... visit a few of the more upmarket establishments.'

'I suppose perhaps... I don't see why not. There you are, you see, thinking out of the box. That's why the VC knew you were the man for the job.'

'Good,' said Brush, envisaging meals in his favourite eating houses paid for on expenses. 'I'll get cracking on it right away. Just as long as my salary...'

'Naturally, you won't forget the press conference.'

'What press conference?' snapped Brush, glancing at his watch. Was he supposed to be elsewhere? Had he missed something? A freebie... nibbles and over-rated Australian chardonnay with names like Convict's Croak?

'It's to do with the concept of the stakeholder experience...'

The confidence with which Brush had entered the room was draining away, or rather being leeched from him. He felt light-headed, distant, and when he tried to speak no sound came. Kerry, though, was still talking.

'Ownership. Engagement. Our sponsors must feel they relate to the new centre. The VC's all for

190

engagement,' Kerry said, a grin ghosting across his face. 'That's why we need a press conference. Get them to come in... wine them, dine them...'

'Ah...' said Brush, rallying slightly.

'The Earl of Cramcaster might host it. You'd introduce him...'

Brush shuddered. Memories of his failure to persuade Pendegrass to engage with the Earl still rankled.

'Then you could show them the plans...'

'Plans...?'

'And the model. The architect's knocked up a splendid model of the whole site. The press'll love that...'

'The press...'

'Get them hooked... sponsors, the Earl... and the media. Once the world knows there's big names on board they'll all be beating a path to our door, wanting part of it, waving their credit cards. That's what we need.'

'I don't see how it's my job...' Brush began.

'There you go again, Professor Brush. So witty. Of course it's your job. Assistant vice chancellor external relations. Press conferences... the media... right up your street. We can't leave this to a secretary, now can we?'

It was on the tip of Brush's tongue to say this was precisely to whom it should be left, when a fit of foxiness seized him. 'Very tricky, press conferences. Need to get them just right,' he oozed, never in his life having arranged such an event. 'Now... if I had staff I could rely on to sort the details... a decent office from which to operate... then...'

'The VC's working on it. She's well aware you've been catapulted into this post with minimal notice...'

'Yes... and minimal salary,' said Brush, sensing this

191

was his moment. 'I feel my duties to be hardly commensurate with my salary... I mean...'

'Well,' Kerry said, quick as a flash. 'If that's the way you feel it's clear we're not keeping you sufficiently busy. This press conference is just what you need.'

'But...'

'That's fine, then, Professor Brush. I'm glad we agree. I'll inform the VC at once.'

'I thought you said she was out of contact... not to be bothered...'

Kerry winked. 'We have our ways, professor. We have our little ways.'

**

Wang gazed at his tutor with a mixture of pity and horror. He and Lina had pulled Pendegrass from beneath the desk and propped him back on his chair. There was a cut on his forehead, which was bleeding slightly, and Lina gave him a tissue from her bag. Pendegrass, though, seemed not to know what to do with it, and gazed round the room in bewilderment. Wang told Lina he thought there was something wrong with Pendegrass's vision: he didn't seem able to focus. Lina waved her hand in front of his face, which startled him.

'Go away,' he said, feebly. 'Can't see anyone just now. Teaching...'

'He says he can't see,' Wang said excitedly to Lina. 'I was right. Perhaps we should...'

'I don't think that's what he meant,' Lina said doubtfully. 'But he's not teaching. It says on his door he's free all morning.'

She turned to Pendegrass. 'No teach. Timetable on door say: Free. Consultation hour. We want consult.

192

Please.'

Pendegrass groaned.

'Haaar… if professor sir not right we come back…'

'Yes,' said Pendegrass, perking up. 'Come back. Tomorrow. Next week. Or talk to someone else.'

'Haaar… not someone else. You good professor. We want talk you. Not Professor Jordy. He bad professor. He not talk clear.'

Wang caught a glance of disapproval from Lina.

'Haaar… clearly.'

Pendegrass rolled back in his chair. He had no idea what they were talking about. He racked his reeling brain for a Professor Jordy past, present or pending, but thought pained him. And now the girl was talking again. He tried to focus on her.

'We very sorry. We give professor great shock. I get drink for professor…'

'No drink,' Pendegrass mumbled. 'Nazareth and Ewesbottom Repentant Sinners…'

Lina's spectacles flashed angrily at Pendegrass. 'Professor need drink. Good for professor. I get.'

It crossed Pendegrass's mind that if he volunteered to get the drink himself he might escape, seek sanctuary somewhere. Anywhere. He tried to stand but the office began to spin crazily around him. He flopped back onto the chair.

'What professor want? Professor say. Water, juice, tea, coffee, chocolate, Cola, Irn Bru, Doctor Pepper…'

Pendegrass wondered if Doctor Pepper was a colleague of Professor Jordy, if the school of management had been hiring staff and he hadn't noticed. It wouldn't surprise him. Or, alarmingly, perhaps the doctor was a medical man, and the injury to his head more serious than he imagined.

'No fuss,' he croaked. 'Don't want any fuss.'

'Drink machine not have fuss. Just water, juice, tea,

193

coffee...'

'Tea. Tea... anything...'

As Lina turned to go she rounded on Wang and, Pendegrass thought, from her tone of voice, appeared to be giving instructions. Wang, however, cut her off, raising his hand to stem the flow, and the girl stepped back, mild surprise on her face. Wang grinned at her and almost, it appeared to Pendegrass, his vision slowly returning, seemed to dismiss her. At any rate the girl, with a last look at Wang, left the office without another word. Wang watched her go and then drew up a chair before his tutor's desk. Placing himself on it, he stared hard at Pendegrass.

'Haaar,' he said.

Pendegrass was unsure how to respond. The room fell silent. Outside, from below, a lorry, reversing, began bleeping like an alien invader. Overhead, distantly, aircraft engines roared as a plane wheeled on its path to Cramcaster International Airport. Pendegrass wondered if it was bringing more Chinese students. To exclude this possibility, and to avoid Wang's gaze, he shut his eyes and felt himself drifting, lightly, easily, as a balloon. He found himself floating above the university, wafted westward towards the flatlands beyond the city; below him...

'Professor sir... professor,' an insistent note in Wang's voice brought Pendegrass rapidly to earth. 'I have to say you...'

Pendegrass opened his eyes, briefly, and squinted at Wang.

'Not now. Not up to it. Not feeling quite myself. Sorry.'

Wang looked as if he was about to speak.

'Forty winks. Must have forty winks. Essential.'

'Forty...? Haaar... you wait for tea.'

'No. Yes... I'll wait for tea. So, in the meantime,

please… just leave me be. Sit there if you must… but don't disturb me. Do not disturb… like in a hotel.'

'Haaar… hotel. Note on door. Okay… I sit.'

'Good. You sit. And I'll… whatever you do, just keep quiet.'

So saying, he shut his eyes once more, and was instantly lost. When he awoke, well into the afternoon, with a slight headache, he was puzzled to find a beaker of cold tea on the desk in front of him. He frowned. How had it got there? He had no idea. And why were his plant, and soil, and bits of broken pot strewn across the floor? That was even more of a mystery. Pendegrass wondered if the cleaners would clear the mess – they had been very particular of late regarding what they would and would not clear up – and, rubbing his forehead, which for some reason seemed especially tender, he set off, groggily, for the car park and home.

30

From her office in Wole Soyinka, Christine Reeve – standing idly at the window, trying to summon the courage to tap out another page of her hardly-thrilling thriller – looked out across a rainswept campus. What a dump, she thought. A complete mishmash, ranging in style from solid and grubby Victorian to flimsy and equally grubby 1960s, with the Cram, almost an open sewer, snaking its surly, sluggish way through it. Apparently a king, possibly one of the Jameses, had crossed the river at some point here. Probably all fields in those days... not a factory, derelict or otherwise, in sight.

Two students, bending into the wind on the path below, caught her attention. She rubbed at the slightly misted pane to get a clearer view. It was as she thought. The girl with the spectacles, Emmeline – she could remember her name – and a boy from the English class. That would be William, the one the girl was worried about, and who, according to Pendegrass, had arrived with a case full of money, and whose very name sent the usually placid Pendegrass into paroxysms of rage. Christine wondered if he had seen his tutee, if whatever problems the boy was facing had been resolved. She doubted it: Pendegrass had probably forgotten all about their conversation in the car park. Christine thought she might email him with a reminder, but decided against it. It would be unlikely to do any good and, besides, given Pendegrass's apparent antipathy to the student, could even be counter-productive.

Christine rubbed again at the window, and looked out. There was no sign of the boy or girl. She turned away and, staring disdainfully at the half-finished sentence from her thriller, teasing, taunting her on the computer screen, she stabbed the 'delete' key. Then,

196

flopping into her chair, she seized a pile of papers and began marking.

**

Wang was not in the best of tempers. Despite his understanding that his relationship with Lina was on a more equal footing, he had been persuaded by her to ring Mr Wu and say he was still not fit for work. Instead, Lina told him, he should see Professor Pendegrass and get the business about not attending class, about working, sorted out as soon as possible. Wang knew she was right, which was why he agreed, but all the same it was galling that the suggestion came from her, not him. Nevertheless he was grateful when, after Pendegrass's human resource management lecture, together they were able to corner him and cut off his escape.

'Please... we talk. Wang talk,' Lina said, as Pendegrass eyed the door. 'Now.'

'Ah,' mumbled Pendegrass. 'Bit awkward. I've... er... got a meeting.'

'No meeting,' Lina said. 'We check. Professor sir free until three o'clock.'

'It's a meeting... an appointment,' Pendegrass said quickly, in a flash of inspiration. 'About this...' and he pointed to a plaster on his forehead.

Lina stared at him. 'When appointment? Time...?'

'Soon,' said Pendegrass vaguely. 'In fact, very soon. So... sorry...'

'Haaar... we visit professor yesterday... professor sleep. Not good. We visit professor today... professor say meeting. But no meeting. Not on timetable...'

'Doctors' appointments aren't on timetables...'

'You my tutor. You good man. You listen.'

'I need to go to the toilet.' Pendegrass ventured,

197

attempting a grimace. 'Very urgent.'

'Toilet wait,' and spectacles flashed menacingly in Pendegrass's face. 'What Wang say more urgent than toilet. Besides... we Chinese student. We customer. You teach customer always right. Pay good money... big fee... to British university. No big China fee, no student. No university. No job...'

Pendegrass rolled his eyes in despair. As other students began filing into the room for the following class he told Wang and Lina that, yes, if they wished to go back with him to his office he would listen to what they had to say there. Wang and Lina exchanged a triumphant glance.

At least, thought Pendegrass, reluctantly gathering his lecture notes and remnants of self-pride, he'd be able to have a pee on the way. And possibly effect an escape. He tried to recall how large the windows were in the cubicles of the gents. Then he remembered the toilets he usually used were on the fourth floor. Perhaps not a good idea. Though, as a last resort...

**

As it happened, escape was impossible. Wang and the girl were standing guard outside the gents after Pendegrass, having skulked in the toilets as long as decently possible, nervously ventured forth in the hope of finding the coast clear. No such luck. So now, several minutes later, he found himself in his office, longing for a nap, but required to concentrate on his tutee's tale of... well, what?

'I'm sorry,' Pendegrass said for what seemed like the umpteenth time, 'but I'm really not following this.'

'What my friend say...' the girl with the spectacles began, but fell silent as Wang turned and glared at her.

'This my problem,' Wang told Pendegrass. 'Not

198

problem of good friend Emmeline. So I say. Not she say. And now I say you… I work. Work hard.'

'Good,' said Pendegrass, cautiously, wondering if he had missed something. 'I mean… excellent. Work hard. That's why you're here.'

'Haaar… professor not angry…?'

'Why should I be? I wish we had a few more students who worked.'

'Few more student. Haaar… professor want me find job for few more student?'

'I'm sorry…?'

'Haaar. Not sorry when I find job for student like professor say.'

'I don't think we…'

'I ask Mr Wu. But I think many British student not like. Hard work in field.'

'Fieldwork? Well… sometimes that's very good. I mean… in our line of work we all have to do fieldwork sometimes…'

'All do field work? Professor sir do field work?'

'Well, yes. A bit. A long time ago… for my dissertation.'

'Haaar… professor do field work. Like in China. Many professor and student do field work in China. I think… not much different in two country China and Britain.'

'Well… I don't know…'

'And professor do field work for dissertation. Now I do field work for dissertation.'

'It's a bit early to start thinking about the dissertation.'

'Bit early… not. I ask question. Many question. I say… why you here? What you do? When you go home?'

Pendegrass wished Wang would go home. And that girl. In fact, the lot of them. Students, staff, the whole

199

university. Especially Brush. Just get off his back. Then he could… could write his letter to Lynne Truss. Meet her, fling himself at her feet, offer his services… more, oh yes… but these were not sinner-like thoughts. Or were they? They were actually extremely sinner-like. Hence the need for repentance. In this way he was both a good sinner and a bad sinner. But this was confusing. What was he doing here? What was it all about?

Wang was still talking. He was saying something, if Pendegrass heard correctly, about harvests, and potatoes, and Bilbo Baggins. He seemed to have met Bilbo Baggins under a cart in the rain, and spat him out – Pendegrass could sympathise: he thought Lord of the Rings overrated – but the whole story made no sense. The student was clearly mad – the incident with the suitcase full of useless banknotes was the first clue – and he should never have been admitted to the university. Pendegrass resolved to write a stiff note to the admissions department, after Lynne's letter had been safely despatched, until he recalled with a shudder that responsibility for accepting Wang rested entirely with him, as postgraduate admissions tutor. He groaned.

'Excuse,' the spectacles broke in on Pendegrass's reverie. 'I think… we get nowhere.'

Too true, thought Pendegrass grimly.

'I explain,' the spectacles said, adding something in her native language which Wang, with a slight frown, seemed to accept. 'I explain to professor sir what is situation with Mr Wang. Situation bad. Situation very bad.'

What's new? thought Pendegrass, settling back into his chair and waving vaguely at the girl to indicate she had the floor. At least he might get more sense from her than from Wang.

The girl began speaking. In floods, in torrents, an

outpouring of Wang's financial worries. How he was in debt not only to the university but also to Mr Wu and someone called Qi, how Wang had to miss classes and work long hours, on some farm, with other Chinese workers, way out in the country, how he wanted to turn this to advantage and use his experience to research the labour market, in particular the exploitation of overseas and possibly illegal workers, and write this up for his dissertation, and how...

'Whoa,' said Pendegrass, having caught the word 'research', and conscious of something stirring, a ghost of an idea, a flicker of inspiration. 'Whoa... hold it right there.'

He shut his eyes, concentrating, focussing on everything and nothing, shadows, shapes, flitting through his mind, including repentant sinners with their bulging bank balance.

'Let me see if I've got this straight,' he said, opening his eyes and looking hard at Wang. 'I know you're in debt to the university. All that's going to have to be sorted. But now, in addition, you owe money to this Mr Wu, or his boss, and you're trying to pay it off by working on the land. Somehow I can't see that happening. But... I think there's a way around it.'

No-one moved. The faces of both Wang and Lina were expressionless. Pendegrass felt suddenly very sorry for them. They were children, lost in a strange world, someone else's world. He looked at them with new-found pity, sympathy and tenderness. To his surprise he felt his lower lip quivering, and a tear rise to his eye. He blinked it away. Yes, there was a reason to be a sinner, after all.

'I think,' he said, 'we can kill two birds with one stone. That is... I can help you, if you help me. Listen...'

201

31

The press conference, Brush thought, looking round the room, was remarkably successful. At least, for a first attempt. Private dining area number three was full; there was standing room only; and the buffet, provided at no small expense by the Bay of Bengal, was, as Brush expected, outstanding. He noted with satisfaction that the specimen menus the restaurant had thoughtfully laid out on the tables next to its curries and spices were being removed almost as quickly as the food. The prospect of several evenings of complimentary dining at the restaurant lifted Brush's spirits.

Of course, the evening was not without its difficulties. Although the Earl of Cramcaster, unable to attend, had promised to open his chequebook for a suitable sum, the vice chancellor had been forced at the last minute to cancel. An urgent meeting in London with some Whitehall mandarin, Pat Kerry told Brush. The vice chancellor was extremely disappointed not to be able to talk about the new arts and media centre herself but, Kerry said, she knew she could rely on Brush. A mixed blessing, Brush felt. On the one hand she would not be present to witness his organisational triumph; on the other she would be less likely to discover the majority of people in the room were there under false pretences. Despite a mail shot to firms and businesses, promising an exciting evening of award-winning Indian food and the chance to shape the future of the arts in Cramcaster, the response from would-be sponsors was almost non-existent. In fact, the only reaction was a curt letter from the head office of a chain of bookmakers asking whether Brush knew there was a recession on and, if he didn't, saying he shouldn't be employed at a so-called university. In despair, Brush had been about to hire a coachload of resting actors to masquerade as sponsors, when he realised he could fill the room more cheaply. Using his wife's contacts he flung open the invitation to the membership of Cramcaster City Council, sensing that, like academics, no self-respecting representative of the people would pass up free food and drink. Next it was the turn of the school of management, whose long-suffering staff were dragooned under pain of extra administration duties to attend. The numbers were completed by several of Brush's neighbours, the milkman, two Jehovah's witnesses and a Big Issue seller: in short, anyone Brush could lay his hands on. As far as numbers were concerned, the evening could not be faulted. Besides, Brush convinced himself, these people might not be sponsors now, but any one of them might be in the future. Even the Jehovah's witnesses. Then again...

True, there had been a misunderstanding over the model of the proposed centre that was supposed to take pride of place in the room. Marcus Dunlittle, wearing his health and safety cap over his customary head of physical plant and resources, refused to sanction the displaying of the model. He emailed Brush, saying that 'strictly no modle is to expose itself where foodstufs is being severed on the grounds of hygeine'. In vain Brush pointed out that the man had the wrong type of model in mind. Dunlittle was adamant: regulations stated there should be no modelling where food was present, and that was his last word. Brush backed down with bad grace. At least if there was no model it would make it easier to field questions from the press.

As it happened, the local radio station failed to turn up – the reporter was sent to cover the rescue of a family of hedgehogs stuck in a drain, Brush learned later – and the only media representative was the Cramcaster Evening Herald and its trainee reporter, Jason Hackley. Hackley, thought Brush, was drunk.

203

Either that, or extremely... what was the word?... brash. The reporter wanted to know why there were so many councillors at the launch which, after all, was about sponsorship. Brush mumbled something about partnership, about building bridges with the community, whereupon Hackley said the best bridge that could be built was to leave the College Arms alone. Then, after Brush had delivered his hastily cobbled speech – ill-prepared, because he understood the vice chancellor would do the honours – and invited questions, Hackley asked what the university felt about the 'Hands Off Our Arms' campaign. Brush, wondering what this had to do with the arts and media centre, but flattered to be invited to comment on what was evidently a news story of international importance, said he thought that as a punishment for theft the cutting off of hands was overdoing it – but if those countries where this was practised insisted on physical retribution then perhaps a good stoning would be sufficient. From the corner of his eye he noticed hands rising to mirthful mouths, while several people began openly to laugh including, Brush observed, Dozy Pendegrass.

'Excuse me, Professor Brush,' Hackley intervened, 'but the 'Hands Off Our Arms' campaign is the campaign to save the College Arms... to save the College Arms from the arts and media centre you want to put there. I wonder...'

Damn it, thought Brush. How could I have missed that one? That's the trouble... not been in the Arms for ages because of trying to sort this goddam evening. And why didn't anyone brief me?

'No comment,' he growled. 'And that's quite enough questions, thank you.' Too pushy by half, that kid, Brush thought. And obviously biased. Wants putting in his place. Like Pendegrass, who was very cocky of late. Perhaps he'd joined the union, something

204

subversive like that. He'd have to find out. In the meantime it would serve Pendegrass right – serve anyone right – to introduce him to his wife who, Brush saw, appeared to be sharing a joke with a fellow councillor he knew vaguely as McGurkin, something like that. Didn't think she liked the fellow. Scottish, and all the rest. But I'll break up their little shindig. Elbowing his guests aside, he ploughed his way across the room to Pendegrass.

'I'd like you to meet my wife... she's a councillor,' Brush hissed, steering a startled Pendegrass towards Mrs Brush. 'I'm sure you'll get on well... so much in common. Darling... I'd like you to meet a colleague... Dozy... Mr Pendegrass.'

'Delighted to meet you,' Brush heard Pendegrass say with unexpected confidence, as he backed away towards the buffet to assuage his humiliation at the hands of Hackley with seconds of sweet and sour. 'Actually I was hoping to have a word. About illegal immigrants in Cramcaster and the council's response...'

'Illegal immigrants? Here? Oh, hardly, Mr Prenderghast. I am quite sure...'

'On the contrary. I happen to be doing...' – here Pendegrass raised his voice so Brush might hear – 'a spot of research into the subject. I have reason to believe there is a cell, or whatever you call it, in Compton Park...'

Councillor Mrs Rosalind Brush, having just taken a generous and unladylike sip from her third glass of Chardonnay, spluttered her indignation, which splashed over Pendegrass's one and only suit, his chapel suit. What if the elders...?

'I can assure you,' Mrs Brush boomed, 'there are no illegal immigrants in Compton Park. I should know. I live in Compton Park. I represent Compton Park on the council. Compton Park is highly respectable... much sought-after...'

Brush wondered what on earth Pendegrass was on about. Had he mentioned research? The fool didn't do research... that's why he'd asked his staff to come up with ideas, knowing for the most part they couldn't, which would make it easier to fire them when the cuts came. He was about to move back to Pendegrass and his wife when from the corner of his eye he saw Pat Kerry bearing down on him. Kerry... the evening was beginning to unravel, like one of those awful lopsided baskets he used to make at primary school. You think it's done when part of the weave pops out and the whole thing falls apart.

'Now, here's a thing for you,' Kerry began. 'It can't have escaped your notice there don't seem to be many would-be sponsors here. In fact, I haven't spoken to anyone who might fall into that category.'

'There's the Bay of Bengal.'

'Ah, well, you see... that's just a catering firm.'

'On the contrary. High class restaurateurs. Look. Have you tried this chicken korma? Exquisite. I can really recommend it. Here...'

As Brush leaned across the table to spoon a portion of chicken onto a plate, he was pushed violently from behind. Lurching forward, he put out his hand to prevent himself sprawling across the table. The hand landed in the chicken which, overturning, splashed onto Kerry before running down his trousers to the floor. Brush turned to see Hackley behind him.

'Sorry,' said the reporter, a malicious grin on his face. 'Someone bashed into me. One of your... er... sponsors. Hardly room to swing a...'

'You...' roared Brush, waving his chicken-covered fist in the direction of Hackley, showering those around in droplets of sauce. 'You did that deliberately.

206

Deliberately pushed me...'

'Careful what you say,' Hackley said nonchalantly. 'I think you'll find that's slander. No shortage of witnesses. Okay?' And with that, he sauntered from the room.

Something was wrong. Desperately wrong. Nothing was in its place... everything, everyone... Pendegrass, his wife, now this trumped-up little newspaper reporter; Kerry, Dunlittle; even the dish of chicken korma... all were trying to humiliate him, all plotting, conspiring against him. What was going on? Brush had no idea. But he knew he had to get a grip. Fast.

**

Across the campus from where Professor Arthur Brush was managing to boost the profits of the Bay of Bengal, and not much else, a weary figure was dragging tired and aching limbs along a corridor in the Martin Luther King hall of residence. The figure stopped outside one of the rooms and rested itself for a moment against the wall. Then a grubby, grit-grained hand tapped feebly at the door.

'Come in,' a voice said.

Wang pushed open the door and saw Lina, as expected, hunched over her desk, surrounded by books and papers, and scribbling furiously. She glanced up as he entered.

'Honestly... I despair,' she said, throwing down her pen, and rocking back on her chair. 'I mean... look at you. You're a wreck. And you stink of that awful place.'

'Sorry,' Wang mumbled. 'But I just wanted to see you.'

Lina sighed. 'Yes... but I do think you might have a shower first.'

207

'Too tired,' Wang said, flopping onto the bed.

Lina gave a shriek, leaped up and hauled Wang to his feet. 'That's where I've got to sleep. Look at that filth. It's disgusting.'

'I just wanted to...'

'Shower. This second. In the meantime I'll make us some tea. I suppose you're hungry...?'

'Ravenous. I could eat a...'

'Good. But, first things first. Shower.'

Thrusting a towel into his hand, Lina opened the door and bundled Wang back onto the corridor he had just left.

'If you can't find clean clothes I've two shirts of yours I washed when I did my stuff.'

The door to Lina's room shut behind him.

**

'Did you know they're having a launch of this arts and media centre tonight?' Ed asked Christine as she walked into the College Arms. 'To drum up support from sponsors.'

'As a matter of fact, I did,' Christine said. 'For some reason I got an invitation from that Professor Twat... now assistant vice chancellor for public relations or some such thing. No way I'd go.'

'Perhaps you should have and then you could have reported back. But no matter. I've got my spies there. Or spy. Agent provocateur, more like. I don't reckon it'll come to much, this launch.'

'You seem remarkably chirpy this evening, all things considered,' Christine said.

'And you seem remarkably unchirpy, if you don't mind me saying so. What you need is a drink. Let's see...'

'What I need is inspiration,' Christine said and, as

Ed produced two tumblers of whisky, she told him about her writing and the spy thriller going nowhere. She refrained from adding that the hero was based loosely on him and that, perhaps if she knew him better, the whole thing might take off.

'Forget the thriller,' Ed said. 'Write about what you know.'

'I only know about teaching...'

'Nonsense,' retorted Ed. 'You know about life. What goes on around you. For instance... you should write about this place.'

'The College Arms?'

'No, silly. The university. I mean, surely, that's what you know best. There must be dozens of things you could tap into.'

'I think one or two others got there first. The university novel...'

'What if they did? There's always a fresh angle. Come on, Chris. Think positive. Give it a go. And while you're thinking it over... drink up.'

He'd called her Chris. Chris. She'd never liked the short form of her name: it was too... too crisp, too masculine. But now, the way he said it, it was like melting snow... Christine reached for her whisky and took a gulp. The liquid hit a spot somewhere in the back of her head, charging her brain with momentary exhilaration, before finding the throat, cascading downwards, making her splutter.

'Sorry,' she said, putting the glass down and dabbing with a crooked forefinger at her mouth.

Ed grinned. 'It has that effect, doesn't it? Something a bit special, I think.'

What was? The whisky? Or something else? Was this his way of saying...? But no. Flustered, she averted her gaze and studied the polished wood of the bar. There was a constancy, a permanency in the grain,

209

which reassured her, steadied her. How many troubles had been poured out over that venerable surface; how many secrets spilled, emotions uncorked? All wiped clean, leaving just the wood; smooth and silent, witness to the woes of a worrying world. Christine thought she caught her reflection in the wood, shimmering faintly in the glow of the light over the bar. She ran her fingers over the surface, as if to capture the image, burnish it, but it had gone. Perhaps it was never there. She looked up.

'It is,' she said. 'A bit special. But one I could get used to.'

'Ah,' said Ed, his eyes sparkling. 'Plenty more where that came from.'

**

Showered and freshly shirted – wearing one of the garments Lina had washed – and with a full stomach, Wang was in expansive mood.

'I thought perhaps this weekend we might go out. We could have a meal... and then there's a film I rather fancy down in Chinatown...'

'I've too much to do. I've an essay... and I'm trying to sort these notes for you...'

'That's why you need a break. And I want to treat you... say thanks...'

Lina's face contorted and she tossed back her head. 'It doesn't seem right. Spending all this money. One moment you haven't two yuan to rub together, and the next the professor's paying all your fees and you're wanting to throw money round like nobody's business.'

'It's okay. The professor... those kind and generous friends of his... they won't mind. The professor said after all I've been through... the worry, the uncertainty... I deserve to spend a bit on myself.

Anyway... it's not as if I'm not earning it. I am.'

'I know you are. And I half-wish you weren't. Honestly, I'm worried. It's all very well doing this research for Professor Pendegrass, but asking all those questions is going to get you into trouble. These are nasty people.'

'I'm being careful. Besides, I'm almost done. The professor's more or less got what he wants... and I've loads of stuff for my dissertation. Soon I'll be able to give Mr Wu the money I owe and tell him I don't need the job. Then I can get on with the course... just like an ordinary student.'

Lina frowned. 'What bothers me is when the professor publishes this book, or whatever it is he's doing. I mean... it'll all come out. They'll know you were... sort of... undercover. Spying.'

'When that happens we'll be safely back home. And...'

'These people have connections. They must have. Everywhere. Especially China. That's what worries me.'

'Look. It's only a bit of research. To help the professor. Which in turn helps me, because as his research assistant...'

'Not officially...'

'Whatever. But as his assistant, he's paying my fees. Anyway, research... the only people who look at research are other researchers. Professors. Students. People who have to. No-one else can be bothered. They've better things to do.'

'You've some funny ideas, Wang Ti. I hope you're right.'

'Of course I am. And here's another funny idea. What about that film this weekend...?'

'Out. You need your sleep. Especially if you're up again at the crack of dawn.'

211

'Please say you'll think about it...'

'I'll think about it. But only if you go now so I can get on with my essay.'

32

Whether it was warmer working outside, in the fields, or inside, in the distribution centre, was difficult to say. Wang couldn't make up his mind. When the wind dropped and a watery, early-winter sun shone languidly over the rows of celery or Chinese leaves – the potato crop was now in – Wang preferred to be outside. It was less claustrophobic, somehow liberating, and a welcome contrast to the walls which seemed to constrain him; whether in his room in Martin Luther King, a lecture theatre, the library (when he could get there), or, indeed, the entirety of the drab, grey, featureless buildings that comprised the campus of Cram Vale University.

On the other hand the distribution centre, a concrete and cladding construct on a neighbouring farm, was permanently chilly. It had to be, for here the crops were brought to be vacuumed, cooled, sealed and kept in refrigerated conditions before dispatch. Wang wondered why the refrigeration plant was needed. If they just opened the doors, let the damp, slightly salty wind blow through that gusted in from the coast, then they could keep the place cool and save huge sums on electricity. And, if they needed electricity, why didn't they use wind-power to generate it? Wang had seen windmills in China in places where there was a fraction of the wind that swept across the former marshlands to the west of Cramcaster. But the British were so backward, Wang was learning, so reluctant to move with the times. Gone was the spirit of enterprise and innovation that built empires. That spirit had moved elsewhere. Back home where it belonged, where it was nurtured. Back home to China.

At least in the distribution centre there was protection from the elements, and for this Wang was

213

grateful. He felt Mr Wu had taken pity on him, telling him on more than one occasion not to leave the minibus with the other workers but to stay on board until he reached the distribution centre. It was as if Mr Wu had realised that Wang, slightly built, clearly unaccustomed to manual labour, was not cut out for toiling on the fields. Perhaps, Wang reasoned, Mr Wu wanted to protect his assets: if Wang fell ill again, unable to work, his boss would not able to recoup the money he said he owed. The first time Wang was taken to the centre he waited outside while Mr Wu, having gone into the building, could be seen through a window waving his fist and pointing outside in Wang's direction. Wang, feeling awkward, averted his gaze and, looking around, spotted a brass plate next to the door by which Mr Wu had gone in. It read: Earl of Cramcaster Estates. Registered Office. The word 'earl' – pronounced, presumably, as in 'ear' or 'year' – was unfamiliar to Wang. He made a mental note to check his electronic dictionary when he returned to his room that evening, or else ask someone who might know. That, of course, in the immediate future was unlikely: almost all the people he encountered on the farms spoke little or no English. As he was rolling the word 'yearl' around his tongue, Mr Wu stepped out of the office and told him that from now on, for the most part, he would be working here. The duties were less onerous, Mr Wu said, than out in the fields, but with more responsibility, involving quality control and making sure everything was properly packaged before sending to customers. Then, telling Wang he would pick him up at the usual time, he got back into the minibus and drove off.

The work was, indeed, lighter. The processes were largely automated and, apart from shifting cartons and crates, required little brute strength. The routine of the distribution centre also made it easier to talk, to

214

communicate: those words and phrases which, out on the fields, remained half-said, half-heard, and then cast to all points of the compass, could be readily reformed as dialogue, enquiry. Besides, there were different people in the distribution centre, not the same mournful souls who came each day in Mr Wu's minibus. They came in different buses, with different drivers, and it was an opportunity for Wang to broaden his inquiry, to collect material for his tutor and for his dissertation from fresh sources.

The morning after Wang had invited Lina to the cinema, Mr Wu had not dropped him off at the fields but had taken him, as promised, to the distribution centre.

'Looks like a storm,' Mr Wu had said. 'You'll be better off in there.'

Mr Wu was right and, later, with the rain pinging on the roof above him, Wang found himself surveying a seemingly never-ending succession of bundled and packaged Chinese leaves jostling along a conveyor to their waiting cartons.

'Odd, isn't it,' Wang said, to the man standing opposite him, performing apparently the same task, 'that what we've got here are Chinese leaves... so far from home.'

The man looked briefly at Wang, and said nothing. His faced was lined, wrinkles etched into dry, flaky skin. He looked old, but his bearing was that of a younger person. It was impossible to tell his age.

'I mean,' Wang said, 'we come all this way to find just the sort of thing we get back home.'

The man stared across at Wang and fixed him with a look of boredom and resignation. He was not one of Mr Wu's workers: Wang had not seen him before. He had a scar beneath his left ear, extending towards the throat, which Wang found both fascinating and frightening.

'Stir-fry,' the man said.

'I'm sorry...' Wang replied, lifting his eyes from the scar.

'Stir-fry. Very big in England. Supermarkets, restaurants... can't get enough of it.'

'Oh,' said Wang. 'I see.'

Then, having opened communication, Wang sought to press his advantage.

'Ni hao,' he said, holding out his hand across the conveyor. 'Wang Ti. Pleased to meet you.'

The man said nothing, and gazed balefully on the passing packs of Chinese leaves.

'Tell me,' Wang said, 'if you don't mind... but where are you from? And how did you get here?'

The man frowned, which creased his face even more. It reminded Wang of an old wash-leather, the sort of thing his uncle sometimes used for cleaning bicycles. He wondered briefly what Uncle Peng would be doing. What time was it in China? Would he be in bed? Cooking rice? Washing Chinese leaves...?

'Cramcaster,' the man said. 'I came by minibus.'

It was Wang's turn to frown. The man thought he meant now, today, whereas what he wanted to know was where in China he came from, how he had reached England, what he had experienced on the way, how long it had taken – these were the missing pieces in Professor Pendegrass's jigsaw. Wang sighed. This was the problem. No-one he'd spoken to ever wanted to give details. Either that, or they had put the horrors of a journey halfway round the world firmly behind them.

'What I meant,' Wang said, spotting a pack incorrectly sealed, and setting it aside, 'was how you came to end up here. In Britain. Doing this. I mean...'

'You don't want to know.'

'But I do,' Wang said eagerly, too eagerly, then checked himself. 'I mean... everyone has a story to

216

tell,' he ended lamely.

'Stories… pah. There are too many stories in the world. They get in the way of life.'

Wang seized his opportunity. 'Tell me about life, then.'

The man curled his lip into a sneer, which exaggerated the scar, burnishing it red and raw.

'Love. I fell in love with the wrong woman. Actually, the right woman. Divine. Perfect in every way. Except…'

'Haaar,' said Wang, unsure if he wished to be privy to the man's love life.

'She was the wife of a party official. Twice her age. When we were found out… betrayed… that was it. They said if I wanted to stay alive there must be no more contact. I was to leave the province, the country. The shame, they said. They told me I could work overseas… they would see to it.'

'And did they?'

'After a fashion. I was expecting an airline ticket… these were wealthy, powerful people. I was an engineer… I would work in Africa, I thought, for one of their companies. Instead…'

'Instead…?'

'I end up here.'

'But… I mean… how did you get here? By plane…?'

'You ask a lot of questions, young man. Why do you want to know?'

The man's voice, his features, had suddenly hardened. The scar was standing proud on his neck, pulsing, throbbing. Wang became aware the rain had stopped, or at any rate abated; he could no longer hear it drumming on the roof. Apart from the steady hum of the conveyor, the shed was quiet.

'Come on,' the man said. 'It's your turn to answer

questions. Why do you want to know?'

Wang felt the ground tremble beneath his feet. The Chinese leaves seemed no longer to be flowing smoothly, seamlessly, but to be riding great rolling waves which threatened to wash them away. At the same time the building was closing in on him, and he knew he needed fresh air.

He turned for the door. His way was immediately barred by Mr Wu, standing directly behind him.

'We need to speak,' Mr Wu said. 'Come with me.'

33

Lina was not unduly alarmed when Wang failed to call in to see her that evening. There were many times when he was working in the fields and he didn't come. Sometimes he was too tired, and went straight to bed; sometimes he took himself off to the library and tried to concentrate on his books. Besides, she had been immersed in her essay, hadn't noticed the time, and when she stopped she decided she needed a shower, to wash her hair, something to relax her. It was possible Wang came when she was out, in the washrooms at the end of the corridor. It was no matter: she would catch up with him the following morning.

However, at breakfast time the next day, there was no sign of Wang. Again, this was not especially worrying. Lina knew, if he was working for Mr Wu, he would have left long before anyone was stirring. On the other hand she didn't think today was one of what she called his Wu-days. The trouble was, she couldn't remember. She reproached herself for not paying more attention. She had been too preoccupied with that essay, hadn't taken in what Wang had said, ought to have known what he was doing. None of the other students using the communal kitchen had seen Wang, and no-one seemed particularly bothered. Jingen, still wondering what Lina saw in a loser like Wang, told her he thought he had done a runner because the showers were too clean.

'What do you mean?' Lina asked, archly.

'You always know the little runt's around because, if he tried to clean himself the night before, there's half the farmyard – soil, earth – clogging the place next morning when we want to use it. It's a miracle the cleaners don't complain. Anyway, this morning, it was okay. Like a new pin.'

219

Lina pursed her lips. Perhaps Wang had been so tired when he came in last night he hadn't bothered with a shower and taken himself straight to bed. Men, Lina realised, were like that. They didn't worry about dirt like women did. Why, Wang would wear the same shirt, the same underpants for days if she didn't take him in hand. As for the shower, Jingen was probably exaggerating. It couldn't be as bad as he made out. Besides, that's what showers were for. To wash the dirt away. There was no way he could tell if Wang had used the place or not.

Seeking further evidence of Wang's presence, or not, as the case might be, Lina opened the cupboard where Wang kept his food. Tea, rice, noodles – all in their place. Lina thought hard to recall if anything had been moved since she last looked. She'd used his tea... when? yesterday? the day before?... but couldn't recall precisely how she'd put it back or whether it had been moved since then. There was nothing to indicate whether Wang had been to the cupboard either that morning or the previous day.

Still pondering, Lina left the kitchen and made her way to Wang's room. It was entirely reasonable, she reckoned, that if it wasn't a Wu-day then he was fast asleep, utterly exhausted, and was having a well-deserved rest. All the same, if he was to come to classes, he would need to be stirring. A wake-up call would surely be appreciated. Reaching his door, she tapped lightly on it. There was, as she half-expected, no response. Clearly he was asleep, dead to the world. She tapped again, this time more loudly, more insistently. Again, no response.

'Wang,' she called, this time rapping hard on the door. 'Wang. It's me. Time to get up.'

The sound had a curious empty, echoing quality which reverberated, hollow, dull, in her ears. She knew at once, instinctively, there was no-one there. Then, as if holding the room responsible, she began to beat on the door with her fists, shouting, wailing, 'Wang... where are you? Wang...'.

Figures, some dressed in pyjamas, one wearing nothing at all, began to emerge from neighbouring rooms. The students in the kitchen, finding the commotion more appetising than any breakfast, came to see what was going on. Among them was Jingen, who thought it highly amusing.

'He couldn't hack it,' he crowed. 'He's done a runner. I said he had.'

Ceasing her drumming, Lina whipped round and glared at Jingen with such contempt that for a moment he thought she was about to fly at him. Instead, summoning her dignity, she marched up to Jingen and the others and stood before them.

'Wang Ti has not done a runner,' she said. 'He's not like that. He's more guts than the lot of you.'

Someone began to laugh, but a look from Lina cut the perpetrator dead.

'Mark my words. More guts than the lot of you.'

**

Christine Reeve had spent a sleepless night. She had stayed up until two in the morning, hunched over her keyboard, trying to find a way in to the campus novel Ed had said she should write. Vague story-lines involving elderly professors flirting with lascivious female postgraduates washed round in her mind, before beaching themselves ignominiously, where they remained high and dry and refused to relaunch themselves. Anyway, that sort of stuff had been done before. It sounded very Mills-and-Boonish, and Christine knew neither her experience nor her

221

imagination enabled her to write convincingly about passionate embraces in the stacks of the university library, interrupted when the postgrad's best friend – ostensibly looking for a volume on Chaucer, but also wildly in love with the professor (who unknown to her, is her uncle) – happens upon the panting pair. Write about what you know, Ed said. That was fine, but Christine's knowledge of university life revolved round staffing and budgetary cuts, redeployment, ever-increasing class sizes, paperwork, and an environment that grew steadily more shabby.

Then she had slept fitfully. Apart from scenes from the would-be novel churning in her mind, she found herself with Ed on a desolate Scottish island. He was clutching a bottle of whisky, offering it to her, and trying to say something, but the wind and the rain blew his words away and she couldn't make anything out. Eventually, at around six, she awoke with a start, drenched in sweat, and was forced to get up to shut a window that was banging. There was no point going back to bed. She made herself a cup of tea, read the foreign pages from the previous day's newspaper, did the quick crossword, and set off for the university earlier than normal.

She was still yawning as she crossed the campus, and debating whether she should have gone back for an extra hour's sleep, when from one of the halls of residence shot a small, swiftly-moving figure, spectacles glinting even in the grey damp of morning, and cannoned into her.

'Professor... professor,' it panted. 'Help... please help. Wang Ti... he gone. Not there. In great danger...'

The first thought that crossed Christine's mind was that it was not Wang Ti who was in danger but the girl, Emmeline. She was wearing no coat, just a flimsy blouse and skirt, and if she stood around like that for

222

too long she'd catch her death of cold.

'Take it easy,' Christine said. 'Tell me again... slowly... what is it?'

A stream of words poured from the girl, of which Christine caught perhaps one in ten. If she understood correctly, the showers in the hall of residence were not working and Wang Ti had gone to repair them but had not come back. For a moment Christine thought perhaps the student had drowned but, unless showers had changed since her own days in halls of residence, she dismissed this as unlikely.

'Look,' she said, feeling rain beginning to fall, 'why don't we go to the cafeteria and get a coffee. I could do with something warm... I daresay you could, too.'

'But Wang Ti...'

'Mr Wang will be much better served if we get out of the cold and wet and we know exactly what's going on. Come along.'

The cafeteria was busy, but subdued. It always was at that time in the morning. Students were more intent on breakfast, on the day ahead, than on chatter. Christine sat Lina at an empty table and went to get her, as requested, a coke and donut – how anyone could stomach this so early in the day was beyond her – and herself a coffee. On impulse, and not something she normally did, she seized two sachets of sugar to stir into the coffee. She had a feeling she might need the extra energy to face whatever lay ahead.

Lina, chomping at the donut, which all but concealed her face, and which left something white and sticky round the bottom of her spectacles, appeared calmer. Gradually, Christine was able to piece together Lina's story. Wang, working for Mr Wu, was also working for Dozy Pendegrass who – despite his shambolic appearance and museum-piece of a car – now seemed rolling in money and able to pay Wang's

223

bills. The student, however, had gone missing, and might be in danger because of the double role he was playing. That was it... a double role. The student Wang was a double agent... just the sort of hero she had been looking for when trying to write her thriller. But Ed had said to write about the university... and now the two things were coming together. Or were they? Christine felt her brain begin to churn. Something, an idea, a plot, was forming... and to aid the process, she tipped the second sachet of sugar into her remaining coffee.

'Please... Professor Christine... what we do?'

'Eh...?' said Christine, nudged from fiction to fact, and attempting to focus on the spectacles across the table from her.

'I'll tell you what we'll do. We'll go and see Dozy... Mr Pendegrass straight away. He needs to be told. Let's hope he's around. But in the meantime... go and find yourself a jumper and a coat. You might need them.'

**

Christine and Lina, now more suitably attired, were waiting at the lift in Wole Soyinka when Pendegrass, puffing and panting, hands covered in grease and oil, came up to them.

'Sorry,' he said. 'Bit of a state. The car...'

'Don't know why you don't get yourself a new one,' Christine said. 'I know you can afford it.'

Pendegrass stared stupidly at Christine. Lina saw her opportunity, and launched into a monologue about the missing Wang. Pendegrass took a step back and muttered about having left some papers in the car and needing to go back for them. Christine said there was no point fetching papers with hands covered in oil. He should go and wash and then hear what Lina had to say.

At that point the lift came, and Christine pushed Lina and a protesting Pendegrass inside.

With hands suitably scoured, and ruefully contemplating his black and broken nails, Pendegrass found himself some minutes later at his desk listening to Lina's tale of woe.

'This is awful,' he said. 'It's all my fault. If anything happens to him... the repentant sinners will disown me. As for the university...'

'Get a grip,' Christine said. 'I'm sure it's not as bad as you're both making out. For a start, we don't know definitely what's happened. We haven't any facts. I mean... there might have been some minor accident. He might be in A&E somewhere...'

'Ehanee...?' Lina echoed.

'Accident and emergency. A hospital...'

'Hospital...? Wang hurt. Wang hurt bad... we go hospital. Find...'

'Hold on. We don't know. The first thing is to check his room. After all...'

'Check room. No Wang.'

'You said you hadn't been in. There might be a note... he might have said if he was going somewhere.'

'Wang say me if Wang go. Wang not go. I know.'

'Mr Pendegrass will ring the porters to get us into Wang's room...'

'Me?'

'Yes. You're his tutor. Then we'll have a look round the campus. See if he's in the library... computer rooms. International centre.'

'Wang not in library. Wang in danger...'

'Then, if we can't find him, we give him until this evening to come back...what time does he usually return if he's working?'

'Depend. Seven... eight o'clock. Sometime later.'

'Okay. We wait until then. Then, if there's still no

225

sign of him, we ring the police.'

'Why not now?' Pendegrass said, thinking it would be less effort if the police were involved.

'Come on. Do you think they'd take us seriously? We need to have looked for him ourselves. And he's only been gone a couple of hours.'

A sombre stillness fell, broken by Lina.

'So... why we wait? Professor Christine and me go library. Search bottom to top. Professor Pendegrass... he walk over campus. All over. He look. Find Wang. Now...'

'I think I'm teaching...' Pendegrass began.

Lina drew a sharp intake of breath, and her body tensed. At the same time she cast Pendegrass such a withering look that he shrank back in his chair.

'No... perhaps not,' he mumbled. 'Free all day. To find Wang.'

34

The journey back to Cramcaster passed in silence. At first, Wang tried to make conversation. After all, Mr Wu had said they needed to talk and here they were, just the two of them in the minibus. What better opportunity? But Wang's attempts to draw Mr Wu out met with a scowl. His hand rose from the steering wheel, causing the bus to jerk violently. The gesture was as if swatting a fly.

'Time for talk later,' was all he would say.

Wang's hopes rose slightly as they approached the university, and the spot where the minibus would pick him up or set him down: perhaps Mr Wu had taken pity on him, rescued him from the farm, and would deposit him so he could return to Martin Luther King, perhaps spend some time with his books. Or with Lina. But the bus stuck resolutely to the outside lane, with no chance of stopping, and swept past the university, heading towards the centre of Cramcaster. Was it Wang's imagination, or did he catch a glimpse of Lina and a few of the others coming out of one of the buildings? It was entirely possible: this was around the time they would be leaving Professor Jordy's class on... whatever. Wang couldn't quite remember. He sighed. He had to get back to his studies as soon as possible or he would be left hopelessly behind.

Progress in the city centre was slow. Several times the bus stopped at traffic lights or pedestrian crossings. Wang thought perhaps he should make a dash for the door and leap to freedom: the atmosphere in the bus, particularly since they passed the university, was increasingly tense, indeed hostile, and Wang was suddenly filled with fear. Every time however he was about to rise from his seat, the bus lurched forward and the opportunity was lost. Besides, he reasoned, what would be the point? The door was almost certainly locked and, even if he managed to escape, Mr Wu would come after him, find him, and then who knew what might happen. No. Better to face what was coming, bring it into the open, sort it out. After all, he could tell Mr Wu he would be able to pay off what he owed and would no longer need to work for him. And that would be the end of the whole thing.

Leaving the city centre behind, the bus took the long straight road leading to Compton Park, which Wang remembered from his first day in Britain. Drawing up outside the familiar house, with all its security, Mr Wu pressed something on the dashboard and the heavy gates swung open. The bus crunched its way to the back of the house, where it stopped.

'Out,' ordered Mr Wu.

Wang was only too willing to oblige, to stretch his cramped limbs, to replace the stale air in his lungs from the minibus with something fresher outside. But there was little chance to stand around taking deep breaths. Mr Wu prodded him in the small of his back towards a door which seemed to open as if by itself. Once inside, Wang was surprised to see the man with the scar on his throat push the door shut behind him, and securely bolt it.

'All set?' Mr Wu asked him.

'Yes, boss,' the man said. 'And I've contacted...'

'Good. When?'

'Tomorrow afternoon. The flight gets in just after two.'

Mr Wu grunted his approval. The two men turned to Wang and looked at him with a mix of disgust and pity.

'You've got twenty-four hours to do some thinking. Then we're going to want some answers,' Mr Wu said.

'But what...?' Wang began.

'Take him away,' Mr Wu motioned to the man with

the scar. 'Make sure he's nice and comfortable.'

**

The cellar was damp and dingy and in stark contrast to the bedroom Wang had been given soon after he had arrived in the house. Wang's mind was pulsing as he cast his eyes over what he could only describe as a cell. A mattress with a blanket lay along one wall, a table and a chair, occupied one of the corners, while a greasy, grey light filtered through a narrow, oblong window, covered with a mesh grating, set at roof height above what had been a chute. Possibly for coal, Wang thought. He could also make out a hook, or something similar, set into the ceiling in front of the window – perhaps for a pulley to lower goods into the basement. The cellar was sealed, however, by a stout wooden door which, when he leaned on it, tugged at it, failed to budge. It was locked, and possibly bolted on the other side. He sank onto the mattress, which smelled of urine, and buried his face in his hands.

He wished he had listened to Lina. She was right: he had asked too many questions. He had raised the suspicion of persons who would stop at nothing, especially – a thought struck him – since he knew too much. What would they do to him? He had heard all sorts of tales, delivered in hushed and furtive tones, about strange disappearances, violent and sudden deaths. There was mention of mysterious boat trips, fishing expeditions, along the coast, from which people failed to return. Once a body had been found in a drainage ditch, badly mutilated. Its teeth had been pulled and fingers were missing which, it was rumoured, had been parcelled up and sent back to China. Fell into machinery: very tragic, must take more care. That was what Mr Wu had said. It was even

229

whispered that on a neighbouring farm someone who complained was forced to drink petrol, and then set alight. Wang had only half-believed these stories – they were too fanciful, too fantastic – but now, on this filthy mattress, in a dank, airless pit, they assumed a terrible and final reality.

Was this what was in store for him? Fed to fishes? Found face-down in a stinking ditch? Burned alive...? Then, battered and broken, flung forgotten into an unmarked grave, unmourned, unloved? Was this, in the end, what it would all come down to?

A sudden spasm – pain, anguish – wracked his body and jerked him upright. For a moment he sat rigid, petrified. Then he began to tremble, at first gently, soon violently, uncontrollably. He felt very cold. In an attempt to warm himself he pulled the reeking blanket around him and curled up, like a dog, on the equally reeking mattress. And fell into fearful, fitful slumber.

35

The search for Wang had drawn a blank. Pendegrass, after much dithering and several wrong numbers, had managed to reach the correct extension to get someone to come and open Wang's room. Lina led them to Martin Luther King where they waited for a janitor who, scowling, let them in.

'I'm nights,' he told them. 'Should have knocked off hours ago. Short-staffed… that's what it is.'

'You very helping man, Mr Nights,' Lina said, as he pushed open the door. 'Thank you.'

The room smelled of socks and sweat, and Lina was faintly ashamed. Of Wang there was no sign – no note, no evidence the bed had been slept in, nothing.

'That's sorted, then,' the janitor said, shooing them out. 'Can I get off to bed now?'

Outside, on the corridor, Lina reissued her instructions. Pendegrass was to walk round the campus, while she and Christine investigated buildings. Pendegrass mumbled that his leg was bad and said something about gout, but Lina frowned hard at him, which he felt might be a harbinger of something more sinister. He wondered if the girl was into karate. Or was that Japanese? He set off with bad grace, telling himself that even teaching was preferable to this. After an hour, having circumnavigated the campus, even – he thought – showing initiative by poking around in a shrubbery, only to be called a pervert by a pair of passing students, he decided enough was enough. He slunk into the library, which he fervently hoped Lina and Christine had already searched, and found a quiet corner among the periodicals where he enjoyed an uninterrupted two hour nap before returning to his office.

Meanwhile Lina, increasingly agitated as the day wore on, had dragged Christine into buildings and

231

offices she hardly knew existed. Any door was fair game for Lina. It had to be opened, the space behind it explored, those who dwelt behind it quizzed, interrogated and, when they protested their ignorance of Wang, quizzed and interrogated again to make sure. By late afternoon Christine was in a state of exhaustion, the caffeine and sugar from earlier having long worn off. She almost wished she had joined Lina in a donut – that would have boosted her stamina.

Eventually, as arranged, late in the afternoon, they tramped back to Pendegrass's office. Christine flung herself into a chair, relieved to take the weight off her feet. Lina was buzzing like a fly in a jam jar and seemed even more active, more charged, than before. Christine wondered if the energy that had drained from her had been transferred to Lina. Perhaps the amount of human energy was finite, traded on some invisible cosmic exchange. If so, her stock was at an all-time low, while Lina's was in the ascendant.

'So, now we make more plan. I think...'

Christine held up a weary hand. All day she had gone along with the girl's endeavour to turn the campus upside down in the quest for the missing Wang – accepted it partly out of pity, partly because she had no better idea of her own. Now, however, she was in no mood to fall in with another of Lina's schemes.

'As I said before, what we do is wait. We know Wang might not be back until eight, possibly later. We need to hang on until then. So...'

'Chinatown. We go Chinatown. Ask... in shop, in restaurant...'

'You go to Chinatown if you like,' said Christine, increasingly exasperated. 'But I'm not going with you. I'm going to the College Arms, and...'

Pendegrass tut-tutted and looked as if he were about to say something.

232

'And you'd do much better to stay here... on campus, in halls... to see if Wang turns up. Then, if he does, you give me a ring. Here's my mobile number.'

She took a post-it note from Pendegrass's desk, wrote on it, and handed it to Lina. 'And, while you're waiting, you might try and get some rest,' she added.

'But... if Wang not come...?'

'If Wang doesn't come then, say, around half eight, you ring me, let me know, and Mr Pendegrass rings the police.'

'I don't think I...' began Pendegrass.

'Of course you can. And you must. Firstly, you're his tutor. The university owes a duty of care to its students and you... God help us... are that care. Secondly, you're the one who got him into this mess.'

'That's unfair. And there's no need to bring God into it.'

'There's probably every need. Mind you... if this student is in danger then your God must have been looking the other way.'

'Please, professor Christine... why God...?'

'A good question,' Christine snapped. 'Why God? But we'll leave that for another time. For now... you're going back to your hall, and Mr Pendegrass is coming with me to the College Arms.'

'What...?'

'You heard. You can't stay here...'

'But... '

'They lock this building at six and turn the heat off long before that.'

'I can't go to a public house. It's... it's...'

'You're coming with me. I need to make sure you're around to phone the police.'

'A place of sin. Licence. Drunkenness and depravity...'

'Rubbish. Anyway... when were you last in a pub?'

233

Pendegrass stared in horror at Christine. He'd never noticed before but, surely, those were horns... or was it her hair? Or a trick of the light?

'I'll have you know,' he said, nervously, never having met a demon, a she-devil, in the flesh before, 'that as a respected member, an elder, of the Nazareth and Ewesbottom Repentant Sinners, I have never entered a public house in my life. Nor do I have any intention of doing so...'

'Fine,' said Christine. 'So you're talking through your backside. I thought you people were all about knowing your enemies. Here's your chance to find out.'

'Not knowing your enemies... loving them. But as I said... I have no intention...'

'Professor Pendegrass do what Professor Christine say. Not talk through backside. And go place of sin. For sake of Wang. Or else...'

Pendegrass swallowed hard. A she-devil on the one hand, possibly a karate expert on the other, left him little choice. Besides, there was a distinct chill in the room. The she-devil was right. The heating had turned itself off, unless – Pendegrass shuddered – she had exercised her evil to turn it off herself. He raised his eyes heavenward, and offered a silent prayer. His God would surely protect him during the trial about to begin. Perhaps, after all, this was a chance to prove he was truly a worthy sinner. And an even more worthy penitent.

'Okay,' he said. 'You win.'

36

Wang was woken by the minibus returning from the country. Presumably Mr Wu had gone back for the others after returning him to Cramcaster. Or perhaps it was a different bus. Wang didn't care. But through the grated aperture above his head he was briefly aware of lights, muffled voices, a banging door, and then all fell quiet. A little later the man with the scar brought a cup of water and a bowl of lukewarm rice, and put them on the table.

'Here you are,' he said. 'To help you think.'

Wang was ravenous. He'd had nothing since the morning, and his stomach felt as if it were populated by spiders. He dug his fingers into the rice and stuffed it into his mouth, barely chewing, washing it down with a deep draught of water. He was about to repeat the procedure, when a terrible thought struck him. The rice, the water, were surely poisoned. It was a trick, a ruse: his captors expected him to eat it and roll over and die. He'd seen that in films. They would drag his body from the cellar, wrap it in chains, and drop it from a bridge into the river. He wondered how deep the Cram was as it wound its way through the campus. Probably not deep enough.

All the same, he could take no chances. He rammed two fingers into his throat and wiggled them round. Wasn't this how you were supposed to make yourself sick? But nothing was happening, except he was starting to choke on his own saliva, and his mouth had a funny taste. Of course... if he'd eaten poisoned rice his fingers would be contaminated. Far from getting rid of the poison, he was adding more. He withdrew his fingers at once. He listened: his stomach was rumbling, which must surely be the killer inside him going about its murderous business. But wasn't his stomach trying to tell him something before he ate the rice... making the same sounds, the same gurgling? Perhaps... but he could take no chances. The rice, the water, must remain where they were. He pushed the containers from him.

Meanwhile, if he were to die a lingering death, shouldn't he use his remaining time to scribble a message implicating his captors? Again, as in the films, where the dying victim starts to daub the killer's name by using his own blood? Then the police could get on the trail of the man with the scar, arrest him, bring him to justice. Except that here there was no blood. Wang raised a hand to his mouth; no, nothing dripping from his lips, which always seemed to happen in a cinema murder. So if he couldn't use his own blood, he would have to scrawl a message onto the wall. He dropped to his knees and groped on the floor of the cellar. There must be a nail or a bit of old brick he could use to carve his last will and testament, his accusation that would send his killer to the noose, if that's what the police used in England. But there was nothing. Anyway, what would he write? All he wanted to say, and the world to know, was: Lina – I love you.

Wang lifted himself from the floor and sat at the table. He wondered what Lina was doing. Whether she'd missed him. Whether she'd been waiting for him, to boil water for their tea, tell him what they'd done in class, give him notes from the day's lectures. Suddenly the university, the course, the essays, all seemed easy. And irrelevant. And a long way away... a make-believe world where there were no men with scars, no damp and freezing cellars, no poisoned rice. Would Lina miss him when he'd gone... when he was at the bottom of the river, or encased in concrete on a building site? He'd seen that in a film, too. He tried to imagine what it would be like, tied and trussed, a rag in the mouth, cast into a trench, concrete tipped on top. Would you choke or suffocate? How long would you last? Seconds, minutes? And, years later, when the building collapsed or was demolished, and the foundations dug up, would they recognise you? Would someone chip you out and say: 'Ah! This was the student who vanished all those years ago. His name was Wang Ti'? And would there be a proper funeral... with Lina, tearful, bent and wizened, supported by children and grandchildren, saying: 'I knew him. He was my love. Things might have been so different'?

Wang's eyes filled with tears. Above him were footsteps, as someone passed overhead. Dust, dislodged from creaking joists, fell about him, into his hair, causing him to itch. Voices, faint. Impossible to make out what they were saying. He fell into a light sleep at the table, his head on his arms, which was broken only by the man with the scar, who came to take away the bowl and cup.

'Still here, I see,' the man said.

So it was true. They were trying to poison him. By rights he should already be dead. He shrank back into the corner of his cell and wrapped the blanket round him. He must remain vigilant. He could not afford to sleep. Who could tell what they might do?

More lights. Outside. An engine starting up. It was the minibus about to depart. Despite his resolve, he'd been asleep. How long? But it was morning, though not yet dawn. He'd survived the night, fought off the poison. That, in itself, was something. It gave him hope. Surely, if they had wanted to kill him, they would have done it by now.

A faint grey day appeared at the window. The man with the scar brought more water and rice. Wang was tempted to drink – his throat felt like gravel – but he resisted. Perhaps this was the real poison; having lulled him the first time into a false sense of security, this

237

food would knock him out. Oh, no... he would outwit them. To banish the cramp from his limbs, and to try and keep warm, he began pacing up and down. How long would they hold him? How long could he survive? Perhaps this was their plan. Give him food they knew he wouldn't eat. Then he would waste away. Die of natural causes. And, if his body were found, there would be no trace of poison. Oh, they were cunning, these people.

The light filtering through the mesh grating was beginning to strengthen, when the man with the scar thrust open the door.

'It's time,' he said. 'They're ready for you.'

**

Wang, blinking, his eyes adjusting to the light, was thrust into a small room which looked as if it might serve as an office. There was a desk, with a computer and a phone, some papers, a battered filing cabinet in a corner beneath a window, barred on the inside. Around the walls, apart from a door, presumably to an adjacent room, were shelves – mostly empty, except for a ring-binder and a couple of shoe boxes. The man with the scar, who had led Wang from the cellar, pushed him onto a chair in front of the desk.

'Sit,' he said, unnecessarily, for the grip on Wang's shoulder as he forced him down left no doubt what was expected.

The man walked across to the internal door and opened it.

'All ready,' he said.

In marched Mr Wu followed, to Wang's amazement, by Qi, suave, as neatly dressed as ever, who sat himself behind the desk. Wang half-rose in greeting, but the man with the scar, who had resumed station behind

238

him, pushed him back onto the chair.

'Haaar,' said Wang.

Mr Wu, standing behind Qi, began talking. 'As you can see, Mr Qi is here to listen to what you have to say. Mr Qi... an extremely busy man... has flown in specially for this meeting. This shows how seriously he regards the matter...'

Qi held up his hand to silence Mr Wu. For a moment he sat looking at Wang, studying him, a look of concentration on his face. Then he leaned back and spoke.

'I have to say... I am disappointed. Disappointed in you, if these allegations are true, disappointed in me. I regard myself as a good judge of character and, when we met at the airport, I imagined here was a young man I could trust. Keep an eye on... perhaps, at some point, as a future employee. My business interests are such that I always have need for intelligent, honest people, with an unblemished record, to help run my affairs. However, when I learn there has been carelessness...'

'I can explain about the vase,' Wang interrupted. 'It was an accident. I've spoken to Mr Wu, and I'm paying off the damage. In fact...'

'The vase is a trifle. I have no interest in the vase. What concerns me is your questioning. Questioning your fellow workers about matters of no concern to you. Raking over past history, spreading discontent, undermining confidence, and trying to discover things which, in the wrong hands, might endanger my operation. What have you to say?'

Wang stared blankly at Qi and at Mr Wu. His mouth felt hot and dry and he almost wished he'd drunk some water, poisoned or otherwise. He felt his lips move but no sound emerged.

'Let me help you,' Qi said. 'It's quite simple. I want to know who you're working for.'

239

It was as if time stopped. No-one moved, no-one breathed. Everything was suspended, expectant, nervous anticipation. The only sound was the humming of the strip light above their heads.

Wang's mind was racing. If this was all they wanted to know, he was off the hook. It was easy. He was working for himself, his dissertation. Best, perhaps, to leave Professor Pendegrass out of it. He wasn't really working for the professor... more with him.

'Haaar...' he began.

'Tell me,' Qi said, 'what do you think about the coast around here? The seaside?'

Wang was taken aback. That was an odd question. What had the coast... the sea... to do with anything? Unless they were thinking about those fishing trips from which no-one returned.

'Haaar,' he said cautiously. 'Very wet...'

Of course it was wet. It was the sea. It was bound to be wet. Why did he always make a fool of himself in front of Qi? He floundered on.

'I mean... wet and windy. There are great storms... with waves washing over the beach... onto the promenade...'

'So you admit you've been? To the coast?' Qi asked.

'Yes. The place with a tower...'

'Anywhere else? Along the coast? Further up, perhaps?'

'No. Just the place with...'

'And whom did you see when you were there?' Mr Wu put in.

'Haaar. Friends...'

'What sort of friends?'

'Friends from the university...'

'Anyone else? Did you see anyone else?'

'No. Yes. When we were there this man came up to us. He wanted... tried to... take one of the girls...'

'That figures,' Mr Wu said. 'I heard they were getting into women. Look. It all adds up. He's working for the Tigers.'

'Steady,' Qi cautioned. 'Let's not jump to conclusions.'

'It's obvious,' Mr Wu retorted. 'Since that business with the cockle-pickers they've had to branch out. If they can muscle in on us, bring us down, they've a perfect cover.'

Wang looked at his interrogators in despair. 'I know nothing about any tigers… cockle-pickers. Certainly nothing about any women. I don't know what you're talking about. I'm just a student…'

From behind Wang, the man with the scar snorted in derision. Qi cast him a disparaging look.

'If you're not working for the Tigers, who are you working for?'

Wang hesitated. 'I'm working for myself. It's for my dissertation. About… about human resource management.'

'A likely story,' Mr Wu interjected.

'It's true. You can ask Professor Pendegrass. I mean…'

'Who's Professor Pendegrass?' Qi shot at Wang.

'No-one. That is… I mean… someone at the university,' Wang said miserably.

'How much does this professor know?' Qi demanded.

'Nothing. I mean… not much. The dissertation… it isn't written yet.'

'He's lying,' Mr Wu said. 'It's a cover… a good one, but…'

'We need to check this out. The professor, for a start. If Wang has been foolish, rather than perfidious, we might be able to stop things before they get out of hand. If not… well, we know the consequences. And what we have to do.'

Mr Wu looked solemn. A shiver ran down Wang's spine. What did they mean? Have to do...? He wondered if he leaped up, jumped onto the desk, flung himself at the barred window, whether the grille would come away and he could smash through the glass to freedom. As if in answer, he felt a heavy hand on his shoulder.

'Take him away,' Qi was saying. 'We'll resume this conversation when we've made some enquiries.'

**

The man with the scar booted Wang down the stairs to the cellar, where he collapsed in a heap on the stone floor.

'There you are, tiger cub,' he said, pursuing Wang down the stairs, and dragging him to his feet. 'Those tigers wouldn't be roaring so loudly if they could see you now.'

Kicking open the door of the cell, the man dropped Wang like a sack of rice onto the mattress. The student felt his legs give way, and he fell awkwardly. His body hit the mattress, hard, and something jabbed into his thigh. He winced. As the cellar door banged shut, he rolled over, groped in his pocket, and pulled out Uncle Peng's universal bicycle repair tool.

He turned it over in his hand, unfolding from their carapace the spanners and screwdrivers and examining them carefully. Of course... Uncle Peng always said no-one should travel without such a tool. You never know, the old man had said, when it might come in handy. Time, Wang felt, to put the theory to the test.

37

The College Arms was sparsely populated. This, Christine reasoned, was for the best: a noisy, lively pub would only confirm Pendegrass's belief that here was a den of debauchery and damnation and make him less likely, despite his promise, to stay.

Nevertheless Pendegrass hovered in the doorway, wrinkling his nose, and had to be led like a small and wondering child into this cavern of magic and mystery. Christine introduced him at once to Ed, and told him this was Pendegrass's first visit to licensed premises.

'Good heavens,' said Ed cheerily. 'This calls for a drink.'

Pendegrass took a step back and said he was a member of the Nazareth and Ewesbottom Repentant Sinners, and would partake of no strong waters.

'Really?' Ed said, pausing in taking down a bottle of single malt. 'Most interesting. Would that be the reformed Nazareth and Ewesbottom Repentant Sinners, who broke away in the 1880s, or the...?'

'You've heard of us?' Pendegrass gasped in disbelief.

'I've come across a few references... local history books, mainly. Quite fascinating.'

Christine found herself wondering once again how Ed knew so much. Were there no limits to this man's knowledge? Nothing seemed to stump him: he was a walking Google. That's it... somehow his brain must be wired to the internet. Or else he was the internet: a giant database receiving and storing all the information that ever was or will be. She wondered if the CIA knew about him.

By now Pendegrass and Ed were conversing like old friends on the history of the repentant sinners. At moments it seemed Ed was better informed than

243

Pendegrass, whose understanding of the breakaway reformists appeared to have several gaps. As they were talking, Ed served Pendegrass an orange juice and poured a liberal measure of whisky for Christine.

'What's that?' Pendegrass enquired.

'Whisky,' Ed replied. 'Purity itself.'

Pendegrass looked doubtful.

'Here. Have a sniff. Just put your nose into the tumbler and breathe in. Deeply. And think of mountains and lochs. Or anything you like.'

Christine shot Pendegrass an encouraging smile. Or was there something dark and demonic behind that look, something leading him on the road to ruination?

'Go on,' Ed said. 'It won't bite.'

The whisky might not bite but that woman, that she-devil, certainly would if he refused. Reluctantly, Pendegrass leaned over the glass and inhaled.

Something warm, slightly woody, singed his nostrils. At the same time his lungs filled with the aroma of peat, of heather, of open rolling moorland, expelling the stale city air that usually dwelt there. His breathing was free and easy. It reminded him of oxygen he'd once been given in hospital as a child.

'Well,' he said, drawing himself upright, and feeling relaxed and cleansed. 'Well...'

A blast of cold air struck them as the door to the College Arms briefly opened. Pendegrass was grateful; it was sobering, it returned him to normality, and he pushed the glass away. The trial had begun, and he had shown he could vanquish temptation. Congratulating himself, he was unaware of Chattermole who swept past, leering at Christine, and demanding in rich and rounded theatrical tones a pint of Old Stinkle. This, when drawn, he carried to a corner table where, with histrionic flourish, he spread before him The Stage and began his usual perusal of the situations vacant.

Christine turned back to Ed.

'Mr Pendegrass and I think one of his students has gone missing. We've tried to find him and now we're making sure he doesn't turn up, before ringing the police.'

Ed asked how long the student had been gone. She told him. She said they were worried because he had fallen in with the wrong people. He had been trying to make some money, she added, having arrived in England with a stack of ancient banknotes with which he tried to pay his fees.

Ed pricked up his ears. 'What sort of banknotes?'

'Don't know. I never saw them. But you did, didn't you?' she said, touching Pendegrass lightly on the arm, causing him to jump and spill his orange juice. Ed produced a cloth and wiped the bar.

'Want another?' he asked.

The she-devil had touched him. She had put the flux on him: he knew it at once. He heard a voice, his voice, coming as if from a great distance, saying if it wasn't too much trouble he'd like to try a whisky. Just a small one, of course. A very small one.

The she-devil feigned amazement. 'Are you sure?' she said.

Pendegrass heard himself say he was perfectly sure. He said he'd led a sheltered life and it was now time to branch out. It was important to love one's enemy... which, since all things flowed from the bounty of the Lord, including whisky, probably wasn't an enemy at all.

He saw Ed and the she-devil exchange glances. He tried to tell them this was all wrong, that it wasn't him speaking, but nothing came out. He heard the she-devil tell Ed to give him just a small whisky, with lots of water, and ice, and to remind him not to down it in one.

A glass was placed before him. Pendegrass gazed at

245

it with a mix of lust and loathing. He could resist, he was stronger than they realised, he would not drink; but the glass was already in his hand, its fragrance inhaled, the first drops tingling on his tongue. He was tasting paradise.

'The Lord...' he spluttered, 'yeah, verily, the Lord is bounteous indeed.'

Christine was about to say the Lord had nothing to do with it when Ed chipped in, wanting to know more about the money. What sort of notes? What denominations? How old?

Pendegrass, savouring the whisky, was vague. He remembered some of the notes were large and white, but couldn't recall more. He said he'd taken them over to accounts with the student, and left them there. 'Not the student,' he cackled. 'Just the notes.' Though if he could have left the student there he would have. But didn't. He cackled again.

Christine frowned. She'd not seen him like this. It must be the drink. Ed, unconcerned, not knowing Pendegrass, was asking if he could recall who in accounts he'd given the money to. Male or female, young or old...? Pendegrass shook his head. No, he didn't know... but perhaps another drink might jog his memory? This time more whisky, less water. Please.

Wait. He hadn't said that. Those weren't his words. It was... it was that she-devil, who was giving him a most peculiar look. She was the one...

The deft hand of the publican had poured another glass before Christine could protest. Pendegrass gulped it down.

'If this is my enemy,' he cackled, 'I'm loving it.'

**

By the time eight-thirty came Pendegrass was in no

246

condition to ring the police. Christine was furious: furious with Pendegrass, furious with herself for bringing him to the College Arms, furious with Ed for plying him with drink.

Ed told her he had his reasons. 'I needed him to talk. I needed to find out about that money. See... I think I know.'

'Know what?'

'That would be telling. I need to ask a few questions.'

This riled her even more. Why wouldn't he trust her? Take her into his confidence? They seemed to be getting on well, making progress... but this was typical Ed. He was his own man... not hers. It was hopeless, ridiculous, to think she could ever become a part of his life.

Now, to cap it all, she had to deal not only with a distraught Lina, who had rung to say there was no sign of Wang, but also with the police, to say nothing of the gently snoring Pendegrass. She wished she could be rid of him, pack him off home, but there was no way he could drive. A taxi...? She'd no idea where he lived. Most likely he didn't, either. Not in this state. She was probably going to be lumbered with him for some time yet.

She told Ed to ring the police. He did so immediately, having the number to hand, and, thought Christine with some satisfaction, perhaps out of guilt at his complicity in Pendegrass's condition. She instructed Ed to ask the police to send someone to Martin Luther King, where they would be given details and a description of the missing student.

Then, she tried to rouse Pendegrass. It was, she imagined, like waking an elephant. It snorted, it grunted, it eventually shambled to its feet.

'Love your enemiesh,' it exhorted the startled

drinkers in the College Arms, as Christine steered it towards the door. 'Love your enemiesh... and make mine a double.'

38

'I've been thinking...'

'Makes a change. Want to finish this lot?'

'Yeah. Don't mind if I do.'

The remains of a portion of chips, laced lavishly with salt and vinegar, passed from driver to passenger. A plump hand gratefully received them and greasy fingers, having disposed of their own portion and dropped the wrapping into the well of the car, pincered a pair of congealing chips and offered them to a waiting mouth.

'Steaming up,' Dutton said. 'I'll put the window down.'

'Not the window,' Gruff said through a mouthful of chip. 'Get the blower on.'

'We need outside air. It stinks in here.'

'If there's a stink, it must be you.'

'There'll be a stink if we return the car like this. Hurry up and finish those chips, and then we can find a bin.'

It had been a quiet, unremarkable evening. The shift was almost at an end and Gruff was grateful for the chance to enjoy a chip supper before returning to the canteen to see if they had any meat and potato pies left over. Policing was a funny old business, he told himself: sometimes out on the job for hours on end, no chance of eating, so it was vital to line the stomach at every opportunity.

The call came as Gruff was swallowing his last chip and wiping his hands on his trousers.

'You take it,' he told Dutton.

The message was clear. A missing student. Proceed at once to Martin Luther King, Cram Vale University, to speak to a Christopher Reeve, who would assist with enquiries.

'Thought he was Superman,' Dutton said, after the call finished. 'You'd think he'd be able to find his own missing student.'

'I wonder if that university place has got a caff... and if it'll be open,' Gruff said. 'I'm still feeling peckish.'

Dutton started the car. 'Wild goose chase, if you ask me. These students are always going missing. Drunk as a skunk, face down in a gutter, if you ask me.'

But Gruff wasn't asking. He was thinking about his next meal.

**

The grating over the window was neither as solid nor as secure as it looked. Standing on the table, which he had dragged across the cell to the wall by the former coal chute, Wang discovered he could just about reach the wire mesh. This had been crudely fixed – partly nailed, partly screwed – but by using the bicycle spanners to lever away the bottom he found he could force the nails out of the wall and then bend the grating upwards. The mesh, though dense, was also old, and rusty in places, and yielded with relative ease. Only the screws caused a problem. They were firmer but, again by leverage, Wang was able to force the wire away from the screws. On one such particularly obstinate fixing a spanner broke, snapping it in two, and a fragment of rogue metal flew past his ear, grazing it and drawing blood.

'Chinese workmanship,' he muttered, feeling his ear sting. 'Not as good as it was in the old days.'

Fortunately Uncle Peng's universal repair tool offered several spanners, of various sizes, so the loss of one was not unduly worrying. Nevertheless, Wang worked more slowly, applying less brute force, more gentle pressure, to prise the rest of the lower part of the

250

grating from the wall. As the day wore on, and the light began to fail, he felt himself beginning to tire and he needed to pause more frequently: reaching up, stretching to free the mesh, was causing his arms to ache. Of late he had felt strength in his arms, in his muscles, through manhandling bags of potatoes, but this was effort of a different kind, and the joints in his elbows and wrists were starting to hurt. But there was no time to rest. He needed to free the fixings along the bottom, perhaps a few up the sides, to fold the mesh back so he could... what? Scrabble up the chute to reach the window, get it open, and make a bid for freedom. Supposing the window wouldn't open? He'd worry about that when he got there. And if the man with the scar came in, found him standing on the table, he'd charge at him, stab him with one of the prongs on the universal repair tool, then try and dash up the cellar steps and out of the house. It was all pretty fanciful... but there was no other choice.

**

Christine and Pendegrass were waiting on the steps of Martin Luther King when Gruff and Dutton eventually arrived. Christine thought the night air might do Pendegrass good, but it only seemed to make him worse. They had seen the police car arrive, whereupon it disappeared behind a building, and it seemed to Christine an inordinately long time before the two officers made their way to them.

'You took your time,' Christine said.

'Needed the toilet,' Gruff lied, having discovered the university refectory bolted and barred and having made his way round the back to see if there was anyone still on duty who could find him a packet of crisps.

Dutton, sensing his colleague to be temporarily

251

wrong-footed, took charge.

'Okay,' he said, looking at Pendegrass, 'you'll be Mr Reeve. We've had a report...'

'Exshcushe me, offisher,' Pendegrass slurred, 'but you've got the wrong pershon.'

'Story of my life,' said Dutton. 'That's why I'll never make sergeant.'

'I think I'm the person you need to talk to,' Christine said. 'I'm the one who called you in... Christine Reeve. And it's Ms.'

Dutton frowned. He could smell alcohol on the woman's breath. Not even a chill, damp night could disguise that. And the man's speech had been slurred. There was something fishy going on. They were told to meet a Christopher Reeve, and now a woman was claiming to be him. It was as if Lois Lane had assumed Superman's mantle. It wasn't right. He wondered if Gruff had noticed.

'In that case, sir,' Dutton said, turning to Pendegrass, 'who might you be?'

'I'm the boysh... shtudentsh... mishing shtudentsh... pershonal tutor. Pendegrash by name.'

'Had a bit to drink, have we, sir?' Gruff chimed in. 'Good evening, was it?'

'Exshellent. Besht of my life. Paradishe.'

Gruff and Dutton exchanged glances.

'Might I remind you,' Gruff said, visions of canteen meat and potato pie rising before him, 'that wasting police time is a serious matter. I'm prepared to overlook it just this once, but if...'

'Just a minute,' Christine said. 'We've got a missing student, whose life could be in danger...'

'You can't shay we've got him... at the shame time he'sh mishing. Doeshn't add up. Either we've got him... or we haven't. What would Lynne Trush... the shainted Lynne Trush... shay about that?'

252

'Now look here, matey...' Gruff began. 'I haven't the faintest idea...'

'Matey... did you call me matey?' Pendegrass lurched unsteadily towards the policeman. 'No-one callsh me matey. No-one. Not even my matesh. Sho...'

As Pendegrass thrust his face into that of the policeman, who recoiled, Christine moved to restrain her colleague.

'Get a grip,' she said. 'You're not helping.'

Pendegrass went rigid. It was the she-devil: again, she had reached out to him. His words, from a distance, tumbled from his lips.

'Pleash... I confesh. No matesh. I have no matesh. No matesh at the univershity. No matesh at the chapel. No matesh... exshept the lovely Lynne. Lynne... Lynne'sh my mate... shoulmate... shoulder to cry on...'

'I don't think your friend's very well,' Dutton said. 'Perhaps we ought to get him inside...'

'Get him down to the station. Charge him. Drunk and disorderly... assaulting a police officer... we'll do him for resisting arrest...'

Christine looked imploringly at Dutton. 'You're right. He's not well. We need to get him inside. Besides... there's someone you need to speak to. Waiting for us. Who can help.'

'Help with what?' Dutton said, having forgotten why they were there.

'Some missing student or other,' Gruff growled. 'No wonder you'll never make sergeant. Come on... if we're not taking this lunatic in, then let's get the rest of it over with.'

253

39

Another broken spanner later, and Wang had succeeded in freeing enough of the mesh to be able to peel it back to expose sufficient window to climb through. At least, in theory. It was all very well standing on the table and reaching up to free the bottom of the mesh; it was another to scramble up the chute to bring his body, or at least his head and shoulders, level with the window so he could worm his way out. Then, of course, there was the small question of the window itself. Either it had to be opened – Wang doubted it would, as he could see no catch – or the glass had to be smashed. That would make a noise... and he would lacerate himself on the jagged pieces as he made his escape.

He wondered what Lina would do if she were in this situation. She would surely have an answer, would have planned her escape to the last detail. But how? He tried to put himself into Lina's mind, tap into her way of thinking. But all he could produce was an image of Lina at her desk in her room, her silky, shiny hair flowing soft and smooth, like the dark waters of the stream above his uncle's village, and falling onto the words before her, to be tossed away with a flick of the head. An image of Lina, flinging down her pen in exasperation at his misdemeanours, however slight; Lina, rocking back on her chair, looking at him through those spectacles...

That was it, the chair. That was the answer. Why hadn't he thought of it before? If he stood the chair on the table, that would give him the height... and there was the hook, the pulley support, in front of the window. If he could... but the chair was rickety, unstable: it creaked alarmingly when he sat on it. It couldn't possibly bear his weight if he stood it on the table and then climbed on to it. The whole edifice would come clattering down, dashing him to the ground: he'd probably break an arm, or worse, a leg. But all the same… it was worth a try. Indeed, it was the only try.

Wang wondered if he should try to escape now or wait, in case the man with the scar came with more poisoned food. Best to wait. Soon the house would settle down for the night, and then he could put his plan into action.

**

Rarely had the room in Martin Luther King accommodated so many people. Most of it was occupied by Gruff, notebook in hand, sitting fair and square on the bed, which sagged alarmingly, much to Lina's consternation. Next to Gruff, squashed by his side, was Dutton. Christine stood by the door, ready to rush Pendegrass to the bathroom in case his stomach decided to repent of its sins, while the sinner himself straddled a borrowed chair in the middle of the room and, under the she-devil's gaze, sipped at the black coffee Christine had made him in the communal kitchen.

'Shinnersh don't do black coffee,' Pendegrass had objected, when Christine told him to drink it. 'Againsht the rulesh…'

'Get it down you,' Christine ordered, 'or those two goons will have you at the police station before you can say Nazareth and Ramsbottom…'

'Eweshbottom. Nashareth and Eweshbottom…'

'Whatever. I knew bestiality figured in it. Drink up.'

Lina, for her part, was seated at her desk, facing her visitors and giving her instructions to the two policemen.

'You find Wang Ti. He very fine student. Work hard.

255

Wang Ti my friend.'

Gruff wanted to check the spelling. He said he thought Wankty was a peculiar name, and no mother in her right mind would call her son that. Christine gave the policeman a look of disapproval – at least someone else is getting the she-devil treatment, Pendegrass thought – and rapped out the spelling, emphasising the g.

'There you are,' Gruff said, making a laborious note. 'Told you no-one would call anyone Wankty.'

Pendegrass roused himself, and told the policemen he thought a description of the missing student might help.

'Excuse me,' Gruff rounded on him, 'but who's running this enquiry? When we want assistance from the general public, we ask for it. Isn't that so, Den?'

Dutton said he thought the suggestion was actually rather useful, and a description would get things moving.

'As it happens,' Gruff retorted, 'it was next on my list. Description... yes. Perhaps the young lady would oblige.'

Lina looked puzzled. 'Excuse... what mean oblige?'

Gruff took a deep breath and, puffing out his chest, launched into an explanation that to oblige was an obligation placed or imposed upon a person to do something that person might not wish to do, but nevertheless was required or expected to do possibly in accordance with a law, a by-law or other statute as laid down by parliament or similar legislative body...

'Shtop...' Pendegrass lunged into action, shooting coffee onto the floor. 'Too legalishtic. Ten commandmentsh... moral obligationsh... shpiritual obligationsh...'

'Strikes me you've already had enough spiritual obligation for one night...' Gruff began.

'For God's sake,' Christine broke in, and Pendegrass froze: the she-devil was speaking, blaspheming, as might be expected. 'Look,' she addressed Lina, 'just give us a description. Tell us what Wang Ti looks like. Tell us what he was wearing.'

'Professor lady know what Wang Ti look like...'

'It'll be far better coming from you. Just tell the policeman. The one with the notebook.'

Lina looked despairingly at the mountain of blue serge beneath which her bed was bowing and bending in a manner for which it had not been designed. She took a deep breath.

'Wang Ti... Wang Ti wear shirt trouser vest underpants sock training shoe. All clean. I wash. Not training shoe. Training shoe not good in wash machine. But some time in go. Field very dirty.'

Gruff stared at Lina in some disbelief. 'That's very helpful,' he said slowly. 'At least we've established we're not looking for a nudist.'

'He could have taken his clothes off,' Dutton said thoughtfully. 'Then he'd be in the nude.'

'This is getting us nowhere,' Christine said. 'I don't think you're taking this seriously. I'm telling you... we've got a missing student, possibly in great danger. We're dealing here with illegal immigrants... '

'Great danger,' Lina chimed in. 'You take seriously. Or Chinese embassy learn of bad police. Embassy cross. Trade deal for China government bail out bankrupt British government... cancel.'

An uneasy silence fell upon the room. Pendegrass, in whose head all the devils and demons known to man had begun to party in riotous, raucous orgy, felt that if he opened his mouth then some might see fit to escape. At any rate, he might – if only for a moment – put the party on hold.

'Shomewhere... I think shomewhere I might...'

257

'You keep out of it,' Gruff snapped. 'I've said before... this is police work.'

Dutton nodded in agreement, but said the lady was right – they were getting nowhere and perhaps they should hear what the gentleman had to say.

'Some gentleman,' Gruff muttered, shifting his bulk on the bed, which creaked ominously. Then, to Pendegrass, 'Go on. What are you waiting for?'

'I wash merely going to remark... before I wash interrupted... that perhapsh shomewhere I have a picture... a photograph...'

'Right,' Gruff said. 'I was about to enquire if we had any pictures. So...?'

'Ah... there'sh the rub. In shtudent recordsh. Filesh. In my offish. And the offish... sho the she-devil... I mean thish lady... reliably informsh me... the whole building... ish locked.'

'Absolutely,' Christine confirmed. 'Can't do any work here at all after 6pm.'

Gruff was about to say he didn't think much work went on in universities anyway, but thought better of it. He needed to keep this woman, who thought they were not taking things seriously, on side. Any whiff of complaint, of negligence, and he'd never make CID.

'No matter,' he said, hauling himself off the bed, which emitted a grateful groan. 'I'm sure we can get someone to come along and open up. Then we can find the picture, get it circulated, and hey presto.'

Lina, relieved of worry about her bed, let out a gasp.

'Picture... I have picture. Picture of Wang Ti. Wait...'

Excitedly, she turned to her computer, click-clicking the mouse.

'Wait... friend take picture... picture of Wang Ti with all other friend. We visit big town... there, see...'

The two policemen, with Christine and Pendegrass

258

behind them, crowded round the computer. A grainy, slightly blurred image of a huddle of people, one of them with Blackpool Tower growing from his head, greeted their eyes.

'Who's this missing one? I mean... which one are we looking for?' Dutton wanted to know.

'This...' Lina said, stabbing at the screen. 'This... Wang Ti.'

They peered at the picture. Suddenly, Gruff bent down to get a closer look.

'Hold on,' he said, squinting at the image, and rubbing an eye with a fat finger. 'That's... I mean... it can't be. Den... quick... who's that remind you of?'

PC Denzil Dutton stared at the screen. 'Dunno,' he said. 'They all look alike.'

'I'll tell you who that is. That's him... that footballer... you remember... that Queer fellow...'

'Don't know who you're talking about.'

'Yes, you do. A month or two back. Had his car nicked... Compton Park.'

Dutton pricked up his ears at the mention of 'car'. 'Yeah...' he said. 'Now you mention it... I think I do. Picked him up outside that Indian...'

'That's the one. Been trying to trace him ever since.'

'What do you mean... trying to trace him?' Christine asked. 'Is this student... has this student been in some sort of trouble?'

'Madam,' said Gruff. 'This is no student. Whatever name he goes under here, I can tell you he's Queer. A footballer – though not, I have reason to believe, with any of our major local teams – who claimed to have a car stolen...'

'That can't be right,' Christine said. 'This is a student who, for whatever reason, is involved with people exploiting illegal immigrants. And I'm certain

259

he doesn't have a car. Lina can tell us. Lina... does Wang have a car?'

'Wang... no car. Wang go with bus to work...'

'There...' Christine said. 'No car.'

'He's bound not to have a car,' Dutton said. 'It's been nicked. Unless he got another on the insurance... or his club coughed up. But that's why he'll be going to his training sessions and whatnot on the bus.'

'Training sessions...what training sessions?'

Gruff snorted. 'Train...it's what players do. But of course... we can't expect a woman to know about football.'

Regretting immediately what he had just said – this female needed to be kept sweet – he moved swiftly on.

'Anyway... we know precisely where he lives. We can pick him up at once.'

'He lives here,' Christine objected. 'You've got it all wrong... the wrong person. This is a student we're talking about... not... not some footballer with a stolen car. Mr Pendegrass will tell you...'

Pendegrass, battling in his head with legions of darkness and depravity dismantling all he held dear, would agree with anything. 'Absholutely... mashtersh shtudent... firsht clash...'

Gruff waved a plump hand. 'Leave it to us, madam. Leave it to the professionals. I can assure you we are on top of this, and have been since this investigation began. We'll have this person in a trice... then we can find out why, when he's not on the field, he's playing the field... if you'll pardon a pun... pretending to be a student. Very dodgy, if you ask me. With all these young ladies about.'

'I'm not sure we're quite on the right track...' Dutton began.

'And if he's running some illegal organisation... exploiting immigrants... then we'll nick him for that as

260

well.'

'You're making a huge mistake…' Christine started, but Gruff had already bundled Dutton from the room.

'Huge mistake,' Lina echoed, bursting into tears. 'Wang not queer… please?'

40

Wang was glad he postponed his escape for, soon after he had hatched his plan, the man with the scar returned with a bowl of rice and a glass of water.

'Don't know why I bother,' he leered at Wang. 'You never eat anything. Anyone would think we're trying to poison you.'

He gave a thin, hollow laugh.

'Look,' he said, scooping a handful of rice, filling his mouth with it, and swallowing with exaggerated pleasure. 'Very tasty... perfectly alright. You don't know what you're missing... though it could do with flavouring.'

So saying, he cleared his throat and spat into the bowl.

'Enjoy. And sweet dreams, tiger cub.'

As soon as the man had gone, Wang was tempted to tackle the window. He told himself, though, that he should wait. The man might return to take away the uneaten rice, check on him; moreover it would be sensible to delay until the house was quiet. This would be soon: everyone went early to bed, because of the pre-dawn start. Besides, if he went now, there was a chance Mr Wu or another driver would be returning with a busload of workers: arrival times were not consistent, reflecting the finishing times at the farms.

Wang settled himself on the mattress, pulled the blanket around him, and tried to rehearse in his mind the escape. The grating was already loose: all he had to do was stand the chair on the table and, using the height, bend the grille upwards. Then he would swing himself from the hook at the top of the chute to wedge himself parallel to the window. Easy. What could go wrong? Well, for a start... but this didn't bear thinking about. He was not going to slip down the chute. The hook looked sturdy and was not going to come loose; and once outside he was going to make a dash for freedom before anyone came to investigate the breaking glass. But what if they were armed? What if the man with the scar had a gun? He'd just have to run for it... reach the gates, squeeze through, or else up and over the wall. The one at the front, he recalled, was topped with steel or metal bars. He hadn't noticed this round the back. But there might be glass, or some sort of electric fence. How many volts? How much of a shock? Enough to kill? Wang shuddered, and huddled more tightly in his blanket. Perhaps it would be better just to stay, try and brazen it out. But no. These people, not even Mr Qi, were to be trusted. In the present circumstances there was just one person he could trust. That was himself. He knew what he had to do.

He yawned. He must remain alert, vigilant... choose his moment with care. Except, perhaps, a few moments' shut-eye would do no harm. It would help him relax, gather his strength. He yawned again.

How long he had been asleep, he had no idea. Minutes, hours... but this was no matter. Banging, thumping... Above his head the ceiling was creaking, jarring, fit to collapse. Dust, bits of ancient masonry, brick, showered upon him, entered his lungs, and he coughed. Footsteps... running, pounding. Voices. Raised, alarmed. Orders. Commands. Instructions. And one word above the tumult: police.

Wang struggled to his feet, casting aside the blanket, feeling for the repair tool in his pocket. Clearly, it was now or never. In an instant he seized the chair, carried it to the table, placed it beneath the window, clambered up. The tower swayed, swung, pitched, plunged as, astride the seat, Wang grabbed the grating and bent it up to expose the window. The chair wobbled; a woodwormed leg gave way, and the chair began to

263

describe the arc that would dash it, smash it, on the cellar floor. Wang flailed at the hook, caught it and, with superhuman effort, slammed his feet, as planned, against the wall by the chute. Kicking off, still clutching the hook, he swung his back against the other wall. The force of his body against the cold rough brick winded him and, relinquishing the hook, gasping for breath, he heard the chair break on the cellar floor below him.

Wedged between the walls of the chute, he reached into his pocket for the repair tool. Take it, open it, smash it against the glass. But the tool was not there. He felt his other pocket: similarly, it was empty. Panic washed over him. He craned his neck to look down to the table, the floor: that's where it must be, having fallen from his pocket when the chair tipped back and he made his grab for the hook. He peered into the gloom below. Nothing.

Despite the chill, he wiped sweat from his forehead. Should he drop down to retrieve it... this gift to a nephew setting out in a world of which an uncle could only dream? But... if he slid down the chute, to look for the tool, he would never get back. The chair was wrecked: he could not reach the window without it. And there was no time. Besides, surely, the implement had done its work, loosened the grating, helped expose the window... there could be no further need for it. Farewell...

Shutting his eyes, bracing himself against the walls, Wang jabbed an elbow at the glass, which shattered. Something stabbed his arm; from the gash spurted warm, wet blood. But the crisp night air invigorated him. He jabbed again and again at the glass, kicking at the parts his arm could not reach, concentrating on blunting the spikes still toothed in the frame over which he knew he must pass.

Reaching out over the frame, feeling the remaining fragments dig into his palm, he grasped the wood and, edging closer to the now virtually pane-less window, took a deep breath and launched himself, hurled himself, rolled himself, to freedom.

It was impossible to say whether the pain from the shards was greater than from the cold, sharp gravel that received him. For a moment he lay where he landed, unable to move, but the clatter of bolts, keys, and a clamour of voices behind a door told him he was still not safe. Forcing himself to stand – aching, cut and bruised in every limb – he loped around the corner of the house, along the side, to the front where, to his distress, across the gravel and beyond the gate, he saw the flashing blue light of a police car and, silhouetted against its headlights, two figures. The larger of the two was shouting, remonstrating, but Wang could not make out the words. Besides, it seemed pointless. The front of the house was in darkness; the security lighting was not on and, as far as Wang could tell, there was no-one to listen. The presence of police, however, quashed the idea of squeezing through the gates, or climbing the adjacent wall. He would have to think again.

Cautiously, he retreated down the side of the house and peered round the corner to the spot where, a few moments earlier, he had made his bid for freedom. A knot of people was standing, huddled, outside the open back door. They were talking animatedly, but in low tones and, again, all Wang could make out was the word police. Mr Wu did not appear to be among them. Fortunately, although the moon was bright – the sky was clear, with a hint of frost – no-one, it seemed, had noticed the smashed window. The open door cast but a small rectangle of light onto the path where the men were grouped.

Remaining in the shadows, Wang turned and made

his way to the perimeter wall. Following it, feeling every brick with his lacerated hands, watching each step, lest he tread on something that might make a noise, he worked his way round to the outhouse where he knew at least one of the minibuses was garaged. The building was partially screened from the back of the main house by an overgrown shrubbery, for which Wang was grateful. Moving silently in front of the garage doors, Wang passed around the side and discovered the building lay in a corner, sharing two of its walls with the perimeter. From the back of the garage, the wall continued along the rear of the property.

Wang hesitated. If he continued to follow the wall, he would eventually end up at the front of the house. There was no point because of the police car waiting there. It was apparent he needed to get away from the house, its neglected garden and grounds, as soon as possible, before Mr Wu, or the man with the scar, discovered his escape. With a shudder Wang realised they could probably trace him: he had seen enough second-rate films with a sleuth who followed a trail of blood to apprehend a murderer. Looking round in some desperation he noticed, in the corner where the garage met the outside wall, a drainpipe. If he could get up there, onto the roof, then he might be safe.

The pipe, cast iron, was cold to the touch, but it was solid, built in an age when things were designed to last. Wang was no expert on drainpipes, never having had reason to scale one, but grasping the metal firmly with both hands, a natural, simian instinct took over which, before he knew it, propelled him up the pipe and onto the roof. From here it was but a step to find himself on top of the outer wall.

From behind him, from the back of the house, an angry roar. They had discovered the broken window.

266

No doubt they would come looking for him, search the grounds, recapture him. There was only one thing he could do. Gritting his teeth, he leaped from the wall into the unknown on the other side.

Something soft, squidgy and smelly cushioned his fall. As he landed he toppled over, face down. Floundering, attempting to sit, he reached out. His hand met something floppy and flaccid. Taking it between two fingers, he held it up. A cabbage leaf. Suddenly he remembered how hungry he was. He stuffed it into his mouth, spitting it out at once. It was foul: slimy, tasteless, faintly gritty. Of course... a compost heap. Just like his uncle, just like all the villagers had. Extricating himself, brushing himself down, he made out among the leaves and eggshells a mosaic of carrot and potato peelings. He wondered if the potatoes were those he had harvested.

From over the wall more shouting, calling. He heard his name: it was the man with the scar who was calling. If they thought to look over the wall... no. It couldn't be. He began running. Running as best he could, a body sore and suffering, gasping for every breath, leaden in every limb, in a strange and gloomy garden. Before him was a huge house, not unlike the one he had just left, with an opening, a drive, to one side. This, surely, would lead to a road, to safety.

As Wang drew level with the house on the drive, and could see the road beyond, a car swung in, catching him in its headlights. Wang froze. He was blinded, could see nothing, had no idea where to turn. The car screeched to a stop, a door opened, and a woman's voice... 'What's this? What's going on? Who are you?' Footsteps, rapid, urgent... he should get away, move, anything, but there was no response from a body, a will, shrivelled and played out.

A mighty blow to the side of his head knocked him

askew. As he collapsed, deflated, punctured, he heard the woman's voice: 'Always thought these council agendas had another use.'

**

The two policemen were standing at the gates to the Compton Park mansion, getting nowhere, when the radio in the car crackled into life. Dutton took the call and relayed the message to his colleague.

'Attempted break-in over in the next street. We're to go at once.'

'No way,' Gruff said. 'Tell them we're on the verge of apprehending a wanted man... illegal immigrants, and whatnot. Get them to send someone else.'

The response from the control room when Dutton gave them Gruff's reply was short and to the point. Some woman on the council had apprehended a burglar, and said if they didn't get their asses in gear she'd see to it the city council would slash police funding.

'Let me speak to them,' Gruff ordered, marching over to the car. 'Look,' he growled, 'we're about to land a big one. Foreigner... comes into the country claiming to be a footballer... in actual fact a pervert, sex maniac, hanging round the university, the women, and running an illegal immigrant racket. Probably into drugs. Porn. Arms dealing. You name it. A nasty piece of work. And... you what?'

A stream of invective rewarded Gruff's oratory. Control was blunt: even if the prime minister and the entire cabinet were staring down the barrels of AK 47s, wielded by Islamist wackos or other fundamentalist freaks, they were to get over to the councillor that instant. Because of cuts, there was no other car in the whole of the north of Cramcaster that could attend...

268

and if the woman stuck to her guns and trashed the budget, they'd all be out of a job.

'But…' began Gruff, as the radio went dead.

'You heard,' Dutton said, climbing into the driver's seat and turning the ignition. 'Best get over there. Now.'

**

The scene that greeted the policemen when they arrived, just one and a half minutes later, outside Councillor Rosalind Brush's abode, reminded Dutton of something he'd seen in a museum, perhaps on a school trip, or on a postcard.

A warrior, female, stood statuesque over – presumably – its vanquished foe. A stately foot rested on what appeared to be a bundle of bloody and shredded rags from which, nevertheless, protruded head and feet. The only thing lacking, thought Dutton, was a helmet, and perhaps a sword, though the figure appeared to be armed with a gigantic wad of paper and a mobile phone. Evidently, these days, the phone was mightier than the sword.

The statue spoke. 'You took your time. I was about to ring and find where you'd got to.'

'We came as quick as we could,' Gruff lied, adding for good effect, 'Councillor.'

The statue snorted and, prodding one last time with its foot at the broken humanity beneath it, said, 'It's yours. Take it way.'

Dutton approached the mound of clothes and shone his torch over it. 'Looks in a bad way,' he said, wrinkling his nose at the whiff of garden compost. Then… 'Good God. You know who this is. It's him. Queer. I'm sure of it…'

'You're kidding,' Gruff said, bending closer. 'It

269

can't be. I mean...'

'He's not... gay? Is he?' Mrs Brush said, examining with distaste the boot which, a few moments earlier, was resting triumphantly on her victim's chest.

'Stand back, madam,' Gruff ordered. 'This is a wanted man... highly dangerous...'

'You're telling me,' Mrs Brush said. 'Filth like this... homosexuals... all those diseases... wandering our streets...'

'I don't think there's much danger here,' Dutton said, examining the motionless Wang. 'This fellow's all in. In fact, what we need is an ambulance. I mean... look at him. Have you done this?' he asked, turning to Mrs Brush.

'Done what...?'

'He's a mess. You realise he could do you for assault... sue you...'

The papers in Mrs Brush's hand quivered menacingly.

Gruff gave a nervous laugh. 'I don't think that's likely,' he said, breaking off his call for medical assistance. 'Not a course of action we'd recommend... under the circumstances. Is it, Den?'

Dutton muttered something under his breath. Then: 'Poor sod. The only time we ever see him is when he's flat out.'

**

By the time the paramedics arrived, Mrs Brush had retreated into the house.

'I have to change my boots,' she told the policemen. 'They're feeling a bit uncomfortable.'

'We can't let her go in,' Dutton hissed at Gruff. 'She's a suspect. She might be carrying vital evidence... victim's blood. If that gets removed we'd

270

never be able to prove...'

'Drop it,' Gruff hissed back. 'Follow this up and bang go my chances of CID. And my pension. And yours. Why are you always on his side?'

'Come on. He's just a kid. This is no underworld Mr Big. And what that woman at the uni was saying...'

'She was drunk. And you're soft. That's what you are. See... that's the difference between you and me. And I understand the criminal mind...'

The paramedics greeted the two policemen like old friends.

'Hi,' the first one said. 'I'm Vikki. Remember? And I know who this is,' she added, bending over the prostrate Wang. 'Never forget a face. It's Harry... something like that. The footballer.'

'Well,' said Gruff, 'rather a lot's happened since then. He might be a footballer, but...'

Vikki was examining Wang and attempting to revive him. 'Pulse weak. Probably lost a lot of blood. Harry? Harry? Are you with me, Harry? Can you hear me?'

Wang opened a bleary eye. A talking cucumber, possibly a banana, was looking at him. He'd been here before, a long time ago, in a different life... and it wasn't pleasant.

'Haaar,' he breathed, and promptly closed his eye.

'Right,' Vikki said. 'Hospital. This time... like it or not... that's where you're going.'

271

41

There was no-one at the reception desk when Christine and Ed, having mastered the labyrinth that was Cramcaster General Hospital, walked into the Thatcher ward.

'Surely they can't have named it after her,' Christine said. 'I mean... I know she said the health service was safe in her hands, but that would be taking things too far.'

'It ought to be the Marie Celeste ward,' Ed said, casting his eye over the open files and folders, the half-drunk cup of coffee, abandoned on the desk. 'There's no-one here. Perhaps there's a bell we can ring.'

The rattle of a trolley, scraping along a door leading into reception, caused them to turn.

'Damn,' a voice said, belonging to a woman in a hospital uniform, half-hidden behind the trolley. 'Mind of its own, this thing.'

'Excuse me,' Ed stopped her, 'but I wonder if you could tell us where we might find one of your patients... a Mr Wang Ti?'

'And perhaps you could tell us how he's doing? When he's likely to be out?' Christine added.

'Don't ask me, love,' the woman said, shuffling off. 'I just bring them their tea. There's an agency nurse about somewhere... perhaps the next ward.'

'This is a disgrace,' Ed was horrified. 'Anyone could walk in and no-one would be any the wiser.'

'The last place I'd want to be ill,' Christine sniffed. 'Where are all the staff?'

'They hide them. It's like a Victorian poor-house. Make the conditions on the inside worse than those on the outside so only the most needy will use it. We come in, think how dreadful it is, and resolve to stay fit. Either that, or go private. Government health policy in

272

a nutshell.'

'At least this is the right ward,' Christine said, pointing to a board with Wang's name on it and, next to it, a colour. 'He's around here somewhere.'

They went through the doors from which the tea trolley had appeared and found themselves facing a corridor with a fire exit at the opposite end. Rooms, all open, led off from the corridor.

'Come on,' Christine said. 'He can't be far away.'

They found Wang in the room next but one to the end. Lina was with him, as Christine thought she might be. She was perched on the bed, and as the visitors appeared in the doorway her hand, which had been holding Wang's fingers protruding from an enormous bandage, shot back to rest demurely on her lap.

'Haaar…. professor lady Christine,' Wang greeted her.

'How are you?' Christine said. 'I mean… how are you getting on?'

Wang cast a sly glance at Lina. 'Haaar… getting on very good. Very well. How you say… like house in fire.'

It was on the tip of Christine's tongue to correct the preposition, but she thought better of it. Instead, she introduced Ed.

'I've brought someone to see you. He's got something for you. Ed runs the College Arms… the pub opposite the university…'

'Haaar… very great honour.'

'And this, Ed, is Lina… Wang's friend. Lina… Ed.'

'Very pleased. And very kind for professor lady come to hospital to see Wang. Great honour.'

Ed went in search of chairs for Christine and himself. Lina remained on the bed – the first time, Christine thought, as she tried to get comfortable on the low, plastic chair Ed brought, that she had ever looked

273

up at Lina. The high hospital bed, from which Lina's legs dangled, lent the student a physical presence she did not normally have.

Christine turned to Wang. 'So... how are they treating you?'

'Haaar... very nice. Bring tea. Every hour. Not good tea.'

'Not China tea,' Lina volunteered.

'No... well...' Christine said. 'But I'm sure they're not treating you just with tea.'

'I wouldn't be surprised,' Ed growled. 'All these cuts.'

'Haaar... cuts. Many cuts. All over body. Like pin cushion, doctor say. Please... what mean pin cushion?'

Christine attempted to explain, but Wang's eyes were glazing over. Lina said they were keeping Wang in for another day for observation. Partly because of the flesh wounds, mainly superficial, but they had to dig glass out of some of them, and partly because of the blow to the head, but mainly because of – and she stumbled over the word – dehydration.

'They seem to be sorting you out,' Christine said. 'I must say, with all those bandages, you look a bit like the Michelin man.'

'Please... what mean...?' and Christine cursed her thoughtlessness. Fortunately, Ed came to the rescue.

'Here you are,' he said, reaching across the bed and handing Wang an envelope. 'A sort of get-well present.'

Wang took the envelope and, carefully examining his name on the front, turned it over to check the other side.

'For me? Present for me?'

'Go on. Open it,' Ed said.

Cautiously, as if embarrassed that everyone was watching, Wang opened the envelope and took out a cheque. He stared at it for a second, and his eyes

274

flashed wide in surprise.

'Haaar... mistake. Big mistake. Terrible mistake. This not me...'

'I beg to differ,' Ed said, smiling, 'but I rather think it is. Ten thousand five hundred and twenty one pounds owing to you from the sale of extremely rare and valuable banknotes, which were stolen...'

'Banknotes...?'

'The money you brought with you from home, far from being worthless, was a collector's dream. The crook at the university you gave the money to realised they could be worth a bit and starting selling them off to members of the coin club that meets at my pub. I realised large amounts of money were changing hands and, when Christine mentioned your problem with paying the fees, I put two and two together.'

'This my money...?' Wang said, staring incredulously at the people grouped round him. 'All of it?'

'All of it,' Ed said. 'Every last penny.'

'But... no bank account. Cheque no good... no bank...'

Ed laughed. 'We can soon sort that out. Besides... there might be a bit more to come.'

'More...?'

'I understand there might be some sort of payment ... a reward from the public purse, for helping round up a criminal gang.'

'Haaar...'

'You're something of a hero, you know. A celebrity. The reward would be compensation for what you've been through in collecting the evidence Mr Pendegrass passed on to the police. Apparently, there've been some arrests at the farms.'

Christine broke in. 'They went to where you were working. Interviewed farmers, managers – including

275

the Earl of Cramcaster, who owns the estates. Mr Pendegrass is over the moon. For some reason, he doesn't seem to like the Earl.'

'Haaar... but Mr Wu... Qi...?'

'According to Mr Pendegrass,' Christine said, 'the police found your friend Mr Wu in the small hours of the morning by the side of a motorway with a broken-down minibus full of workers. Apparently the police wanted to take them in, but there was no back-up at that time of night and nowhere to take them. All the police stations for miles around were closed. So they took their names, told them to report the next day to the immigration office in Cramcaster, whereupon they all cleared off over a fence and disappeared.'

'No wonder the country's the mess it is,' Ed said.

'But Mr Qi,' Lina wanted to know. 'He boss man... very dangerous.'

'No sign of him,' Christine said. 'At least, not yet. Apparently they're watching the airports.'

'Mr Qi... not bad man,' Wang said slowly. 'Mr Qi help. Mr Qi give room in house... give job. Mr Qi believe when I say not work for Tigers. Mr Qi not steal banknotes like very bad man at university.'

'You needn't worry about him.' Ed said. 'He's got his comeuppance all right.'

'Haven't they all?' Christine said.

'Excuse... what mean comeuppance?' Lina asked.

'It means they've got what was coming to them... what they deserved,' Ed told her.

Lina looked blank.

'Ah,' Ed said, a faint smile playing on his lips. 'Perhaps you haven't heard. Look... it's all here. You can read all about it.'

So saying, he pulled a rolled and crumpled Cramcaster Evening Herald from his pocket and, smoothing it open, laid it on Wang's bed.

'There,' he said.

Wang stared at the headline splashed across the front page. 'VC fiddles as Uni earns,' he read. 'Exclusive by Jason Hackley. Please... what mean...?'

'It doesn't matter,' Ed said, airily. 'Just read. Then you'll know what's being going on while you've been breaking up an international gangmaster organisation and getting locked up and beaten into the bargain. In the meantime... we need to be off. I've a business to run, and a couple of things to sort out.'

He stood up, taking his chair back to where he had found it.

'Come on,' he said to Christine. 'I need your help. Crucial, in fact. Besides... these two need to be by themselves. And they've a newspaper article to read. Practise their English.'

Christine scraped back her chair and stood up. 'I could come again if you like.'

'Wang soon out,' Lina said. 'Wang back with friend in Martin Luther King. Start study...'

'Haaar... professor Christine. I ask... please... you find Uncle Peng universal repair tool. Professor Pendegrass... he know. Tool in house... house of Mr Qi... room under house... dark... please bring. Uncle Peng say have bicycle repair tool all time. Cheque... much money... good. Repair tool... more good than all cheque in world.'

Lina put out her hand to Wang and began tenderly to stroke his fingers, protruding from a swathe of bandage.

'I'll see what I can do,' Christine without conviction. 'Leave it to me.'

As Ed and Christine left the ward, they all but collided with the tea trolley.

'Find that nurse?' the tea-woman asked.

'No,' Christine said. 'But I think our patient's in

277

very good hands.'

**

The photograph illustrating the front page spread, together with its caption, was rather more informative than the headline. The picture, slightly grainy, and presumably shot from a distance, showed an elegant middle-aged woman leaving a casino. The caption read: 'Vice chancellor's vice: six-figure sums are missing as Cram Vale uni boss Barbara Redwell-Nope lives it up on her paradise island, leaving her toy-boy lover in charge.'

'What's that word... vice... mean?' Wang asked Lina.

She giggled. 'Plenty of time to find out,' she said, adding hastily, 'but not here.'

They read on:

'A university boss is believed to have embezzled hundreds of thousands of pounds of public money to lead a life of luxury on the paradise island of Mauritius.

'Police have issued international arrest warrants for Cram Vale University vice chancellor Barbara Redwell-Nope and her toy-boy lover, personal assistant Pat Kerry, who was left in charge of the university, its hundreds of staff and thousands of students.

'The Cramcaster Evening Herald, following a tip-off, can reveal exclusively that:

⌃ Barbara Redwell-Nope ran the university in name only, while living the high life at top hotels and casinos in Mauritius.

⌃ With her toy-boy lover, Pat Kerry, she created a web of lies and deceit to siphon hundreds of thousands from the university budget.

⌃ Her lover appointed staff, sometimes to senior positions, and took executive decisions, such as

278

commissioning a new arts and media centre.

'University governors are now calling for the resignations of key members of staff. It is understood several employees have already left.

'The governors have also asked for senior academics and administrators from neighbouring Cramcaster University to take over at Cram Vale, as a temporary measure to help put the stricken university back on its feet.

'Projects such as the proposed arts and media centre, on the site of the popular College Arms public house, will now be put on hold as the university struggles to restore its finances.

'A spokesperson for the Department of...'

Wang threw down the paper. 'What's all that about?' he said. 'Who is this Barbara Redwell-Nope? I mean... what's it to do with us?'

'Well,' said Lina, 'what's it's saying is...' and she paused. 'You're right. It's nothing to do with us.' She squeezed his fingers in affection.

'Ouch,' said Wang. And grinned.

**

Dozy Pendegrass needed no reminding that it had been a tumultuous couple of days. He was exhausted, drained, and could barely keep his eyes open, but for some reason found it impossible to sleep. It wasn't just the constant pressure from the police – visiting, phoning, demanding further and ever more specific details from the information Wang had supplied him. Going through his own notes was bad enough, but deciphering Wang's hastily scrawled references, written in his own and very distinctive Cambridge proficiency English, and collating them, was a nightmare. Then there was the continuing saga of what was becoming

279

known at the university – with some hyperbole – as the mystery of the missing millions, with its resultant sackings, dismissals, resignations. It was all very Stalinesque. Talk to someone one day and there was no guarantee they'd be there the next. To cap it all was the shameful evening in that cesspit of licence and liberty, the College Arms, when he had walked in – nay, had been led into – the valley of the shadow of the demon drink. And not just the shadow, but the demon itself, in human form, in the shape of that temptress, that siren, that vixen, whose very name – Christine – was a travesty of the Good Lord himself. He should have seen it coming, should have been more alert: had countless Sundays spent in chapel so ill-prepared him? At least now his head was more or less his own. The devils had departed, painfully, under protest, but the experience had weakened, wearied him. His sole consolation was that, verily, he had known sin, had tasted of it, believed it for one debauched night to be noble, enlightening. His credentials as a sinner, his need for repentance, were – so to speak – impeccable.

A knock at the door interrupted his reverie. Without being asked to enter, a tall man, wearing a crumpled suit and an air of harassment, came in.

'Peter Jamieson,' he introduced himself, extending a hand to Pendegrass. 'Your opposite number, I believe, at the other place... Cramcaster University. Sorry to barge in like this... it's really a bit awkward... but I'm here... a sort of troubleshooter, after all that business with... what was his name?... Brush.'

'Ah... Professor Brush. Very sad,' Pendegrass said, more out of form than sincerity. 'How can I...?'

'I won't beat about the bush... the brush, as it were,' Jamieson said, helping himself to a chair and seating himself. 'We need someone to take over the reins of the school... at least on a temporary basis... while things

280

sort themselves out.'

'Ah, well...'

'We're looking for someone who's an original thinker, can take a lead, who's not frightened of banging heads together. You're the ideal person. You appear to have a good record... this business with those illegals proves that... and I understand there's a couple of good publications in the pipeline. So...'

'I think you've got the wrong end of the stick...'

'Nonsense. As it happens, there's no choice. So we're putting you in as head of school with immediate effect. Pro tem, of course... but who knows what it could lead to if you play your cards right?'

'I don't play cards,' Pendegrass said. 'I'm a member of the Nazareth and...'

But the door was already closing behind Dr Jamieson.

42

Wang, freshly released from hospital, but still bearing scars and plasters from his ordeal, was uncertain how to respond to Ed's invitation. The College Arms was hosting a celebration to toast its escape from the wreckers' ball, and Ed wanted Wang and Lina to be there.

'You're a key player in this drama,' Ed told Wang, having come across to the university to deliver his invitation in person. 'That business with your money was another nail in the coffin of an institution rotten from top to bottom.'

Wang's brow creased in a puzzled frown. 'Haaar... you want me go College Arms?'

'That's the idea. With Lina.'

'Haaar... not know English public house. Never go. Never have been gone.'

'What? Not someone else who's never been to a pub...?' said Ed, recalling Pendegrass's visit. 'No wonder the licensed trade's in the state it is. All the more reason you should come... experience a vital part of British culture.'

'British culture... good.'

'Yes... and the beer's even better. You do drink, don't you?'

'Haaar... China beer very fine.'

'I think Old Stinkle will give it a run for its money.'

'Please... what mean Old Stinkle?'

'Come along and you'll find out. I assure you... you'll like it.'

**

The College Arms party was in full swing. The regulars had turned up, as well as those who used the place in

282

the evening. The Old Labourites were in full force; also the Women for Kosovo; the Esperanto-speakers, at a table where, to great wonder, they laughed and joked in a language that many wrongly assumed extinct; and several members of the Coin and Stamp Collectors' Colloquium – though, as Ed noted, rather more philatelists than numismatists. All, of course, enticed by Ed's promise of a pound a pint.

'It's not every day we have something as big as this to celebrate,' he explained, breezily. 'I want everyone to have a night they'll remember.'

Wang was at a table with Lina, Christine and a brooding Pendegrass, who had allowed himself, under sufferance, to return to this pit of perdition partially to support Wang, but mainly to punish himself, to atone for his lapse. He sat clutching a glass of orange juice rather as he might a crucifix, or other totem, to ward off evil. The juice, he told himself, would send a clear message to the she-devil opposite that he could resist her sundry and manifold wiles.

Wang, for his part, was finding common cause with Old Stinkle. He took to telling anyone in earshot that Old Stinkle was very fine, almost as good as beer in China, but not quite, and when he finished his MBA he would set up a company to import the products of Cramcaster Brewery to his homeland. Lina looked concerned, and wondered how long it would be before Wang ended up on the floor.

The only person who put a damper on festivities was Greg Chattermole, the performing arts lecturer.

'It's all very well saving the pub,' he grumbled, 'but all this business has put the kibosh on our arts and media centre. We'll be stuck in our old place for ever.'

Ed, however, cheered him up.

'I'd like to pay special tribute to our good friend Greg,' he said, climbing onto a table to get everyone's attention. 'Without Greg, we wouldn't be here.'

A cheer went up, and cries of 'Good old Greg.'

Ed continued: 'Most of you will know Greg as the person who sits over there reading The Stage...'

'Didn't know he could read,' a voice called.

'Reading The Stage and the job ads... to further his already illustrious acting career...'

Jeers greeted this appraisal of Chattermole's one-off appearance in a long-forgotten soap.

'However... I can tell you that in the drama that has unfolded... that is unfolding... at Cram Vale University, Greg has played a major role... a leading role...'

Wolf-whistles, whoops.

'He might not be aware of it... but his part has been a veritable turning point... what the Greeks called perepitea...'

Catcalls, jeers.

'In this tragedy...'

'Comedy, more like,' someone ventured.

Ribald laughter.

'Hang on,' Chattermole was heard to exclaim, over the hubbub. 'I still don't know what I'm supposed to have done.'

More laughter.

'Well,' Ed waved his arms for silence, 'not exactly done...'

'What then...?'

'Perhaps it was something you said.'

'You see...?' Chattermole struck a histrionic pose, patently pleased with himself. 'The art of the actor... the power of the spoken word...'

'Tosser,' someone said.

'Please...' Wang turned to Christine. 'Tosser... what mean?'

Christine opened her mouth to venture an

284

explanation, but Ed, still on the table, was holding up his arms for quiet.

'While we're still in the formal phase of proceedings, I want you to give a big hand to Jason Hackley...'

Beer glasses, hands, fists, thumped on tables, as Hackley stood up to take a bow.

'Without the unerring investigatory talents of young Jason... without his polished prose...'

'Wait a moment,' Hackley remonstrated. 'If it hadn't been for you...'

'Without the tenacity of this young reporter,' Ed carried on, 'prepared to pursue this matter across continents, oceans, again, we wouldn't be here tonight.'

More table thumping, cheering, calls for another round of drinks.

'You can get to the bar in a moment,' Ed said. 'But before you do... a round of applause for someone, through no fault of his own, who's become an expert on the health service... our guest Wang Ti. Wang, up you get, please.'

Lina pushed him to his feet, as the room around him erupted in clapping, cheering and table-banging. Wang blinked at the faces around him, and began to regret his last pint of Old Stinkle.

'As a token of our esteem... our respect...' Ed continued, 'we have a small gift for you. A memento. Mr Pendegrass, if you please.'

On hearing his name Pendegrass started, and some of the orange juice spilled onto his suit. He stood up and stared around at the clientele in the College Arms.

'Ah', he said. 'I'm not used to... to addressing people in a house of ill... a public house. I'm not sure...'

'Just get on with it,' someone said.

Pendegrass flinched, and looked as if he might bolt.

285

'Er, yes,' he said. 'Quite.' Then, rallying, and at the same time fishing in his pocket, continued: 'I... that is, we... feel this should be returned to its owner... where it belongs...'

'Haaar,' gasped Wang, gazing on the universal repair tool as Pendegrass held it out to him. 'Haaar.'

A huge grin extended over Wang's face as he felt his hand mould itself once more around the familiar metal. Tears of joy, of happiness, began to roll down his cheeks, as cries of 'Speech! Speech!' rang through the pub.

Choking back his emotion, Wang seized Pendegrass's still-outstretched arm and began pumping it for all he was worth.

'You great man,' Wang burbled. 'You bring tool... gift of Uncle Peng to Wang Ti. Without tool... Wang still in house of Mr Qi... in prison. You... you help Wang. You pay Wang university when money no good... which Mr Ed bring Wang in hospital. You good man... Mr Ed, he good man. And professor Christine... very good teacher. Wang learn much English. Now speak fine.'

A cheer went up, but Wang was still talking.

'All people very fine. I thank all. But one people I thank better than all other. That people... Lina... walk with me... always by side... always here...' and Wang gave his chest a mighty thump '...in heart of Wang Ti. So I say... in front of professor... in front of all friend... Lina... Wang Ti... he love you.'

A collective 'Aaaah,' sighed through the pub, followed by sporadic applause, and a shout of 'Give 'er a kiss, then,' with an echoing 'Kisu! Kisu!' from the Esperanto table.

Wang needed no second bidding. The international language of love he understood as well as the next person. He scooped Lina off her chair, who squealed in mock protestation, seized her in his arms, and planted an enormous kiss on her lips. And another. Lina wriggled and writhed without conviction, and the more she squirmed the tighter Wang held her. The audience loved it, drumming on the floor with their feet in an ever-quickening frenzy of appreciation.

Pendegrass stepped forward. 'Please,' he quaked. 'I don't think that's altogether right…'

But no-one was listening.

'Okay,' Ed roared into the crowd. 'Bar's open.'

Postscript

Cramcaster International Airport is as Wang remembers it. Perhaps more security, more men in uniform, more intrusion, probing, at immigration; but the same air of general decline and neglect. He ignores the baggage carousels, the lost luggage window. They are as he recalls, but now he travels light, carrying his smart executive suitcase with him, rather than entrusting it to others. As he passes through the baggage reclaim area he looks around, not without apprehension, for a suave, well-manicured figure, a countryman, whom it might be best to avoid. All he sees is a Frenchwoman of indeterminate age – elegant, poised, attempting to explain to a shabby official that her case has gone missing. Again. But Wang is away, through the baggage area, past unmanned customs desks, past people bearing signs – Amikaro Plc or Car For Mr Schneckenfresser – and out into the terminal concourse.

Wang is in Cramcaster to do business. His solar-powered bicycle company flourishes. It is founded on his uncle's enthusiasm and, more significantly, on start-up monies from his friend and business partner Professor Pendegrass. The professor refuses to be drawn on the source of the funding, saying it comes from a venerable charitable institution intent on saving souls and, since saving the planet will help save souls, investment in solar-powered cycles is in accordance with its ethical principles.

Pendegrass – now a full professor at Cram Vale University and dean of the faculty of social sciences and management – is to meet him at the airport. There is, as yet, no sign of him. Wang wonders if he has a new, or at any rate newer, car. Probably the old one has broken down. Why the professor continues to rely on a vehicle with which, in China, not even the poorest

288

peasant would be seen dead, is a mystery. Something to do with atonement, whatever that is.

Wang checks his Rolex. If the professor does not turn up soon, they will miss their meetings. Wang is here to investigate business premises, with a view to setting up a distribution centre in Cramcaster. Perhaps even manufacturing. The market for solar-powered bicycles, Wang feels – despite the gloom and the grey, the damp and the drizzle in this Northern city – is as good in Britain as in China. Chinese people are not interested in bicycles, solar-powered or otherwise. Bicycles belong to the past: everyone wants cars. The slicker, the sleeker, the better.

But in Britain, as cars, as fuel, fall beyond the finances of the ordinary citizen, the demand for cheaper alternatives will grow. That's why, Wang believes, it will make sense to manufacture in Cramcaster. Costs are rising in China, workers are demanding ever fatter wage packets, benefits: the time is ripe to outsource to cheaper, poorer, struggling countries. Such as Britain.

Wang looks at his watch again. Trust the professor to be late. He checks his mobile, to see if Pendegrass has left a message. Unlikely: the professor is the last person to use mobiles, messaging. While Wang has his phone in his hand, he sends Lina a text. He's arrived and waiting for Pendegrass. She should rest, take it easy. An expectant mother cannot be too careful, he reminds her. And adds three kisses.

Still no professor. Wang decides to find a toilet. He misses the signs in the arrival area and sets off along a series of corridors, which brings him to a different part of the airport.

He eventually locates a gents – not the most salubrious – and, emerging, notices a book shop opposite, facing the toilets. Posters proclaim: The No. 1 bestseller! Now an amazing film! He stops. It is a while

289

since he read any English. A book would do him good. Especially if he is to spend time on this trip waiting for Pendegrass.

He advances towards the shop and is at once rammed by a cart, laden with brushes and other cleaning materials, heading for the toilets.

'Watch where you're going,' rasps the creature – a crabbed thing, with a shaggy beard – propelling the cart. Then: 'I know your type. Think you've got it made. But you haven't. I had it once. Job, house, wife... all gone. You've got to think of it like spider solitaire...'

A voice of authority, of supervision, rings out, causing the thing to jump. 'Arthur... you're behind schedule. Get in there this minute.'

The creature curls its lip at Wang, revealing decaying, browning teeth. Smirking, it manoeuvres its cart around Wang and disappears into the toilets.

Disconcerted, Wang forgets about the No.1 bestseller, the amazing film, and sets off to return to arrivals.

In this way he fails to see that the No. 1 bestseller sports an illustration on its front cover of a Chinese youth, looking lost, with a suitcase, in what is evidently an airport.

In this way he fails to see on the rear cover that the author, Chris Reeve – a talented newcomer to the world of fiction, having given up a teaching career – lives with her partner in Scotland, where they manage a small distillery.

In this way he fails to see the critics' comments that this is a 'comic novel of wit and discernment', a 'sardonic look at higher education', an 'oblique glance at a clash of cultures,' a 'wry comment on the state of present-day Britain.'

In this way he fails to see the disclaimer that names

in the novel have been altered and that any resemblance to persons living or dead is entirely coincidental.

However, back in arrivals, he does not fail to see Pendegrass peering forlornly at the sombreros, the baggy shorts, the hungover hen parties, the duty-frees, the Cram United strips, disgorging themselves into the arms of waiting relatives, friends and neighbours.

He goes up to Pendegrass, who turns around, surprised.

'There you are,' the professor apologises. 'Sorry I'm late... car trouble. You know how it is.'

Yes, thinks Wang, accompanying Pendegrass to the car – which, on double yellow lines, is receiving a parking ticket, as well as increasing interest from armed anti-terrorist police officers. I know precisely how it is. And how it will be.

'Oh,' says Pendegrass, oblivious to the drama about to unfold, 'I almost forgot. I've something for you. A book. A bestseller...'